BLACK MARIA, M.A.

When Ralph Black, chain store mag-nate, was found shot by his own gun in his locked library, the New York police pronounced it as suicide. However, family members believe it was murder. His sister in England, Maria Black, M.A., Headmistress of a girls' school, wants to discover the truth. She travels to America, and with her penchant for solving crimes, sets to work to trace the mysterious plot against her brother to the final unmasking of the amazing truth.

JOHN RUSSELL FEARN

BLACK MARIA, M.A.

Complete and Unabridged

LINFORD
Leicester

First published in Great Britain

First Linford Edition
published 2008

British Library CIP Data

Fearn, John Russell, *1908 – 1960*
  Black Maria, M.A.—Large print ed.—
Linford mystery library
  1. Women school principals—Fiction 2. Murder
—Investigation—Fiction 3. Detective and
mystery stories 4. Large type books
  I. Title
  823.9'12 [F]

ISBN 978–1–84782–187–4

Published by
F. A. Thorpe (Publishing)
Anstey, Leicestershire

Set by Words & Graphics Ltd.
Anstey, Leicestershire
Printed and bound in Great Britain by
T. J. International Ltd., Padstow, Cornwall

This book is printed on acid-free paper

1

The students of Roseway College for Young Ladies were intrigued: the Headmistress intended spending her summer vacation in the United States! How would the inexorable ruler of this South England School react to American life . . . ? Significantly, Miss Maria Black, M.A., intended leaving before the summer holiday break-up. Might there be an easing up in the usual implacable discipline?

The climax to the hint-and-whisper campaign came when a command was issued for a complete gathering of the school in the Assembly Hall one morning. The teachers and Housemistresses gathered on the dais. The girls themselves kept quiet, awaiting Miss Black's inevitable appearance from the rear door of the hall — a melodramatic entrance she could never resist.

She swept in a breeze of black silk down the central aisle. The girls glanced sideways and saw that famous bun of black hair speeding towards the dais. A moment later Maria Black had mounted the four steps and then moved to the platform centre, her compelling calm pervading the great room.

Her age was fifty-five, but only the Board of Governors knew that. She stood as erect as a general surveying a conquest, the no longer graceful curves of her figure somewhat camouflaged by the sweeping dark gown she invariably wore, relieved only by the gold of a slender watch-chain. Some might have considered her handsome. One got this impression from her long keen nose and strong lips that stopped short of being cruel. Chiefly though it was her eyes that always got their victim — frosty blue, unwavering.

Had she allowed her hair to fall softly instead of scooping it back in an old-fashioned bun she could have possessed a mellow if rather aloof beauty.

Suddenly she spoke, with perfect diction.

'Young ladies, in the two weeks before you depart for the summer vacation Miss

Tanby will become temporary Headmistress in my stead . . . '

All eyes turned to Eunice Tanby — a calm, pale-faced, highly algebraical spinster.

'Therefore,' Maria resumed, 'you will cease to regard Miss Tanby as Housemistress after today and will direct all matters of higher jurisdiction to her.'

There was a respectful silence. Maria fingered her watch-chain and swept her eyes over the assembly.

'I hope, young ladies, you will have an enjoyable vacation and will return here fully prepared for another term of work. You may dismiss . . . ' She turned. 'Miss Tanby, please come with me.'

The talking girls scattered immediately as Maria swept through their midst into the long, cool corridor outside the Hall. She entered her study, settled at her desk. She looked up at the pale-faced Housemistress who had followed her and nodded for the door to be closed.

'Please sit down, Miss Tanby . . . I would like to explain to you my immediate departure for the United

States. You see, my late brother's lawyer has summoned me. My brother died quite recently.'

The Housemistress murmured a condolence and smiled in pale sympathy.

'This lawyer,' Maria went on, 'asks me to present myself at the earliest moment in order to clear up certain details of identity and so forth . . . My brother, Miss Tanby, was no ordinary man.' Maria coughed slightly. 'He was the first man to produce tinned broccoli.'

'How remarkable!'

'My brother went to the United States at the time I became a junior teacher here. I have moulded girls and he moulded broccoli. The essential difference seems to be that he made a fortune whereas I — No matter! The fact remains that my brother is dead and there is a bequest to me which I must claim personally — But there is also something else!'

Maria's eyes took on a gleam.

'My brother committed suicide. I tell you this because the details are bound to leak out sooner or later into the Press, and if there should be any reflection upon me you will have the good sense to counteract it. You see, my brother was by far too important a man for the affair to be dismissed lightly. The official verdict was that he committed suicide. But my nephew thinks it was . . . murder!'

'Good heavens!' Miss Tanby exclaimed.

'It may only be a young man's theory,' Maria mused, 'but if he has the vaguest ground for his assertions I shall spend every second of my vacation getting to the bottom of the problem. Mysteries intrigue me immensely, Miss Tanby. I held my brother in high esteem for his purpose and energy, and if he did not die by his own hand — which I for my part cannot credit — then I consider it my duty to discover the real facts.'

'But — but Miss Black, isn't that a job for a detective agency, or the police?'

Maria smiled the special smile she kept pigeonholed for moments of surpassing triumph. 'I have not devoted all my life to the teaching of girls, Miss Tanby. Observe to the right of my bookcase . . . '

Miss Tanby looked at an array of titles

she had never noticed before. She whispered them — 'Crime and the Criminal, Brains and Passion. Alderman's Theory of the Recessive Unit — Good heavens!'

'The skeleton in my educational cupboard,' Maria sighed. 'Frankly, I have quite a penchant for crime — in the right sense, you understand. I am positively fascinated by the hundred and one methods of committing a murder! My greatest interest is Van Furber's treatise on forty-two different ways of producing strangulation. A most enlightening work, I assure you. Incidentally, I might remark here that I placed the Langhorn Cinema out of bounds for the girls because of the number of crime films they exhibit. I allowed the girls to have three local cinemas and kept the Langhorn for my especial patronage. I am — ah — not very well known there.

'I have seen many interesting crime films. I find there is a snap in the American 'racket' film that is most satisfying. And my weakness is one which I can now perhaps really turn to account.'

Tanby hurdled on the uptake. 'In regard to your late brother, you mean?'

'Exactly! I understand crime, crime's methods, and criminals. I am aware from what I have seen of American films that methods over there are very different from ours — that a man in my brother's position, for instance, might have been the target for numberless enemies. I do not say,' Maria finished modestly, 'that I should become a detective. But at least I could look into the details of my late brother's death. I am taking a vacation and a business trip and I shall turn them both into an experiment . . . Now you know why I must leave so quickly.'

'Yes, of course . . . ' Miss Tanby hesitated, then: 'Miss Black, maybe your hobby is not so secret as you imagine. I'm afraid — er — you are known among the girls as 'Black Maria'.'

Maria smiled icily. 'So I am aware. But I fancy that is because the reversal of my two names lends itself naturally to our slang term for a prison van, not because my hobby is generally known.'

'I can promise you everything will be

treated in strictest confidence.'

'Naturally. I shall expect that. You have entire authority from now on, Miss Tanby. I shall be back here again for the next term. During the rest of my time here today I shall draw up a timetable for you to work from . . . '

★   ★   ★

Maria departed from the College by car, and was driven to Southampton by the school chauffeur. Then she was glad to relax within her cabin aboard her ship . . . It seemed to her as the liner sailed on the late evening tide that the receding coastline of England in its soft glow of summer dusk was also taking away a mountain of cares and responsibilities.

She stood at the deck-rail and watched the seething activity of the quayside fade slowly into a blur. It all became a mist, vanishing as though it had never been.

The next morning the ocean had completely replaced the land, and for five days and nights Maria forgot all about curricula, classes, and girls. She went through a round of sedate deck walks, lounged awhile, listened to the orchestras, read her favourite treatise on crime, went for more walks — That nobody ventured to strike up a voyage-acquaintance with her was no surprise. She knew she looked forbidding, and preferred it that way. Romance to her mind was only for the young.

Altogether the trip was calm and uneventful; the weather perfect. By the time the towers of Manhattan loomed on the horizon Maria was reflecting on the benefits the trip had conferred upon her. The cabin mirror proclaimed she was browner, stronger-looking, well fitted for the private experiment she intended making.

She watched the quayside draw near, saw for the first time the grey symphony of stone and endless windowed towers which up to now she had only seen on the cinema screen. Now it was real! Soon she would set foot in it —

The liner docked forty-five minutes later in the brilliance of the afternoon sunshine. A porter lumbering behind her with her smaller bags, Maria walked down the gang-plank, and the exertion convinced her that her mannish black costume was not the ideal outfit for mid-summer New York.

The press of surging people was bemusing to her. It looked as though everybody was looking for somebody else — which they probably were. There was clangour, a hooting of tugs, grinding of cranes, blaring of taxi horns, and the grander, deeper throb of excited humans and their conversation. It was distracting, just a little crazy — then it all began to make sense for Maria as a young man in a soft hat and a lounge suit edged through the crowd. Up went his hat from his dark head and a wide smile broke the tan of his broad, good-natured face.

'Aunt — It *is* Aunt Maria?' he asked uncertainly, as the cold blue eyes swept him.

'Of course,' she said, rather brusquely; and at that he gripped her hand firmly.

'I knew it! I never pull a boner with faces. Photograph at home, you see.'

Maria smiled. 'I suppose it is silly of me

but I have never visualized you as a grown man, Richard. In my mind you have always remained at two years of age, when you were brought to visit me in England.'

'Some people still think I'm only that old, and not twenty-five,' he grinned 'Say, I'll take your bags.' He clutched them from the porter and flipped him a tip. 'Come on, Aunt, I'll see you through the barriers. They're the devil!'

Maria was silent as he propelled her with ardent haste through the mysteries of the Customs. Once through the ordeal she was glad to sink into the cushions of the monstrous Packard Dick Black had waiting for her. He plumped down beside her. Effortlessly the chauffeur eased in the gears.

Maria was aware of Dick's quick eyes studying her. He was quite handsome, she reflected. Never do to tell him so: he was probably conceited enough already. A very straight nose, strong chin, black hair . . . then her attention became absorbed by the canyon of street through which they were moving, with its brooding giants of buildings on either side.

'Have a good trip across?'

'Excellent, Richard, thank you.'

'Oh, call me Dick! Sounds more friendly!'

'You were christened Richard. Where was the purpose of it, if it was not to be used?'

'You got me there,' Dick admitted, then relaxed and watched from under a raised eyebrow as Maria resumed her survey.

'Remarkable! The size and extent of it — !'

'I guess this place sort of knocks strangers for a loop the first time they set eyes on it. But I like it!' Dick went on. 'I was born and brought up in it. Full of all sorts of people doing all sorts of things. There's both poetry and power in it. Something happens — all the time.'

'Including . . . murder?' Maria murmured.

'Yes. I hope it didn't sound too horrible a suggestion to make in my letter, but I'm sure I've grounds for my suspicions. Don't spring the murder news on mother too quickly, will you? For all she knows at the moment you are here just to see the family lawyer — Say, see that place?'

He broke off and excitedly indicated an

immense façade of granite and chromium across which sprawled six-foot letters proclaiming DICK BLACK'S TWELVE RHYTHM LOVELIES to the myriads. 'Mine!' he announced proudly.

Maria glanced at him sharply. 'You mean you own that theatre?'

'Gosh, no — only the dames. In polite circles I'm called a revue producer. I run late night cabarets, experiment with plays and things off the beaten track — You know!'

'So that is what you have become. I rather expected that your late father's business — '

'Not me. I'm not cut out for tinned cabbage. And if it comes to that I'm not so exclusive in my inclinations. Theatricals seem to run in the family. There's Janet, for instance. She's a professional singer with a high C that can knock your eye out. She's just finished a New York circuit and is resting up for a day or so before taking on a fresh engagement . . . Then there's Patricia; she's a professional dancer. Adagio stuff.'

Maria nodded slowly, telescoping

intervening years. 'Let me think now. Janet was the first child — '

'Right,' Dick acknowledged. 'She's twenty-eight. Pat was the last one. She's twenty. Rather a funny kid is Pat . . . Very headstrong and determined. Once she gets an idea nothing can shift it.'

'Perhaps,' Maria reflected, 'her father is being repeated.'

'Possible. He was a tough old nut, though I say it — ' Dick broke off, realizing his remark was two-edged.

Maria smiled. 'Don't apologize, boy. I know you cannot dissociate me from a Headmistress, think of me perhaps as a frowsy old girl full of Latin and mathematical formulae. Maybe it's even true — but maybe not. Believe it or not, Richard, I have had my moments . . . Tell me, how is your mother?'

'Only so-so. Bit run down after the tragedy, I'm afraid. You will see for yourself in a moment.'

The car moved in to the curb outside a vast Fifth Avenue residence . . .

★ ★ ★

14

As she stepped into the hall of the Black residence Maria was reminded of Waterloo Station at home. The place seemed to have the same tendency to recede into infinite distance, where it finally resolved itself into panels, mirrors, armoury, a gigantic staircase, and innumerable doors. She was adjusting herself to the magnificence when the manservant returned from the front door, took her bags, then departed like a black-coated ghost into the distance.

'What's the matter, Aunt?' Dick asked, smiling.

She turned. 'I was just mentally computing how many tins of broccoli it must have needed to indulge — this. I always knew your father had an extravagant streak but — '

'Here's mother,' Dick interrupted; then he raised his voice. 'Here we are, mum — all in one piece.'

Alice Black came sweeping forward from one of the endless doorways with her hand extended. It looked as though she were dancing the Lancers solo.

'Dear, dear Maria! So many years! So

many miles!' She only came to a halt when she reached Maria. Gently she kissed her, then stood back and smiled. 'So much has happened since we last met . . .'

'Twenty-three years ago,' Maria said, rather grimly.

'Twenty-three years! Well, well! Yet you have changed so little, Maria.'

'Needless flattery, Alice. I have changed — and so have you. Responsibilities and cares have left their mark on both of us. You were a slender girl then, with golden hair. I remember it so well. Now look at you!'

Alice looked down at herself in regret. She had avoirdupois in the wrong places and her hair was greying to whiteness. Only in one thing was she unchanged — her eyes were grey, always steady. They seemed to be the lie to her habitual manner of feathery, pointless gushing.

'Such a pity you could not have come at a happier time. Poor, poor Ralph! He lived so hard and died so — so suddenly. But there, the winds of heaven blow on us all when we least expect it. But this isn't the time to talk of our troubles! Come along upstairs.

'The girls are out right now,' Alice went on, as they began to mount the staircase. 'They promised to be back for dinner this evening so as to meet you. In between you'll want a rest perhaps and — and a cup of tea?' she added slyly.

'Thank you, Alice.'

'You see, I remembered your quaint British custom! Being an American I prefer coffee, or else I have just gotten that way through habit. Habits are hard to break, I think, because when you break one you sometimes form another in order to break it.'

'Yes, I suppose it is so,' Maria agreed rather irritably. She was wondering if the staircase went up to heaven.

'Terrible thing about poor Ralph,' Alice went on. 'Such a shock to us all! We never even suspected he had financial worries of any kind. But we found out afterwards. Awful debts in some cases.'

'Recalling Ralph in his early days I cannot say I am surprised to hear of his debts. And from what I have seen of this place he did not practice any great economy.'

They had reached the vast corridor at last. It seemed full of stained-glass windows.

'But, Maria dear, why should one practice economy when one is wealthy?'

Maria's eyes narrowed. 'You said Ralph was in debt.'

'He was — but quite considerably below the amount of his assets. The proving of his will not only paid off the various debts but it also left each one of us wealthy . . . You'll hear about your share from Mr. Johnson, of course. He's our attorney.'

Maria surveyed her own room and mentally compared it with her modest though comfortable quarters far away in Roseway. Her bedroom seemed to be all mirrors and salmon-pink draperies. The bed was by the wall in the distance. The furniture was rosewood, polished nearly as brightly as the mirrors themselves.

'I don't think you'll find it noisy,' Alice said, noting Maria's all-encompassing survey. 'New York is a rowdy city, of course — but then sounds are a lot worse when you deliberately set out to listen to them.'

For answer Maria closed the window sharply. 'Noises do not worry me, Alice, but draughts do. I am rather subject to sinus trouble . . . '

She crossed to the nearest mirror and straightened her severely drawn hair. Through the reflection she saw the manservant come in, set down a loaded tray, then depart again.

'Milk or lemon?' Alice asked brightly.

'Milk, Alice, thank you . . . ' Maria turned and came forward. 'I cannot say I admire your choice of servants, Alice.'

'Walters?' Alice looked surprised as she sat on the divan. 'But how absurd, Maria! He is an excellent servant. He was with the family who formerly owned this place and so we — we just sort of bought him in with it.'

Maria took the teacup handed to her. 'You have traced his connections?' she asked.

'Of course. He is from a line of servants who originated in England. His father was employed by Lord Glendarlow

. . . But Maria, what on earth does it matter what sort of a servant he is?'

'Don't be alarmed at my questions, my dear,' Maria said gravely. 'You see, my profession has demanded of me that I find out all and everything about everybody. You would understand that if you had a college to control. I have developed a positive mania for knowing the inner affairs of all people with whom I come in contact — And I still say your servant does not impress me. For one thing his eyes are unsteady.'

'Just a nervous affliction, I'm sure.' Alice said, astonished. 'It doesn't make him drop any dishes or anything like that.'

Maria finished her tea, then got up and moved to her luggage. Alice rose too and began to drift towards the doorway. She felt strong hints of dismissal in the air. It was the same 'Get Out!' aura that had afflicted many a Roseway inmate.

'Mr. Johnson will be here tomorrow.' Alice spoke from the doorway. 'Once that little matter is settled you'll want to see New York, won't you?'

'In my own way,' Maria acknowledged.

'When I am on holiday, Alice, I relax completely. The Headmistress is back in England embalmed among her books of learning. I shall go anywhere the mood takes me in this city of yours.'

'Well, we can talk of that later. See you at dinner.'

Maria resumed her unpacking and finally unearthed a strong tin box. Unlocking it, she withdrew a black bound book and opened it at the first blank page. She put the date, then began to write swiftly in her neat, scholastic handwriting —

'First impressions are variable. Richard seems to be a likeable boy with a penchant for young ladies — both in and out of his shows, I should imagine. A rather wicked smile, and much D'Artagnan in the eye. Alice still makes rather inane remarks, but she answers my guarded inquiries with an ease that makes her seem innocent of anything ulterior. It is this innocence that I feel compelled to question, in view of De Vanhart's 'First Impressions of a Criminal.' I shall test this thesis for myself . . . Walters, the manservant, is a

strange, impassive being with unsteady eyes. *I begin to wonder if he is looking for something. So far as I can gather all have benefited financially from Ralph's death. I have yet to meet Patricia and Janet. The time is 5.10 p.m.*'

2

In the lounge prior to dinner Dick Black found himself called upon to answer questions as he tried to prepare a brandy and soda for himself.

Patricia was his cross-examiner. She was dressed in a close-fitting gown of green, a colour that matched her eyes. A certain lack of development about the shoulders still testified to her twenty years — but certainly nothing else was undeveloped. Her face was cast in a shrewd, coldly beautiful mould. The green eyes offset the straight nose and firm, full lips. The blonde hair swept back in shimmering waves from her high forehead gave her an odd, robot-like appearance. In fact, as Dick had often observed, if he ever needed anybody in his show to portray the spirit of the future he had only to ask Pat to hold a lamp over her head. But this was a piece of cynical humour that had so far found no inroads to Pat's forthright soul.

'If you'd put that darned siphon down for a moment and start talking maybe we'd get somewhere!' she exclaimed irritably, flinging herself down on the divan. 'Come on, give! What is she like? She's an English headmistress — that's all I hear.'

Dick got his drink down at length. 'She's all right, Pat. A bit hardboiled, maybe, but I can't blame her if the girls she teaches have anything in common with you . . . Try to imagine dad as a woman, then you have it.'

'Still smells bad to me.' Pat got up and moved to the siphon herself. 'I still think it is a piece of confounded nerve her coming here — She came to see Johnson: we know that. Why couldn't she do it by proxy? Why travel three thousand miles just for that?'

'Maybe she just wanted a holiday . . . What are you beefing about anyway?' Dick asked. 'She isn't going to upset your arrangements, is she?'

'She'd better not try!' Pat's lips tightened as she considered her drink, then she turned as Janet came in.

It was not Janet's fault that she entered like a mannequin at a dress salon. Years of concert platforms had instilled it into her — the measured tread and well-poised head. She had a regal calm, an intense and unshatterable assurance. Her dark colouring lent a touch of the Juno to her. Raven-headed, black-eyed, the taller of the two girls. When she spoke her voice was richly mellow.

'What's the matter, Pat? Don't you like the advent of Aunt Maria?'

'No, I do not!'

'Suppose you wait and meet her before opening the sea-cocks? After all — '

Dick interrupted: 'Take no notice of her, Jan. She's been nuts for some time now, but I'm dashed if I can figure out why. Maybe the hot weather.'

'Dick,' Janet said, turning to him, 'what is she like?'

'Holy cats, do I have to start in all over again? She is — '

'Can it be that I am the cause of this little argument?'

Maria had come quietly into the room.

Undoubtedly the girls of Roseway would not have recognized their empress this evening. The bun was still there unfortunately — but the rest of Maria, exquisitely gowned and matronly, was divorced completely from the sombre college ruler.

Dick jumped up, caught Janet's arm. 'This is Janet, Aunt. Remember her? She was five when — '

'When we last met,' Maria nodded, and stood gravely as the girl kissed her lightly on the cheek. Then she went on, 'So this is the five-year-old who ate all my butter-creams when she came to England? Well! Amazing — ! And now you are a public figure — a singer . . . You make me feel quite old, my dear.'

Janet smiled. 'One just grows up, and there it is. You've never actually met Pat, have you? Her photographs don't do her justice, you know — Come on, Pat!' she insisted. 'Don't stand sulking over there.'

Patricia shrugged and came forward rather sullenly. She returned Maria's calm, blue-eyed gaze with one of equal power, and infused into it a definite challenge. Finally she held out a hand indifferently.

Maria ignored it and said calmly, 'You may kiss me, Patricia.'

Pat hesitated, then administered a peck. She stood back uncertainly, colour mounting slowly in her cheeks as Maria stared at her.

'I was just thinking how very beautiful you are, child. The photographs I have seen of you haven't done you justice in the least. I can see a lot of your poor father in you.'

'Isn't that a trifle pointless?'

'I don't think so. It is not uncommon for a daughter to inherit some of her parents' characteristics — Yes, indeed,' Maria mused. 'I see it in all three of you. Like a cross-section of your father with part of your mother. In you, Dick, I behold your father's reckless ambition without its hard side. In you, Janet, I see the calm repose your father cultivated in his later years. I too have that characteristic — And in you, Patricia, I see something different. Even a part of me, as I might have been had I ever been as beautiful as you.'

Patricia's long lashes masked her

insolent green eyes for a moment. 'We didn't expect to be psycho-analyzed, Aunt. All you are seeing are two sisters and one brother. So what?'

Dick glanced at her irritably. 'You trying to start a war, Pat? Come down off your pedestal! Now that you have met Aunt you can see she isn't what you thought.'

Janet said: 'I have a day or two free, Aunt, before I resume my work. Perhaps you'd like me to show you around? Plenty to see, you know.'

'Yeah, Grant's Tomb,' Patricia agreed bitterly. 'Or maybe that would be too thrilling. There's Empire State, Battery Park — '

'Ah, so here we all are!' Alice Black came in with her usual Lancers movement, gowned in black as became her widowhood. Now Maria came to notice it only Patricia had disdained mourning by wearing bright emerald green.

'So sorry I have been rather long, Maria dear,' Alice went on, patting her hair. 'I had one or two things to do and the time just rushed away. Now, you must meet Janet and — .'

'We've been through all that, mother,' Patricia butted in. 'Right now our main concern — mine anyway — is dinner. When do we start?' Then her lovely young face suddenly lighted as Walters appeared.

'Dinner is served,' he pronounced gravely.

'May I?' Dick asked, drawing Maria's arm through his own. 'I've long wanted to feel what it is like to meet a Headmistress on equal terms. I sort of get a kick out of taking one in to dinner.'

Maria's eyes moved to Pat's elegant form preceding them. 'I'm glad you don't think I'm an old dragon, Richard.'

'Don't let Pat get in your hair. She talks like a chump at times . . . Look, after dinner maybe we can get down to cases a little. I still think dad was murdered, you know. You have met the family now, seen the boss of the domestics in the form of Walters; so what next do you want to do?'

'If possible I would like to see the room where your father died.'

'Okay. You shall!'

★   ★   ★

29

During dinner Maria skilfully steered the conversation away from the commonplace of her profession to the subject closest to her heart. Long the expert technician in rooting out details she began to feel almost as though she were back at Roseway with a bunch of guilty pupils on the carpet.

'I suppose,' she said, 'that it is not very easy for us to sit here in a family group and try to forget what is uppermost in all our minds? I know I cannot.'

'Do we have to go through it all again?' Pat groaned.

Maria's cold blue eyes wandered to her. There was a venom in this girl she could not quite understand. She was too intelligent, too gifted by nature, to be a natural spitfire.

'I think,' Maria said, 'that you have overlooked my absence, Patricia. I have come three thousand miles for first-hand details, not only to see attorney Johnson. I want to know just why your father did such a dreadful thing. What really did happen?'

'Most of us got the news second-hand,'

Janet said quietly. 'I was not here on that evening. I was giving a singing recital at the theatre and Dad had promised to listen in to my concert — as indeed he always did on the first and last days of my recitals. He said he could tell by doing this how my voice had improved, or deteriorated, in the interval . . . ' She gave a little shrug. 'When I got home around midnight the thing had happened. Mother gave me the full details . . . It was a terrible, dreadful shock!'

Alice took the story up. 'Walters was the first to discover things were wrong. Ralph used to ring for his wine in an evening, you see. Sometimes early, sometimes late. He used to lock his door when listening to Janet . . . Well, he rang for his wine all right, but when Walters arrived the library door was still locked. Walters got alarmed at length, asked me what should be done. In the end we broke in by the French window . . .

'There was Ralph in his armchair, a bullet wound in his temple. It was horrible! Horrible! The radio was going full blast too. I remember Walters switched it off, then he sent for the police. As you are aware, however, the final verdict was suicide. It could hardly have been anything else. It seemed queer he should ring for his wine and then shoot himself; that was why we had a police enquiry just — just in case somebody — But it was suicide. Ghastly, I know — but it had to be faced.'

Maria glanced at Patricia and Dick. 'Did you two lend any sort of assistance?'

'I was out with my town show,' Dick shrugged. 'I didn't get home until long after Janet.'

'I was out too,' Patricia said, with a defiant little smile. 'I spent the evening with friends . . . '

'So,' Maria murmured, 'everybody was out except you, Alice, and the servants?'

'Good Lord, are you trying to read something else into the horrible business!'

'No — not yet.' Maria shook her head. 'But when we are finished I would like to see his library. I'm not a morbid woman but I am a stickler for details and I want to know exactly how and where he met his end.'

'Sounds like going over old ground to me,' Patricia sighed. 'Anyway, you won't need me, will you?'

'I would rather have liked all of you to co-operate,' Maria said. 'I've still one or two things to get absolutely clear in my mind.'

'But why?' Genuine fury blazed in Patricia's green eyes. 'Just why do you have to come here and rake up this tragedy again? Why do we have to suffer it all over again just because you want a — a reconstruction? The police went over all the ground and the thing's finished with. You know just as much as we do!'

'Just what's the matter with you tonight, Pat?' Dick snapped. 'What are you going off half-cocked about? After all, Aunt's entitled to some explanations. As she says, she wasn't here when the thing happened.'

Janet said: 'I'm sure we're all willing to do what we can to give you a true picture, Aunt. Of course, I don't much care myself to have old unhappy memories revived, but I also know what is common sense . . . That's for you, Pat,' she added dryly.

33

'All right!' Pat threw down her serviette impatiently. 'But I still resent the insinuation that we're all a bunch of criminals or something! Here are we, a perfectly respectable family with our private tragedy — then along comes Aunt Maria from England to question us all and rake up old dirt . . . Good Heavens, Aunt, one would almost think dad was murdered!'

'What makes you think he wasn't?' Dick asked quietly. 'You might as well all know now as later on . . . I asked Aunt not to spring it on you — not to tell you that I sent for her as well as attorney Johnson. I told her that I did not like the circumstances of dad's death. It looked like suicide: the police were satisfied it was suicide . . . But I'm not!'

'Don't you think you're making rather a dangerous statement, Dick?' Janet commented.

'Why am I? We're all innocent — we know that. It was an outside job, if anything. As we all know, dad had lots of enemies. So I told Aunt Maria I suspected murder.'

'And what for?' Patricia snapped. 'Aunt is a headmistress, not a detective.'

'She happens to be father's sister and therefore entitled to our views.'

Alice Black made a rather bewildered movement. 'I never even thought of such a horrible possibility . . . I begin to think you've been reading too many of those plays of yours, Dick.'

The silence fell back and one looked at the other. Maria finished her meal with calm detachment, then as there was a general rising to feet Dick spoke again.

'Come along to the library, Aunt, and see things for yourself.'

Maria accompanied him through the lounge and across the hall. The two girls and Alice followed. Finally all of them had collected in the library in the sombre twilight.

The place was well but plainly furnished. There was a massive writing desk, a heavy hide armchair drawn to face the old-style fireplace, a radiogram in the corner alcove near the window, a richly thick carpet, and hundreds of books lining the walls. The lighter furniture was in modern steel tubing fashion . . . Maria took in most of this at a glance then directed her attention back to the fireplace.

At either side of it, on the out-jutting wall produced by the chimney breast, fixed at right angles to the fireplace itself, were ancient crossed swords and pistols, shields, armoury trifles, and other examples of antique art.

Patricia glanced round wearily. 'Well, Aunt, I guess there isn't much in the place, is there?'

'It's not the room, Patricia, it's the memories,' Maria said quietly, gazing round her. 'Yes, standing here I can almost feel Ralph's presence. I can imagine how he must have loved this room.'

'I feel that too,' Alice said soberly. 'I often come in here and sit — and sit. I seem to feel again Ralph's blustering assurances, his overwhelming strength of purpose, his ruthless ambition — for which he paid with his life! Well, Fate always has the sledgehammer in her hand . . .'

'Confoundedly depressing, I call it!'

Patricia said. 'I could never understand what dad wanted with a dump like this room. It's — it's medieval!'

Maria's steady eyes fixed on her. 'Patricia, you seem to have no happy memories of your father. Why is that?'

'Would you have any happy memories of a parent who balked your dearest wish? I had no affection for father — none whatever. He insisted on treating me as an irresponsible crackpot, as a money-blown heiress with no sense of duty. I didn't like it, and I'd be a hypocrite if I said I were sorry he died.'

'Pat!' Her mother was aghast.

'It's true!' Pat insisted defiantly. 'And you know it — all of you!' She stopped, gave a slow, bitter smile. 'I'm tired . . . I think I'll go up to my room.' She went out and slammed the door.

'I don't quite know what to say about Pat, Aunt,' Janet apologized. 'She's been unaccountably nasty ever since dad died. Says she sleeps badly. Anyway, she's always going off to bed early in the evening like this.'

'But the doctor can't find anything

wrong with her,' Dick grunted.

'At least she is honest about herself,' Maria reflected. 'Tell me, Alice, can you remember in what position Ralph was found?'

'Yes. I'll show you.'

Alice Black moved to the leather armchair and slumped into it so that her head just angled over the top of the big square back. She lolled her head sideways and tapped her right temple significantly.

'The wound had slight powder marks about it,' Dick explained. 'That indicated fire from pretty close range, of course. The revolver was on the floor, about two inches from where mother's left hand is dangling now. The only fingerprints on it were dad's own. His own gun, of course, a pretty hefty thirty-eight automatic. He used to keep it in the desk drawer, mainly for his own protection. It's in the drawer again right now if you're interested. Fully licensed, of course. One bullet had been fired from the gun, the one in his head . . .'

Janet said: 'He had apparently been listening to the radio because Mother told me it was blaring away when Walters broke in here. I suppose dad had been listening to me singing . . . I guess I'll never know now what he thought of my voice on the last night of the tour.'

Maria went over to the radiogram and studied it. Presently she turned and asked a question. 'Then the shot was not heard?'

'I was upstairs in my room,' Alice responded. 'I was there all evening, reading. In any case I could not have heard the shot from my room. You know how big this house is. The only one who might have heard it is Walters — but he didn't. So he said.'

'Hmm . . . ' Maria began to prowl, regarded the French window with its newly-fitted glass, then walked to the door of the room and studied the lock. It bore no signs of tampering. At length she stood erect again and fondled her watch-chain.

'The windows and doors were locked. Nobody was at home except you and the servants, Alice. And yet . . . Tell me, Richard, what made you think it was murder?'

'I'll show you. Look here!'

He crossed to the desk, unlocked one of the drawers and hauled a batch of papers to light. Quickly he sorted out about half a dozen and handed them over. Maria took them, sat down and read carefully.

The first one was a highly complicated business letter referring to the negotiation of loans and private securities. The amounts involved rather startled Maria; then her face became grim as she read the companion letter to it. It was brief but threatening, demanding the honouring of the debts immediately.

'I admit a certain suggestion of threats here, Richard,' Maria said. 'But hardly enough grounds for murder.'

Dick pointed to the memorandum. 'See that name? V. L. Onzi? That man calls himself a financial expert — but actually he's a loan shark of the lower breed, and when he doesn't get what he wants he resorts to strong-arm tactics.'

'But why on earth was your father mixed up with such a man?'

'He could hardly help it, Aunt,' Janet said. 'As you know, dad started out with canned broccoli. From that, the business flourished. All sorts of canned things were added. A flock of chain stores developed . . . Well, with such numberless organizations up and down the country dad could not possibly give each one his individual attention. That was why some of his branch managers fell into the wrong hands — and one of them into the grip of Onzi in particular. I don't know the exact circumstances, but it looks as though this manager needed a loan to carry over immediate liabilities. He got it. But Onzi, when the time came for payment, did not apply to the manager but to dad, the fountain-head . . . Isn't that what you mean, Dick?'

He nodded. 'I believe that Onzi singled out dad as a possible victim to serve his own mysterious ends . . . Oh, I know it sounds vague,' he admitted, seeing Maria's unconvinced look, 'but it can at least establish a motive for murder . . . Besides, there may be others too! Look at the rest of these papers and you'll find dad and his managers were mixed up with all kinds of unsavoury folk. His vast business made that unavoidable. Briefly, these documents show that at least six or seven people had a good reason for wanting him out of the way. He was a pretty ruthless sort of man, as you may know. He allowed nothing and nobody to balk him. His death must have relieved quite a few people.'

Maria glanced through the documents, finally tossed them down. 'If all this is true why didn't the police follow the obvious trail to a proper conclusion?'

'They said the idea was illogical,' Dick grunted. 'They interpreted the documents as clear proof that dad was beset by numberless difficulties and chose suicide as the only way out. Besides, the locked room, the total absence of any clues to suggest murder, made suicide the only solution. Only dad's fingerprints were on the gun. There were no signs of anybody having been near the house — But Aunt, I still think one of these many people mentioned here, and Onzi in particular, might have had a motive. Don't ask me how it was done. I'm no detective.'

Maria got to her feet. 'Frankly, Richard, I can't help feeling you have based your conception of murder upon a very flimsy pretext. One cannot base a murder motive on nebulous threats.'

'Why not?'

'I am assured of it from my private study of criminology . . . Of course, there is a certain interest attaching to this Onzi person — Would it be possible to meet him?'

'Lord, no! At least not in safety.'

'I am not concerned for safety; only for facts. Where can I find him?'

Dick reflected. 'The Onzi Financial Building is on Fifty-Sixth, but whether you'd find Onzi himself there or just an assistant I don't know. So far as I remember dad was about the only person who ever saw Onzi personally — excepting for a few business big shots of course.'

'Is this Financial Trust illegal?'

'Not as you'd notice,' Dick answered dryly. 'There are dubious quantities in every great city. How long they operate without making a slip-up depends on the cleverness of their legal advisers. So far

Onzi has gotten away with it.'

'I see. Fifty-Sixth, you said? I shall probably visit the place before long.'

'Which means you do believe Onzi may have had something to do with dad's death?' Janet asked quickly.

'I did not say that, Janet. Accusation is a dangerous thing. One must first make contacts: that is the first law of investigation.'

Dick gathered up the documents and returned them to the desk. Janet glanced at her puzzled mother. Then Maria turned to them again.

'Who is in charge of Ralph's business now?'

'Flock of directors,' Dick said. 'But they're all reputable. Dad was only the nominal head.'

'They would not, for instance, gain anything by your father's death?'

'No; on the contrary I think it's put them in rather a spot. It means a whole mass of complication sorting things out. That will be done gradually in conjunction with attorney Johnson. You'll be seeing him tomorrow anyway: perhaps he can tell you one or two things.'

Maria nodded. 'Were you fond of your father, Richard?'

'Why sure, I liked the old man. Can't say I loved him, though. He was too much like a granite statue for that.'

'A man of tremendous ambitions — dogged resolve,' Alice sighed. 'Maybe he had changed a lot from the man you used to know, Maria.'

'Maybe, though I was always impressed by his desire to master every problem . . . Richard, you told me you didn't go into the business because you preferred the theatrical world. Was there ever a chance for you to go into the business?'

'Oh, yes, but the idea of sitting in an oak chair and directing the destinies of chain stores didn't appeal to me. I wanted the bright lights, same as Jan and Pat. We all burst into stage work — Jan as a singer and Pat as a solo dancer. Incidentally, Pat's between engagements at the minute in case you're wondering why she's at home. Summing it up, Aunt, I don't think dad quite approved of my revue work. He had the oddest notions on convention.

Certainly he would never advance me a red cent to finance anything new. I had all my own spadework to do . . . ' Just for a moment Dick's face set in grim lines; then again he was smiling. 'There it is, right off the record.'

'Could it be that your father's odd notions on convention have anything to do with Pat's complete disregard for his memory?'

'Pat,' Janet said calmly, 'is a little fool. She wanted to marry a man who later turned out to be a thief, and because dad knew it was all wrong and forbade the marriage she never forgave him for it. That's all that's wrong with her.'

Maria mused over that. Then: 'Tell me, Janet, what was to prevent your father visiting your first and last nights personally at the theatre instead of listening in over the radio?'

'Work!' Janet grimaced. 'He never went to a theatre if he could help it. He would listen to my singing over the radio, and when it came to the turn of the other singers he would get along with his work until it came to my turn again. We sing in

46

relays, you see. I am the soloist, with three songs at the commencement and usually three at the end. Father was the kind of man who just couldn't sit patiently through anything which did not directly concern him. So he combined pleasure with business so to speak, and thereby never lost a moment.'

'How could you tell all this if he always locked himself in?'

'Oh, merely from the information he had given me at different times. He was a man of punctilious habits, and never varied from them. For instance, you notice that all the chairs in this room are of what one would call the uncomfortable type: he used them strictly for business. On the other hand, for pleasure, he had this huge armchair fixed just so — in fact immovably, for you can see the castors are in wooden blocks. His idea, I gathered, was so that the chair could directly face the radio. Anyway, I know this was the one chair he always used when listening to me. It comprised one of his main relaxations . . . '

'The chair, then, cannot be moved?'

Maria questioned.

'It can — but it rarely was. I think the staff were afraid to move it without dad's permission for fear of him flying into a rage. It's easily the heaviest and biggest armchair I've ever seen . . . '

'Hmmm . . . ' Maria said, surveying it — but not as closely as she intended doing later on.

'I suppose,' Janet went on reflectively, 'that dad and I got along together perhaps better than either Pat or Dick. However, I always had the impression that he was not half so interested in me as a daughter as he was in my ability to sing. Singing to the public, from his point of view, represented power, money, fame — the things he loved so much.'

'In other words,' Maria summed up, 'he was so busy a man that he had become estranged from his own children. Pat openly resented it: you, Richard, took it more or less as a matter of course but disliked it just the same. But in none of you was there any real love of child for parent.'

'It sounds awful,' Janet said, after a

long pause, 'but I'm afraid you're right.'

'Does — does all this mean anything?' Alice put in vaguely. 'Really, Maria dear, it seems there is an awful lot of talking going on which is leading nowhere.'

'I did warn you that I like to know about everybody and everything, Alice,' Maria said. 'But I'm satisfied now.'

'Then you think dad was probably murdered?' Dick demanded.

'I can perhaps tell you better when I have seen Mr. Johnson tomorrow. Then there is this Onzi person . . . '

'Well,' Janet said, smiling, 'now the third degree is ended maybe we can go back to the lounge. This room is hardly the place for congenial conversation. And time's getting on, Dick.'

'Eh?' He glanced sharply at his watch. 'Holy cats! I'm going to be late for my show. See you later, everybody . . . Good hunting, Aunt!'

★　★　★

It was eleven-thirty when Maria retired to her room — but she did not prepare for

49

bed immediately. She sat thinking, fingering her watch-chain. She heard Alice and Janet, and afterwards the domestics, pass in procession along the corridor to their rooms. Since Patricia had not put in an appearance all evening it seemed that she had made good her threat to be rid of her tiredness by going to bed. This was a point that somehow intrigued Maria. Bringing out her black book she began to write —

'Why should a perfectly healthy girl like Patricia suffer from an extraordinary tiredness? Certainly not because of her work for I am assured she is at the moment between engagements. From a preliminary study of her I have the impression she is hiding something and resents my presence for fear I may find out what it is. Altogether, what I have seen — i.e., documents and so forth, leads me to believe the murder motive as rather unconvincing; unless this has been done deliberately to deflect suspicion from a real culprit . . . Viewing the family objectively, I note that each one, save perhaps *Alice, admits having but little regard for Ralph. Another thing: All save Alice were absent from the house on the night. Was that done to provide an alibi? I have intimated that I do not believe Ralph was murdered, but privately I think he was — though exactly how will provide a neat problem. For instance, why was Dick so anxious to assert it was murder . . . ? Tomorrow I meet Johnson, the family lawyer. I shall also hope to contact one V. L. Onzi, a shady financier, I understand.'*

Maria read the notes through, then locked the book away. Again she meditated, this time upon the library, recalling numerous little things it had been impossible to examine thoroughly in the twilight and with the eyes of the family upon her. Finally she came to a decision.

Quietly she left her room, walked silently down the heavily carpeted staircase and descended into the hall. All was quiet and abysmally dark, but she could determine her position from the friendly pedantic ticking of the massive clock outside the library door. She went across the hall, opened the library door and stole softly inside.

'Who's that?'

Maria recognized the sharp voice as Alice's even as the lights came up. Alice was standing beside the big armchair, dressed in a kimono-like gown and lace cap. A variety of expressions went over her features.

'Oh, it's you, Maria. Whatever are you doing here? Dressed too!'

Maria came forward. 'I can assure you, Alice, that I have a perfectly good reason for being here . . . It simply occurred to me that I might be able to learn a little from a quiet look round.'

'I see — ' Alice stopped, seemed to be trying to get possession of herself. 'You're wondering what I'm doing here in the dark, I suppose?' she asked abruptly.

'You are at perfect liberty to do whatever you wish in your own home, Alice. Certainly I did think I heard you go up to your room . . . ' Maria stopped, studying

Alice's attire. 'But I never heard you leave again.'

'No, these boudoir shoes don't make a sound . . . As a matter of fact I came down to sit and think. Remember how I told you I do that sometimes? Often, especially at night . . . Associations seem to be so near at night. One can nearly feel the other world always so close to us. But I suppose such a strong-minded woman as you can have no time for such silly indulgences?'

'My dear Alice, you don't owe me an explanation for every little foible. I think your sentiment is a very laudable one . . . You were very fond of Ralph, weren't you?'

Alice nodded absently. 'Something went out of my life when he died. I have nothing but the memories . . . But that means nothing to you, Maria, and I expect you want to be left alone so you can look around. Just do whatever you wish. The house is yours . . . ' She turned to the door. 'I'll say good night, then.'

'Good night, Alice.'

The door closed and Maria glanced

about her, mystified. The explanation had sounded logical enough, but she had made up her mind to accept nothing as logical until she had proven it to the hilt. She set about the task for which she had come and began to prowl, her Headmistress's eye not missing a thing.

She made a meticulous study of the walls, examined the bookshelves, went again through the documents in the desk drawer, and looked once more at the No. .38 automatic. Nothing there to add to what she already knew.

She tried raising the armchair, but its weight defeated her. Then she studied the wooden blocks. Besides serving the purpose of preventing the castors cutting into the costly carpet they definitely made that chair a stationary piece of furniture for all practical purposes. From which Maria inferred that her brother could hardly have sat anywhere else had he wished to relax and enjoy the radio.

Then she glanced inside the radiogram and puzzled for a moment. The needle had stopped in the middle of a record.

The record itself was some unpronounce-able Italian aria sung by Janet herself.

Maria frowned. Needle in the middle of the record? The radiogram was obviously a self-player, one of those instruments that handle a dozen records at one operation. Maria turned from it at last, still puzzled, and directed her attention to the polished wood surround-ing the edge of the carpet.

After a long search on hands and knees she came unexpectedly upon something. It had lodged in a crack between skirting board top and wall paneling. For a long time she fished carefully and finally pulled forth a short, powerful spring. It was about an eighth of an inch thick and two inches long. At each end a loop formed out of the spring itself, one loop larger than the other.

Maria stood up, turned her find over and over in her fingers, pulled it gently open and shut and noted that dust had gathered on its greasy coils. Obviously it had been there some little time. The more she looked at it the more she searched round in her mind for something to fit it

— and finally accepted the suggestion that a typewriter was the most likely article. Springs are not common things in a house unless connected with some kind of machine — and the most likely machine in this case was certainly a typewriter.

It started her off on another search but she found no signs of a machine anywhere. Finally she sat down in the armchair and pondered the spring again. Perhaps it meant nothing: but equally it might mean something. So finally she put it away in her watch-chain locket; then she eased herself into the position in the armchair in which her brother had presumably met his death — according to Alice's reenactment anyway.

Maria found herself looking at the radiogram in the corner alcove. That seemed natural enough. Then she altered her position a little and found she was gazing right into the barrel of one of the two crossed guns high up on the right-angled wall of the chimney breast. She frowned, a thought twisting quickly through her head.

She got to her feet, pulled up a small

chair and stood on it. Even now she could not reach the crossed guns, but she stood surveying them from this closer viewpoint. They were very old and clumsy looking, but no doubt valuable as antiques. They graced the wall in an 'X' fashion, with their barrels pointing downward at forty-five degrees. Their support seemed to be comprised of five nails, somewhat rusted now with long standing. The nails supported the guns in five-spot dice fashion, the centre nail passing through the trigger-guard on both guns, and the remaining four supporting barrels and butts respectively. Nothing peculiar about this, and probably it was pure coincidence that one of the guns pointed right at the armchair.

Maria smiled regretfully. 'Keep a grip on yourself, Maria. Always remember Calvin Brown's treatise on *Gradual Conclusions*.'

She prepared to descend, then paused again as she looked at the nails supporting the butt and barrel of the gun pointing at the chair. It seemed as though — She got down hastily, added a cushion

57

to the chair, and climbed again. Now she was quite close. What she saw might have meant anything, but to her inquisitive mind it was not at least a natural thing . . .

Briefly, the rust on the two end nails — but not on the centre one through the trigger-guard — had been scored almost to brightness. The scoring took the form of a pin-thin scratch on the nail supporting the barrel; but on the nail supporting the butt it was wider — much wider.

Maria frowned, looked at the nails from all angles. They projected perhaps two inches beyond the gun itself. And the ends were scored? For a long time she thought, then she fished out her spring again and fixed it on the nail that had the wider scoring. A vague surprise filled her on discovering her guess was correct. The scoring exactly matched in width the smaller loop of the spring.

She climbed down, returned the spring to the locket and fingered her watch-chain pensively . . . Perhaps — She looked up sharply, her meditations interrupted by the faintest of sounds from somewhere in the hall. Instantly she moved to the switch and put out the lights. Opening the door cautiously she peered outside, just in time to see a dim figure with a tiny glow from a fountain-pen torch heading towards the front door. Every move was cautious; there was no necessity to draw back the bolts since they were left back in order that Dick could get into the house in the early hours.

From the slenderness of the figure in its light summer dustcoat Maria judged it must be Patricia. She continued watching intently until at last Patricia had the door open. She slipped phantom-like outside, closing the door with her latchkey to avoid the click of the lock — It was enough for Maria. For a girl to be slipping out long after midnight was suspicious. Besides, Maria had remembered that Pat spent a lot of time sleeping. Why not indeed if this was the sort of thing she was up to?

Maria made up her mind quickly as she crossed the dark hall. It was unlikely that Pat would use a car for fear of the noise of the engine. If she walked there might be the chance of keeping her in sight since the main street outside took a beeline for the town centre. In that case — Maria hurried up to her room, bundled on hat and coat, grabbed her umbrella, then returned to the front door. She had to risk the click of the lock. As she descended the steps into the street she saw the white-coated figure of Patricia in the distance, hurrying along under the street lamps. There was not a great deal of traffic about at this hour; people on the pavement too were pretty sparse, so Maria was able to keep track of the girl's movements. Possibly she was not conscious of how conspicuous her light-coloured coat made her. Maria marched on, umbrella firmly in hand, her pace strong and vigorous despite her tiring day.

Pat's walk took her in a straight line into the heart of the city where the people became more frequent and the sky-signs and late night dance halls blazed their invitations to the dark. It was into one of these latter, to Maria's astonishment, that Pat finally vanished from view.

Maria crossed the street and stood

surveying the garish façade of the establishment from the opposite side. It was clearly not high class, was sandwiched between two edifices that were probably offices by day. Bright neon lights proclaimed —

MAXIES' DANCE HALL

Patricia — the lordly, wealthy Patricia Black — gone in here? And in the early hours of the morning? Maria straightened her hat, took a firm hold on her umbrella, thanked God there was an ocean between herself and Roseway, and crossed the street again. Spurred on by memories of a myriad treatises on criminology, all of which seemed to add up to the fact that a good investigator never loses the quarry, she would allow herself no pause — not even when she got to the box office and spent a few moments reconciling English and American currency values. The maiden behind the cash grille watched her in lambent interest, chewing meanwhile.

Maria found the amount she wanted at last, took a ticket, then marched between the dried palms into the foyer. So far all was well: she would have to rely on her personality for the rest. For a moment she paused, aware of a blanketing heat and the distant cacophony of an indifferent orchestra. She caught a glimpse of a mob of half-dressed women and shiny-faced men drifting round the dance floor ... Looking round her she saw the stairs, went up them to a low-built balcony scattered with wicker tables with glass tops, hemmed in on one side by a badly discoloured wall further mortified by patches of faded gilt. The whole place reeked of cheapness.

A waiter came towards her, stopped short as though mastering an emotion, then asked, 'Table, lady?'

'Naturally,' Maria replied coldly. 'Preferably one overlooking the dance floor, yet not so that I am too much in view. Do I make myself clear?'

From the waiter's leer she gathered she did. He waved to a glass-topped table half-shielded by another of the prevailing dried palms, then stood aside while Maria laid down her umbrella and settled herself.

The waiter became apparent again. 'We've a special supper on tonight, lady — '

'I do not require supper, my man. I'll take — Lemonade.'

'Lemonade!' The man half-opened his mouth; then he met Maria's blue-eyed gaze halfway. 'Lemonade it is,' he agreed hastily, and went off.

Maria sat back and stared unemotionally at the grinning girls and boys at the next-but-one table. The longer she stared, the more uncomfortable the little party obviously became. At last they looked at each other, got up, and hurried off downstairs.

'Sir Charles Napier was right,' Maria murmured contentedly to herself; then shifting her position a little she gazed over the balcony. Below there swarmed a varicoloured mass of men and women working themselves into a state of semi-hysterical riot. They were spinning in circles, wagging their fingers in the air, thumping the polished floor with their toes, all to the accompaniment of the whanging, crashing band.

The smoky air wafting up to her was charged with a surfeit of odours that had an admixture of strong drink, cheap perfume, cosmetics, dead flowers, and perspiration. Her unaccustomed ear-drums were throbbing by now with the din of the 'orchestra'; her eyes were somewhat dazzled by the naked glare of lights from shoddy electroliers. In the distance a sailor was dancing so earnestly he looked as though he were strangling his girl partner.

'Here y'are, lady . . . ' The glass of lemonade descended. 'A dollar,' the waiter added, seeing her questioning eye.

She handed it over and he took it solemnly; then as he turned to go she caught his arm.

'One moment, waiter. Do you happen to know if a young lady named Patricia Black ever comes here?'

'I wouldn't be knowin', lady. I only work here. I don't dance.' He reflected. 'What's she like?'

'Slender. Twenty-two years of age. High

forehead, golden hair.'

'Mmm, swell looker, eh? Nope, I ain't seen her; and I don't know her name neither. I'm rather struck on blondes, lady, and I know most of 'em, friendly like. I've not seen her, 'cos if I had I'd know of it, see?' He nodded briefly and blundered off.

'Amazing!' Maria murmured, and leaving her lemonade untouched for the moment she scanned the floor below once more, searching anxiously for that head of spun gold that was in itself an utter betrayal. There were honey-coloured heads, plastered in ringlets; corn-coloured ones with frizzing; peroxided ones mousy at the roots from this exalted angle — But a head of pure gold? Nowhere! Yet Patricia had come in here. Maria was convinced of it.

Puzzled, she turned to her drink, tasted it, then making a wry face she set it down again. Warm water with amber tinting. But she tried again because she was genuinely thirsty, and as she sipped her gaze travelled across the floor to a distant alcove in a backwater of the sea of dancers. Within the alcove sat three scantily-dressed girls in backless gowns, rather like modern versions of the three little maids from the Mikado. They seemed to be boredly occupied in watching the swirling throngs.

Presently a man with extra large feet and very shiny hair approached them, said something and handed over a ticket. The girl at the left of the trio got up and started to dance gracefully in his arms. Maria lowered her glass slowly, her eyes wide, watching intently from the palm tree's camouflage as the pair floated under the balcony.

That slender body, those green eyes gazing absently into space. Patricia, beyond doubt! But now long black hair reached in curls to the top of her creamy shoulders.

Maria compressed her lips, wondering why the idea of a wig had not occurred to her before. Never once in following the girl had she had the chance to see her hair, and now — Now she wondered at its purpose. Ceaselessly she watched as the pair circled the floor once or twice during the course of the pandemonium that passed for music; then as Pat retired to the alcove again to join her two companions and the dancers streamed off the floor for refreshment, Maria snapped her fingers sharply.

The waiter hurried forward. 'Somethin' more, lady?'

'Yes. Information I mean. Here!' Maria dived in her bag and handed money over. 'You can tell me something which perhaps you may know. Those three girls over there in the alcove: what are they doing? I saw one man hand across a ticket. Are they — ushers?'

'Ushers? What in heck do you think this place is — a church? They're professionals.'

'Professional dancers?'

'Yeah. Their job is to partner guys who come in without a dame to hoof with.'

'Ah! And the girl at the left end with the black hair. Who is she? Know her name?'

'Sure — Maisie Gray. Been here around three weeks.'

'Hmm!' Maria said. 'Who is the

manager of this place?'

'Just who wants to know?' the waiter snapped. 'Want to complain or somethin'?'

Maria flashed him an icy look. 'Kindly be civil, my man! I asked you a perfectly straightforward question.'

'Well, it's a question I ain't goin' to answer. Anyway, the manager ain't here.'

The waiter turned away impatiently and headed toward a new group of customers pouring up from the hall below. Maria sat on, eyes narrowed and lips tight — then she looked again at the alcove where Patricia sat with her two colleagues. A man had joined them now, a big fellow in evening dress with thick greasy hair and a pale, babyish-looking face. At length he sat down and threw an arm about Pat's shoulders. Maria watched intently, not sure whether to be horrified or revolted at Pat's obvious passiveness in his grip. Far from repelling his advances she actually caught at his free hand and squeezed it affectionately.

Maria pulled out her notebook, wrote down a brief description of the man, then put it away again. Grabbing her umbrella she got to her feet, flashed a look of withering scorn on the waiter as he hurried past with a tray full of coloured water, then she descended the stairs and made her way outside again. She stood drinking in the cool night air, thankful for the relief from the fumes and clotted atmosphere in which she had been sitting.

'So Patricia welcomes the attentions of that — creature,' she reflected as she marched steadily along the pavement. 'She goes out at night to this appalling dive and uses her dancing ability to partner those — apes! And the name of the manager remains a mystery . . . We shall see! According to Selby's *Unearthing the Culprit* it is now necessary for me to have an assistant, preferably one versed in crime if possible . . . Hmm — on the East Side perhaps. I understand that is a likely spot.'

She let herself into the Black residence quietly and went upstairs without a sound. She was rather surprised to discover when she came to relax that she was nearly too tired to undress.

3

Maria opened her eyes to the warm glare of summer sunshine streaming through the windows and the pert face of the maid leaning over her.

'Morning, m'm,' she said, smiling. 'It's half after eight and mistress said you'd like some tea.'

'How right indeed,' Maria murmured, rising up to watch the girl's quick hands over the silver tray. Then she added, 'I don't think I know you, do I?'

'No, m'm. I'm Lucy . . . Cream or lemon, m'm?'

'Cream — always cream.' Maria hugged her faithful bed-jacket more closely. She took the tea with a nod of thanks, then asked a rather surprising question.

'Tell me something, Lucy. Do you keep the library in order?'

'Why yes, I do.'

'Do you ever recall your late master using a typewriter?'

70

'No m'm . . . ' Then after a respectful pause, 'Will that be all?'

Maria nodded. 'For the moment, anyway.'

When she had dressed and gone downstairs she found breakfast out on the terrace. Only Pat herself was present, dressed in canary yellow, sprawled in the hammock chair engrossed in the morning paper. She glanced up as Maria approached.

''Morning, Aunt,' she said perfunctorily, and continued reading.

Maria returned the greeting calmly, frowning. Pat looked tired despite her efforts with cosmetics to hide the fact. And whatever she was reading did not seem to please her much for her mouth was screwed into a red pout of annoyance.

'Hallo there! And how is my favourite Aunt this morning?' Dick came in view, dressed in an easy lounge suit. He smiled good-humouredly as he caught Maria's arm.

'Everything going okay?' he murmured.

'Splendidly, my boy, thank you — You look particularly cheerful this morning?'

'I just feel good, that's all. I put over a new group of girls last night, and they're the tops, believe you me. They always make me feel good, bless their hearts! Oh, that reminds me!' Dick frowned. 'As I was coming home in the early hours, some-where around three o'clock I think it would be, I thought I saw you, Pat, ways ahead of me. I hadn't the car else I'd have overtaken you. You had on that light coat of yours.'

'Me?' Pat glanced up and put the paper down. 'You're crazy! What on earth would I be doing out at that hour?'

'Search me; but it looked like you. Can't be sure, of course.'

'You bet you can't!' And Patricia resumed her reading.

'I could have sworn — ' Dick shrugged. 'Oh, be damned to it! What's your plan for today, Aunt? Like me to show you around?'

'That's nice of you, Richard; but surely you're tired after being up half the night?'

'Oh, I can usually get a little shut-eye from seven to ten in the evening; I skipped it yesterday because you arrived.

Skip it again today if you like. Lots of things I'd like to show you — '

'That's my sphere, Dick,' Janet announced, walking in. 'Good morning, Aunt . . . I claimed Aunt last night,' she added, looking at Dick. 'Remember? When Pat made that sour crack about Grant's Tomb?'

'As a matter of fact,' Maria said, 'I have my own plans — I move slowly at my age — slowly, but surely. So I'm going to look round this big city of yours in my own time and in my own way — first. I wouldn't dream of troubling either of you. You are young, have your own pursuits. Forget all about me.'

Dick and Janet glanced at each other questioningly, then Dick shrugged. 'Okay, Aunt, if that's the way you want it.'

'And if you ever do need a guide we stand at the gate like Horatius,' Alice Black said, coming in and administering kisses all round. 'Never forget that, Maria dear . . . '

'Horatius?' Janet queried. 'I always thought he kept a bridge or something.'

Her mother looked astonished. 'Why,

Jan dear, I do believe you're right! I must look it up — I see you slept well, Maria dear: you are positively glowing. Come along and sit down now — And Walters, not too much sugar in the coffee. And tea for you, Maria, of course? Pat! Whatever are you looking so cross about?'

'Who's looking cross?' Pat came to her chair and glared round defiantly.

'You are, sweet one,' Dick murmured. 'Boyfriend stand you up, or something?'

'Don't be so cheap!'

'All right, skip it. What's in the paper then? Hand it over. Might as well see who's pinching something which doesn't belong to him — '

Pat reached for it but at that identical moment what appeared to be a gust of wind whirled it from her grasp. She made a dive from her chair, and missed it. It went sailing over the terrace and floated out like a dismembering kite towards the distant rooftops.

'That wasn't very bright!' Dick snorted. 'You know I like the morning news.'

'Could I help it if the darn thing blew away?' Pat demanded heatedly. 'You sound as though you think I did it on purpose, or something.'

Walters interposed gravely. 'Shall I obtain another one, Mr. Dick?'

'No, it doesn't matter. I'll grab one as I go out.'

Maria drank her tea without apparently taking strict notice of what was going on, but she did observe that the wind that had whirled away the paper had not been present elsewhere on the terrace. Pat had deliberately thrown the paper away, probably in the hope that nobody else would trouble to get another copy. Maria had noted that it was the New York Times.

'You'll be seeing Mr. Johnson this morning, of course, Maria?' Alice questioned presently.

Maria nodded. 'I have also one or two matters of a professional nature which I would like to attend to. I have recalled one or two things I forgot to mention to Miss Tanby before I left Roseway . . . ' Do any of you happen to possess a typewriter? I'm accustomed to one. So much quicker than handwriting if one has detailed matter to convey.'

There was a momentary silence that Dick was first to break.

'I've one at the office. Not much use, though. Big, heavy thing . . . Say, Pat, you've got a portable, and noiseless, too.'

She shrugged. 'No use, the spring's gone. I keep forgetting to have it fixed — Sorry, Aunt,' she finished, with a brief glance.

'I have a portable also, at the theatre,' Janet volunteered. 'I could have Mary bring it over — She's my personal maid and secretary,' she added, by way of explanation. 'Sort of girl-of-all-work, rolled into one. She could — '

'Never mind,' Maria smiled. 'I'll manage. No need to go to all that trouble.'

'Seems to me we'd better buy in a brace of typewriters,' Dick grinned.

'Absurd!' Maria reproved — then she stiffened suddenly at a curt command from a corner of the terrace.

'Wash your necks! Quick! The lot of you!'

'I beg your pardon — ?' Then Maria

relaxed as she beheld a parrot turning somersaults in his glittering cage.

'Meet Cresty,' Janet smiled. 'He was put to bed when you came yesterday, Aunt, in case he went off in one of his screeching fits. He always does when strangers are about.'

'Hio! You're a dozy lot!'

'Hey there, Cresty, lay off!' Dick shouted. 'Don't you know your favourite Aunt is present?' He stopped and frowned over a problem. 'Say, Pat, did you teach him that 'Wash your neck!' line? Sounds like one of your weak-moment specialities.'

'Why should I bother to teach him anything? I imagine he picks up quite enough as it is.'

'Dirty work!' Cresty screamed, feathers bristling. 'I saw you do it! I saw you do it!'

The family exchanged quick glances. Then Pat wheeled round.

'Cresty, be quiet! Stop making that racket, can't you?'

'Oi! What's it to you? Good old Walters! Walters wants a shave!'

'Now you know, Walters,' Dick observed

dryly. 'Better go and find a razor!'

Janet gave a chuckle. 'Before long Cresty will start to sing my songs. He picks them up amazingly. I practice in the room next to the lounge and he's quite good on the top C. A bit strident but all right if your ears are accustomed to factory sirens. Cresty, sing! Come on, sing for momma.'

The result was a wince-making screech.

'Shall I remove the bird, madam?' Walters asked with frozen calm, eyeing Alice.

'No, no, he's most entertaining!' Maria exclaimed. 'He's doing no harm, and at least he's sociable,' she added grimly, glancing at Pat. But Pat did not seem to notice the statement. Rather indeed, she seemed keyed up to a point of tension, as though wondering what the bird was going to say next.

Then, with true ornithological stubbornness, Cresty became silent . . . The meal over, Pat made her excuses and departed hastily. Ten minutes afterwards Maria saw her leaving the house. From the clear vantage point of the terrace she watched her board an uptown 'bus from the distant stopping point at the street junction.

'Looks like Pat's got the jumps these days,' Dick commented, watching as the 'bus started off again. 'Queer,' he went on, puzzling. 'That was a Number Nine — goes out to East Side. I wonder what the heck Pat can want in that direction?'

Maria waited for a possible answer to the mystery; but there was none forthcoming.

'Well, Aunt, if you're sure there is nothing I can do for you I'll hop up to town myself . . . '

'Don't worry about me, Richard. Anyway, I have to stay in to see Mr. Johnson.'

Maria watched him stride off, then she returned to her contemplation of the roof-tops. Half-detachedly she listened to the clear notes of Janet's voice floating out on to the terrace as she practiced in the room next to the lounge. It was a pleasant refrain, clear and sweet, with none of the vocal acrobatics usually demanded of a soprano.

'East Side ... ' Maria murmured, fingering her watch-chain. 'Night in a dance hall; typewriter with a broken spring — Oh, Walters!'

He came out of the lounge. 'Madam?'

Maria studied his unsteady eyes for a moment, then she said: 'Miss Patricia has a typewriter in her room, one with a broken spring: you heard her mention it during breakfast. I'd rather like to see the machine. I am — er — rather expert with springs and I may be able to repair it. I have letters to attend to.'

'I'll see you have it immediately, madam.'

Alice, sunning herself in a corner, looked up in surprise. 'Maria, dear, just where do your talents leave off?' she asked, smiling. 'I begin to think that I should have become a Headmistress in order to obtain a knowledge of everything.'

'Not everything, Alice. It would be so easy if one knew everything.'

'Yes, I suppose it would,' Alice admitted, in a queer voice. Then she went on reading her novel.

Presently Walters silently returned and laid the blue-leather-covered machine on the wicker table, surveying it dubiously.

'I am afraid it is the mainspring, madam,' he said, tapping the unresponsive space bar. 'I remember Miss Patricia asked me if I knew anything about typewriters a few weeks ago — '

'And you don't?' Maria questioned, looking the machine over.

'Unfortunately not, Madam . . . Perhaps I had better have it sent to the repairers?' He cocked his wavering eyes on Alice.

'You might as well . . . No!' Alice seemed to change her mind suddenly. 'No, you'd better not. It's Pat's responsibility. The child must learn to shoulder her own troubles.'

Maria sighed, her study at an end. 'Take it back, Walters. Even my little tricks with typewriters are of no use this time. The mainspring has obviously snapped — Oh, Walters!' He turned at the lounge door. 'I'd like a copy of the New York Times.'

'Certainly, madam . . . ' He paced out

gravely with the machine in his hands.

'Silly of Pat to let the wind blow the other copy away,' Alice reflected, tossing her novel aside. 'You should have let Walters get you a paper when he asked Dick — They may all be sold by now.'

'There is always the public library,' Maria observed calmly.

Alice sighed. 'I don't like newspapers, Maria dear. I always think they are so full of crime and murders, don't you? There are such an awful lot of people in the world doing things they shouldn't. Aren't there?'

'How true indeed . . . ' Maria strolled back to the terrace rail. A thought was drumming through her mind. The spring she had found in the library had not been from Pat's typewriter anyway: that was definitely established.

'Dick's machine? Janet's portable?' She juggled each thought; then glanced up and smiled as Janet herself came into view and leaned against the stonework, sunning herself.

'You have a lovely voice, Janet,' Maria remarked.

'I'm glad you like it. I think it's so hard to tell what a voice is really like when you're the owner of it. I hear it played back on records, of course, and it sounds quite ordinary to me. I practice most mornings between engagements — sort of oiling up. I start again tomorrow night for a two weeks' run at the Criterion. Then — ' Janet broke off, looking round. 'Hallo! Where's Pat gone?'

'She took a 'bus to East Side,' Maria answered quietly.

'East Side!' Janet looked puzzled. 'That's queer! And why the 'bus, I wonder? She's got a new sports car — '

'Which is not perhaps very appropriate for the East Side,' Maria reflected. 'The East Side, as I understand it, is pretty similar to our London East End. High-class material not very welcome.'

'Yes, yes, you're right . . . ' Janet looked up again. 'Yes, Walters?'

He looked at Maria. 'The newspaper, madam.'

'Oh, thank you, Walters . . . ' She took it, opened it out. Janet lay back on the stonework of the rail and surveyed the front page casually.

'The set-up doesn't alter much, does it?' she sighed. 'A man falls down a well; a girl shot dead; a convict escapes from a prison farm and is still on the run — Well, I've a musical score to study. I'll leave you to your baser passions, Aunt.'

Maria nodded, her attention fixed on the newspaper. Janet's quick eyes had encompassed the main details on the front page — and it was an identical copy of the page Pat had been so earnestly reading before she had lost the paper through deliberate 'mischance.' Of all the items presented the only one with any hope of being applicable was the reference to a convict's escape from a prison farm.

Maria read carefully, skipping the main details —

' . . . and the police are now confident that they have a definite clue as to the whereabouts of Arthur Salter, the convict who escaped his guards while on road duty near Jamestown, New York, on the afternoon of June 4, and who has since been at large. This man, serving sentence for fraud, eluded his warders by a clever trick and made a clean getaway, obviously aided by somebody waiting for him on the State highway a mile away, with a car. Despite the dragnet Salter slipped through. But it is now passably certain that the circle is closing in . . . '

Maria lowered the paper thoughtfully. 'Alice, what was the exact date on which Ralph committed suicide?'

'June the fourth. How well I remember — ! But why do you ask?'

'I just wondered, that's all — But there's something else, too.' Maria strolled over and sat beside Alice in the swinging hammock chair. 'Last night Patricia said she had no love for her father because he had balked her dearest wishes. Later on Janet said that that dearest wish was Patricia's desire to marry a man who later turned out to be a thief. Just what was the charge against him?'

'Well, it's a bit involved,' Alice said, thinking. 'The young man — I met him once and rather liked him — was employed by Onzi's Financial Trust. He was a clerk or a secretary, or something — Anyway, it was found that he had embezzled and defrauded company funds for his own uses. His sentence was eight years ... Poor Pat! She was nearly prostrate when the news came out.'

'He was sent to prison then before Ralph died?'

'Of course. But — ' Alice looked surprised. 'What are you getting at?'

'Just this ... And if nobody else in the family notices it the better perhaps.'

Maria handed the newspaper over and Alice's hand went to her lips in sudden horror as she read the indicated column.

'Good — good heavens, Maria, this is he! Arthur Salter!'

'I imagined as much,' Maria said grimly. 'The same man Patricia wanted to marry.'

'Yes — yes! But she never told us! We never knew he had escaped. Oh, I don't begin to understand this — '

'But I think I do,' Maria interrupted. 'Doesn't it occur to you that this young man escaped on the very day during the evening of which Ralph died?'

'Yes, I can see that, but — If anybody knew of the breakaway from the farm it would be Pat, and she never mentioned anything.'

'Does that surprise you?' Maria asked. 'Think back! Patricia was, by her own admission, out with friends all through the evening during which Ralph met his death. Did Patricia ever say what friends?'

'Certainly she did! In fact the police questioned her about it after Ralph's death; but several of her friends all verified that she had been with them. They spent the evening touring the high spots in her new sports car.'

'There is an almost Masonic clanship between schoolgirls, Alice, and it does not end just because schooldays are over. Girls who were pals at school will support each other in trouble in the years that follow. I happen to know that . . . I do believe it is quite likely that these young ladies might have been asked by Patricia to say that she had been with them whereas she had really been busy elsewhere.'

'For instance?' Alice's voice was surprisingly acid.

'Obviously, Arthur Salter escaped so easily because a car was waiting for him. Patricia was an intimate friend. Her car was new — and being a sports car, very fast. During the late afternoon and evening of June fourth she was not in the company of friends but was helping the man she loves to escape, evidently knowing of his plan beforehand by some means or other. I do not doubt that he would find ways and means to get his plans to the outside world, possibly even through his lawyer.'

'Really, Maria, this is ridiculous!' Alice exclaimed. 'Pat helping young Salter to escape — ! She'd never dare! And supposing for a moment that she did how do you imagine she cheated the police dragnet that was immediately thrown out?'

'I don't know,' Maria confessed. 'But one day I may find out. It is inevitable that the police must know of her connection with Salter prior to his imprisonment, and even if they have not got enough proof to question her openly on the matter they must at least have her under observation. That seems logical enough to me.'

Alice got up slowly. 'Maria, I am just beginning to wonder if Pat was not right yesterday when she as good as accused you of poking your nose into our affairs. To be frank, I don't like these dark suggestions about my own children! Pat may be headstrong and outspoken, but at heart she is a good girl. She would never stoop to helping young Salter. After all he was proven a criminal.'

'Alice, a girl in love — and particularly a girl with Patricia's defiant spirit — will risk a great deal. I believe Patricia has taken that risk and so far it has come off — But she's playing a dangerous game. Ultimately the law is bound to catch up with her and then . . . Well!'

Alice began to pace the terrace worriedly. 'There are absolutely no grounds for all this, Maria. You are just building up a case against Pat to satisfy yourself.'

'Then why has she never mentioned

that he had escaped? Why did she throw the paper away this morning? I'll tell you why — because she knows where he is and didn't want to be questioned. And if she knows where he is you can take it for granted she has been helping him all along. And the police are getting on the track: the paper proves it.'

'The wind blew that paper away!' Alice said doggedly.

'It did not,' Maria retorted. 'There was no wind then, and there is none now. Even if it was the wind, why should a wealthy girl like Patricia, possessing her own car and moving in a high social orbit, suddenly decide to take an East Side 'bus after reading that newspaper announcement?'

Alice shrugged, still paced up and down.

'Again, Why does she so resent my being here?' Maria went on implacably. 'Because she is afraid I will find out about her connections with Salter. She has not told you anything but she knows that I am the — shall we say, inquisitive sort?'

Alice's face was genuinely troubled. 'On my word, Maria, I had no suspicion that Pat was mixed up in anything like this. Promise me, whatever happens, that you won't expose her to the authorities! I have had quite as much worry as I can stand already.'

'I imagine, Alice, that anything I may have found out will be well forestalled by the police . . . However, I am not heartless. If I think you should know of anything concerning Patricia, which may come up in the future, I'll tell you, of course.'

'Thank you, Maria — thank you. You've taken a great deal off my mind. When Pat comes home again I will have the whole thing out with her.'

'That wouldn't be very wise, Alice. If you have it out with her she is the kind of girl to blurt out the whole story. Inevitably the rest of the family will get to know of it — Janet, Richard, even the staff. In no time it would reach the ears of the police and then Patricia's number would be definitely up. No!' Maria shook her head firmly. 'Your safest course lies in keeping quiet and seeing which way the cat jumps. At least until there is absolute proof by her own admission — freely given.'

'Yes . . . I suppose you're right,' Alice admitted slowly. 'I'll keep quiet for the time being, but I do hope to goodness everything turns out for the best.'

Two hours later Walters announced the arrival of the lawyer. Maria found him in the library — a tall, thin man with crisp brown hair, a long horse-like face, and pince-nez. His attire was immaculate, his manner infinitely precise. When he spoke it was with a certain didactic certainty that immediately betrayed his profession.

The preliminaries of introduction over, he said, 'I'm sorry, Miss Black, that you should have to be asked to make such a long journey across the Atlantic Ocean, but the law is such an exacting business that — '

'I can assure you, Mr. Johnson, that I do not regret my trip. If you are ready for the business on hand then so am I!'

'Quite! Quite!' He eyed Maria quickly through shining glasses then zipped open a brief case. After much fluttering among blue and green documents he laid down three on the table, traced along dotted lines with an immaculate finger.

'If you would be so good as to sign . . . ?'

Maria complied, her lips compressed. The pedantry of the law was something that always irritated her, despite her own inflexible administration of it at Roseway.

Johnson nodded in satisfaction when it was over, then made a pronouncement.

'I'm afraid I shall have to ask you for some further form of identification, Miss Black. The will demands it.'

'Identification!' Maria stared in surprise. 'My dear sir, is it not sufficient that I am here?'

'Not entirely, I'm afraid. Please do not misunderstand me. A clause in the will insists that you identify yourself to me beyond all possible shadow of doubt before I can proceed further. Your late brother stipulated that clause because you were so far away from him. He wanted to be certain that you alone and not an impostor were contacted. After all, an interval of years changes us all. An impostor might have come in your place.'

Maria sighed. 'An extraordinary conception, but I see your point. Pardon me while I get my bag. My passport should convince you.'

'Splendid!'

She left the library, crossed into the hall, and was just in time to see the returned Patricia heading for the staircase. As she went she crumpled something in her hand, finally threw it into the ornamental basket by the bureau in the hall alcove. Without looking to either side of her she went straight up the stairs and vanished along the upper corridor.

Maria hesitated and looked round. Then she detoured to the paper basket and lifted out the paper strip Pat had thrown away. It was a 'bus ticket, registered from 2 to 5 on Route A-12, whatever that might signify. Maria put it carefully in her pocket.

She got her passport and returned downstairs to the library, and gave it to Johnson. He examined it and finally nodded complacently.

'Excellent, Miss Black. That being settled, it is my duty to inform you that

94

your late brother left you the sum of twenty thousand dollars.'

Maria looked at him bleakly.

'But,' Johnson went on, 'there are further providing clauses . . . ' He fished in his bag again and handed over a heavily-sealed envelope. 'This letter I was instructed to give to you upon your proving your identity. You are to read it to yourself, but in my presence.'

Maria eyed the superscription in her brother's firm hand —

To my dear Sister Maria, to be read in the event of my death in circumstances other than natural.

She tore the flap and read the letter slowly, her brows lowering.

My dear Maria,
Should I die of natural causes this letter will be destroyed by my lawyer, Stephen Johnson, but should I die from any other cause it is to be handed to you . . . You, Maria, are tied closer to me by relationship than anybody

else. We have blood ties that cannot be equalled even by my wife and children.

I write this to you because I know you to be a woman of infinite resource — and because I have reason to believe that certain enemies may at any time try to break my control by liquidating me. Inevitably my journey to commercial domination has forced me to be ruthless, and there are times when I feel that avengers are waiting to strike me down. I expect it. I have been hard, cruel — but it has been necessary to achieve my end.

For various reasons I am not passing on this expectation of violent death to my wife and family. I feel they would not fully sympathize with me. I have felt convinced for some time now that my breaking of lesser factions in order to more firmly entrench myself has not been entirely to their liking. You, however, knowing nothing of my methods and bearing in mind only our relationship, will perhaps see things differently.

If I should die anything other than a

natural death — for I have no intention of taking my own life — I want you, with your single-mindedness and passion for detail to use every means in your power to discover my assassin, should he or she not be apprehended by the law. By this means any stigma on the family, resulting from death on my part by other than natural causes, may be removed. That depends entirely on you. And I warn you, if anybody does plan my demise they will work with great skill, may quite possibly elude discovery. Hence my request to you.

I have instructed my lawyer to release the sum of $20,000 to you for expenses that you might incur in tracking down my potential murderer. Should you arrive at the solution and unmask my murderer, together with a complete exposition of the method used to kill me, you are then to receive a bequest of $500,000. Johnson will be the sole judge of whether you have qualified or not. You may trust him implicitly.

With sincere remembrances,
Ralph.

Maria folded the letter slowly and laid it on the desk. She looked up finally to see Johnson regarding her.

'I suppose, Mr. Johnson, you know what is in this letter?'

He nodded. 'And I think I should tell you, Miss Black, that right up to the last moment your brother maintained his sanity. He was not depressed. Whatever business worries he had were merely in the normal course of handling an immense concern. The police chose to believe that he had enough troubles to make his suicide seem logical . . . but of course, knowing as I did the contents of this letter, I could not help but suspect that it was — murder. I intimated that fact to the family also — vaguely.'

'Which may be why Richard wrote me saying he believed his father was murdered,' Maria said slowly.

'I was not aware he did that. No doubt my hints prompted it. Of course, there was nothing I could say or do. I could not bring my suspicions to the notice of the police without revealing a copy of this letter, and in any case I was completely bound to keep it unmentioned until you came. Your brother arranged it very cleverly in order that a posthumous investigation could be conducted, not by the police but by one he knew he could trust implicitly to arrive at the right solution — yourself, of course. He seemed to think very highly of your — shall I say, investigative power?'

Maria smiled faintly. 'He knew that my one hobby in life is criminology. And in his usual ironical way he evidently decided to put my hobby to the test by withholding my bequest unless a solution to his mysterious death be found. I take it that had he died naturally I would have received my bequest in the ordinary way?'

'Certainly. As it is, however, I am simply under orders. The rest of the family imagine your inheritance is a mere twenty thousand dollars, for of course they know nothing of this letter. Your brother did that so that as near as possible he could keep those nearest to him out of all chance of suspicion or scandal . . . Now you see why I had to have positive identification, why I had to see you personally.'

'Yes, yes, of course.' Maria aroused herself from thought. 'Pay the twenty thousand dollars into a bank of your own selection and send the details on to me here. I shall carry out my brother's wishes if it takes every penny he provided and my own money as well . . . Now I know for the first time that it was murder! Marvellously done! Cunningly executed.'

'Yes, I am afraid that is true,' Johnson sighed. 'Not one in a million would suspect it was murder. Not a single clue to go on, either.'

'It depends what constitutes a clue,' Maria replied. 'And incidentally, I believe you can give me a little help. Do you happen to know where I can get in touch with a man named V. L. Onzi? He is some kind of financier, I believe.'

'The Onzi Financial Trust?' Johnson pursed his lips. 'I should imagine the best place would be at their headquarters on Fifty-Sixth Street. Your brother had many dealings with that firm.'

'So I understand. Do you know anything of them? Their reputation?'

Johnson smiled grimly. 'I'm afraid I know little to be said of them which is favourable. More than once I warned your brother to take care how he dealt with them — but he disregarded my advice.'

Johnson turned to his brief case again, handed over a copy of the will, and collected his papers. Then he zipped the case shut.

'I think that's all for now, Miss Black. I'll get into touch with you again — and if there is anything I can do to help you in your efforts don't hesitate to call on me.'

Maria nodded as she shook hands, and bowed him out majestically. Then she gathered up Ralph's letter, the copy will, and various papers, and hurried up to her room. Locking the door she settled down to make her usual black book entries. Thoughtfully she read what she had already underscored:

'*Patricia, disguised by a black wig, has taken a position as professional dancing partner in Maxie's Dance Hall, a cheap dive in the city. She seems to welcome the attentions of a black-haired, rather sensual-looking person whose name I would* like to know. Have tried to get the name of the dance hall's manager but the waiter withheld it from me. But I shall find it — possibly with the aid of an assistant, for which I feel an increasing need.

'In the library I have found a spring, manifestly from a typewriter. I see no importance attached to it at the moment; but it is perhaps significant that one of the spring loops exactly fits one of the nails supporting two guns in the library. I shall endeavor to discover from which machine the spring came.

'It seems clear that Alice, Janet, Patricia, and Richard all resented Ralph's domination over them.'

Taking out her pen Maria added further notes:

'Now I know it was murder! It is definitely proven! I shall leave no stone unturned to unearth Ralph's murderer. Lawyer Johnson seems trustworthy enough.

'Very significant facts have also come to light in regard to Patricia. She has, I believe, helped her lover, one Arthur

Salter, to escape from imprisonment. Alice's reaction to this puzzles me. Her manner has changed amazingly since I pointed out certain facts. It is as though she fears some hitch in a plan, of which I am at present in total ignorance.

'Patricia has freely admitted a broken spring on her typewriter, so freely it makes me wonder. But it is a mainspring. Janet and Richard also own typewriters. I shall look further.

'Shall try to contact this Onzi person and unravel the dance hall mystery.

'N.B. Walters' eyes are still unsteady. I really begin to think it must be nervous affliction. Time is: 12.40 p.m.'

Maria put the book away, reread her brother's letter, then locked it away with the book. As an afterthought she added the spring she had kept in her locket . . . Then she studied Pat's discarded 'bus ticket. Finally she made up her mind, put the ticket carefully away in her pocket and tidied herself up for lunch.

Her afternoon plans were mature.

4

To Maria lunch was a rather strained affair. She parried Alice's quite natural questions concerning Johnson, while Alice herself was dearly itching to question the silent Patricia concerning her East Side 'bus exploit — but she refrained when she saw the warning light in Maria's eyes. Janet seemed the most puzzled of the group, though maintaining her usual air of composure.

Maria was glad when the meal was over and she could excuse herself on the grounds of an intended stroll through the city.

'Expect me when you see me, Alice,' were her parting words — then off she went, attired in her mannish costume and severest hat, with sunshade to match.

Her first call was at the Onzi Financial Trust — but she drew a complete blank. The president was out of town: no idea when he would be back . . . Temporarily defeated, Maria made her next stop at the Bureau of Statistics. Some searching and paying of fees finally obtained for her the marriage records of the past three months. She settled down to a quiet study, notebook beside her.

There were innumerable Arthur Salter and Patricia Blacks — but in one case there was a Patricia Black married to an 'Archer Slater, Financial Executive,' on April 29th.

Maria studied again, then sat back to think. 'Slater — Salter. Archer — Arthur. Just enough difference to make it sound like another person. Registry office marriage. Hmm, my guess seems to have been right. Patricia risked all the things she did because Salter is her husband. They married in opposition to Ralph's wishes . . . The different name explains why so far the police have not linked up Patricia with the escaped Salter . . . Most interesting! This, I think, is what is known as 'playing a hunch.' And the time has now come for an assistant. I must find this Salter person somehow.'

She returned the records, then inquired

of the clerk the quickest route to the centre of East Side. He gave her four different alternatives from which she chose the one recorded on Patricia's bus ticket. A few minutes later she was boarding a 'bus. The driver eyed her grimly as she handed up Patricia's ticket.

'No good to me, lady!'

'I merely want you to advise me when we reach the point marked on this ticket.'

'Eh? Oh, okay. I get it . . . '

He handed Maria her ticket. She returned Pat's ticket to her bag and then resumed her survey of the outer world. The 'bus 'peregrinations' rather confused her sense of direction since she was accustomed to keeping to the left side of the street instead of the right . . . Then she noticed that the city buildings were beginning to give place to lower built edifices, narrower streets, gaunter façades indicating the vast tenement houses of the lower quarters of the city. Elevateds stretched their clangour past infinities of windows; innumerable men and women were plying their wares in open markets — Then the driver gave a shout.

'Your stop, lady!'

Maria alighted, and found herself left on the pavement in the beating afternoon sunshine. Here indeed was a different world. It seemed to breathe the fetid atmosphere of struggle, the battle of men and women against inexorable squalour . . .

Maria was at something of a loss. The more she looked round on the drab buildings and rearing backdrops of factories the more utterly isolated she felt and the less she admired Patricia's choice of a destination. She stood thinking, until her eyes chanced to catch the sign ICE CREAM SODAS over a distant doorway across the road. She hurried across to it immediately, peered uncertainly through grimy glass doors, then slipped into a semi-underground place where the electric lights blazed in pallid contrast to the glare of sun outside.

The bell of the door still clanging over her head, Maria looked first at a white counter, then at partitions each shielding a table, and finally towards a row of swivel stools lined up before the counter. Only two people were present — a girl of about eight playing with a toy pistol, and a triple-chinned man leaning his flabby arms on the counter. He was enormously fat, curly-black-haired, and perspiring visibly. He shifted his dark eyes from an absent survey of the opposite wall as Maria began to advance.

'Would it be possible to have a cup of tea here, my man?'

'Sure!' He swung aside to a hissing cistern and busied himself with the crockery. The girl with the gun surveyed Maria, made an obviously wry face, then went on with her job of taking point-blank aim at a tattered rag doll. There was a grim implication behind it that filled Maria with a rather vague horror. With an effort she turned back to the counter.

'Very quiet here this afternoon, my man,' she commented.

'Yeah!'

'Trade usually as bad as this?'

'Nope!'

Maria swallowed some tea, then went on, 'I don't suppose you are particular about trade to bring you in money? I'm willing to pay you fifty dollars if you can give me some information . . . '

Opening her bag Maria tossed bills on the counter. 'There it is, my man . . . Now you can perhaps give me the information I'm seeking. I'm looking for a place to find a reliable, tough type of man with preferably a knowledge of the — er — underworld and its denizens.'

'No kiddin'!' A fat hand thrust the notes out of sight under a white apron. 'Ex-con?' he asked abruptly.

'A former convict? Yes, that would do admirably.'

'Oke. Lucy! Fetch Pulp. Quick!'

'O.K., pop . . . ' The child stopped playing, turned and skipped to the door, vanished outside.

'Cute!' the big fellow said, with an admiring wag of his dark head.

'Your daughter, I presume?' Maria asked.

'Sixth!'

'Amazing . . . Tell me, do you mean to say you trust her in safety among questionable characters? Among the type of men I am looking for?'

'Sure!'

Maria finished her tea. 'By 'Pulp,' do I understand you mean a person? That it is a nickname?'

'You betcha!'

Maria gave it up. She paid her bill and sat waiting. At last the bell jangled and the child came scampering back. Behind her loomed an individual in ill-fitting checks, a grey shirt with an open neck, and a green pork-pie hat of the soft variety pushed up on his forehead. His hair, what Maria could see of it, was flaming red, shading away with scarcely any change of colour into his skin. In a broad sense he was not bad-looking — heavy-jawed, strong-mouthed, short-nosed, with the keenest sapphire-blue eyes. Probably, Maria decided, he was a man of tremendous physical strength at the expense of the mental. Yet his forehead . . . Not at all bad.

'You sent for me, Three-Shot?' he demanded, coming up to the counter with easy strides. He wore enormous tan walking-shoes, Maria noticed.

'No. Her!'

'Huh?' The thug turned and faced Maria's calm, steady scrutiny. 'Say, lady, what is this? What in heck would your sort be wantin' with me, anyway? Look at you! Class written all over you or I don't know the upper five.'

'What you know in that direction does not concern me, my man,' Maria replied calmly. 'I sent for you even as — er — Three-Shot said.' She coughed primly. 'I am given to understand that you are a rough, reliable man conversant with the underworld and its denizens.'

'Yeah?' His sapphire-blue eyes narrowed for a moment. 'Okay, you got it straight. I'm Pulp Martin, see, because I never socked a guy's jaw but what I pulped it. Feel them muscles!' he invited proudly, and crooked his huge arm.

Maria eyed him icily. 'I did not summon you here for the doubtful pleasure of testing your biceps, Mr. Martin.'

'You're English, ain't you? A furriner! Not that I holds it against you, mind. I always protects the weaker sex ... ' Pulp's eyes went up and down Maria's

111

mannish costume doubtfully. Then he scratched his head. 'You were saying something about a knowledge of the underworld? You came to the right guy, lady. Three times in and out of the pen — that's me. Once for breaking a guy's head; once for friskin' a trifle from a jeweller's; and once for runnin' a car over a cliff with a guy in it. But they couldn't prove nothin', see, so I got off light. Anyway, that feller wanted bumpin' off.'

'Seth Munro?' the fat one reflected.

'Yeah,' Pulp acknowledged. 'But look here, lady, you was sayin' — ?'

'I fancy you have been doing all the talking, my friend!' Maria compressed her lips, then asked briefly, 'You drink?'

'Nothing that Three Shot sells. I like a kick in my stuff — something to rip your boots off.'

'Extraordinary!' Maria extracted another bill from her bag. 'Here, take this and procure for yourself a screwball — or high-ball, or whatever it is, later on. There will be a lot more dollars for you if you help me and do exactly as I say. All providing you can first give me the information I want — or at least obtain it for me.'

'This on the level? You offerin' me a job?'

'Definitely!' Maria studied him thoughtfully. 'To be frank, Mr. Martin, I like you quite well despite an apparent lack of education. That, however, may prove all to the good. And I may as well warn you now that any attempt to steal from me or to injure me personally will put you in a pretty dangerous position.'

'You're a cop?' Pulp hazarded, pocketing the money.

'No . . . ' Maria gave a grim smile, then she said casually, 'Did you ever hear of — 'Black Maria'?'

'Let me see — Maisie the Wren, Muscle-bound Maggie, Adirondack Alice — No, you've got me!'

'Obviously you have never been in England,' Maria observed gravely. 'Otherwise you would know that 'Black Maria' means the police are somewhere near — Get it?' she asked keenly.

A light dawned in Pulp's eyes. 'Yeah, sure I get it. The police was after you and you took a powder. You sort of got your sugar in a big way over in England. Okay, Black Maria, your secret's safe with me. Now we're acquainted what sort of gravy is it you want?'

'Gravy?' Maria repeated, mystified.

He gestured impatiently. 'Dope! Low-down! Whadda you want to know?'

'Oh, I see! Well, to begin with, I want to know where an escaped convict would probably hide himself if he wanted to be reasonably sure of escaping detection. It will probably be a place where a girl, probably his wife, can reach him without much trouble.'

'Gosh, lady, you don't want much for your dough, do you? Where would a con on the run hide? Might be anywhere from the docks to the middle of the city, and New York City ain't a car park, you know.'

'It is around here somewhere,' Maria insisted. 'Somewhere within walking distance of that 'bus stop across the street.'

'Got things all narrowed down, eh?' Pulp said admiringly, and pondered. 'Seems to me there is only one con on the run at present. He broke a prison farm a while back — Arthur Salter.'

'That's the man!' Maria cried eagerly.

'I figured it must be: can't be anybody else . . . But I don't know where he is. He's not in the regular line of boys who do a stretch and then come back to the family circle. I haven't sort of bothered about him — You're sure he's around here some place?'

'I have every reason to think so, yes.'

'An' supposin' I find him? What do you do — fetch the police? I'm giving it to you straight, lady, I won't have no truck with no cops.'

'I have already told you I am Black Maria,' Maria snapped. 'You will have full protection, I promise you. I have no intention of getting mixed up with the police, either. I just want to know where the man is.'

'Get a raw deal from him?' Pulp sympathized.

'Not exactly that, but — None of your business!' Maria broke off curtly. 'Can you help me, or can't you? That's the issue.'

'Yeah, I figure I can help you. Only places I can think of right now are Bald

Charley's and Clip Wilson's. If he isn't there I've got boys who'll find him, don't you fret. And say, who's the dame? His wife, you say? What's she like?'

'That,' Maria answered calmly, 'does not signify . . . How long will it take you to get some information?'

'I'll start on a snoop right now. By eight tonight I ought to have some dope for you. I'll meet you here again then. Okay?'

Maria nodded. Then remembering the money she had handed over and having visions of the complete disappearance of Pulp Martin she added, 'And if you bring genuine information you'll get twice what I gave you. The more you do the more you get.'

'It's a deal!' Pulp said, beaming all over his rugged face. 'Eight it is!'

He left the café eagerly and slammed the door. Maria sat thinking until Three-Shot broke her meditations.

'More tea?'

'No — thank you.' She got off the stool, straightened her costume and collected bag and sunshade. 'I shall return here at eight tonight, Mr. Three-Shot — '

'Aw, the name's Dolanki!' protested the youngster. Then she pouted, 'Betcha don't know why they all calls pop 'Three-Shot'?'

'I imagine,' Maria hazarded, 'it has something to do with revolvers.'

'Revolvers nothin'! It's 'cos he never goes more 'n three words in one mouth of wind.'

'Right!' her father beamed.

Maria turned to the door, shaking her head perplexedly. 'Amazing! Positively amazing!'

★ ★ ★

With four hours to kill, Maria occupied part of the time wandering in circumscribed limits through the insalubrious neighbourhood . . . From the hot main streets with their traffic and busy human beings she drifted through an area that bristled gasometers and elevated railways. Unexpectedly she came upon a park. Gratefully she sought out a seat and relaxed upon it in relief, her eyes travelling to the sombre, brooding masses

117

of buildings thrusting up from the city proper into the evening sky.

At length she turned her gaze to the children playing on the distant grass; the young men and women lying out under the trees or else strolling along arm-in-arm; the elderly folk like herself reclining on the seats . . . Then her casual eye picked up the figure of a girl on a young man's arm that struck an instant answering chord.

There was something about the erectness of the woman, something about the showgirl carriage —

Maria's eyes narrowed on to the pair approaching slowly along the pathway. So far the girl had been occupied in talking to her companion. He had riotous brown hair, a sweep of forehead, wore shoddy grey flannels. Obviously not a man of money — nor yet for that matter a man of dubious motives. Maria soon dispensed with him anyway: it was the girl claiming her attention. The walk was unmistakable — but the shabby tweeds? The cheap shoes and hat? The heavy, horn-rimmed glasses? These were all unexpected — but the walk, and the voice as she came nearer —

Maria rose and said calmly, 'Good evening, Janet.'

The two stopped dead, glanced sharply at each other. 'Isn't — isn't there some mistake — ?' the girl began.

'No mistake, Janet. Glasses and cheap clothes may blind some people — but the voice and the carriage remain. I'm afraid I'd know you anywhere, my dear.'

Janet smiled resignedly. 'All right, Aunt, you win . . . This is Peter Wade, a friend of mine. Meet my aunt, Miss Black . . . '

'Glad to know you, Miss Black.' He smiled and shook hands. He had eager, intelligent blue eyes but a rather rueful expression.

Maria looked at them both in turn, saw Janet's eyes looked troubled behind the plain-lensed glasses. Then she motioned back to the seat.

'Sit down, both of you. I'd like a word with you . . . ' Then as they complied Maria went on pensively, 'I am really just beginning to wonder why the entire Black family does not move to the East Side and have done with it! First Patricia heads in this direction: now I find you here with this young man. Just why did you try to make out you were somebody else a moment ago?'

Janet hesitated, then: 'I'd rather not be recognized, that's all. And I do not believe I would be by anybody outside the family. I don't want to be seen by anybody in this part of the city. If I were seen it might hurt me professionally.'

'But surely you can do as you like with your private life?'

'Not entirely . . . You see, it's because of Peter here,' Janet finished earnestly. 'Tell her, Peter.'

'At one time I was a pretty big composer,' he explained, as Maria eyed him. 'Just at present I've fallen on hard times. Jan and I were in love when I was up at the top, and she is still in love with me even though I'm down at the bottom. But — and here is the point — if she were seen about with me it might spoil things for her with Montagu: that is her manager, controller, and general man-of-work. He is rather 'that way' about her, and as long as he believes she has no outside ties he gives her all the breaks. But if he once found out that she was engaged to me he's the kind of man to go all out to break her — and he could do it. Even yet Jan is not an absolute top-liner: one slip-up now and the whole lot would come down . . . So, determined to stay beside me when she can she adopts this disguise to prevent any chance of tittle-tattle back to Montagu. Right now I'm busy on a new musical revue, which if it hits anything big will put Jan right in the front rank and to hell with Montagu . . . That is the layout.'

'And you are living in this district, Mr. Wade?'

'I guess I have to,' he sighed.

'You won't tell anybody, Aunt?' Janet questioned urgently. 'That was why I pretended to be a stranger — '

'Because you don't trust me?' Maria enquired dryly. 'You have my assurance that this will go no further. I would not interfere with your career for the world — or try and upset your love affair. Does anyone else know of this — intrigue?'

'Only my maid Mary and she is absolutely reliable.'

'And the only other one is dead,' Peter Wade said grimly.

'He means that only father knew about it,' Janet explained. 'I know dad didn't approve, but he never betrayed our secret.'

'Did you ever meet him, Mr. Wade?' Maria questioned.

'Once or twice,' he shrugged. 'I guess one shouldn't speak evil of the dead, but if ever there was a man of iron, a man who had no soul and a dollar sign for a heart, it was Ralph Black. He was the most ambitious, ruthless man I ever met.'

'Peter didn't get to know him, you see,' Janet put in hastily.

'I'm glad I didn't!' he retorted. 'It has always been a puzzle to me how such a tyrant could ever have had so fine a daughter — But please forgive me, Miss Black,' he went on, with a little smile of apology. 'I'm forgetting he was your brother.'

'I am already aware of his ruthlessness,' Maria said gravely.

An awkward silence fell, then Janet

rose. 'Well, we might as well continue our stroll round. It was too hot tonight to work on Peter's new musical so we decided to walk around instead. Shan't get many more chances from now on. I start on a new recital tomorrow . . . Look after yourself, Aunt.'

'I think I can do that,' she replied, and shook hands with the young man again.

He turned and took Janet's arm. Maria watched them stroll slowly away down the pathway. Her cold blue eyes narrowed.

'Ralph,' she said slowly, 'if you are anywhere around me at this moment you might as well know that I think you have got a lot of awfully queer children! Either they are all very loyal or very dishonest: for the life of me I cannot decide. Nor, from what I have seen, had you any great redeeming qualities . . . A cold, hard man! I hear that everywhere. Well, be that as it may, you were murdered and I shall find out how and why . . . '

Checking her watch, she got to her feet. Walking leisurely through the fast-gathering dusk she regained the streets she had mentally tabulated on her inward journey, traced her way back through wildernesses of frowning tenements back to Three-Shot's underground café. She entered, and the bell clanged noisily overhead.

The place had the same barren emptiness of the afternoon. Presumably Three-Shot had moved in the interval even though there was no evidence of it. He still lay with fat forearms on the counter and surveyed the opposite wall. As he saw Maria out of the corner of his eye he gave a shout.

'Pulp!'

To Maria's surprise Pulp rose from behind the partition round one of the further tables. He came forward, chewing industriously, only differing from his afternoon appearance in that he now sported a butterfly bow of crimson.

'Havin' a spot of mash,' he explained, swallowing. He cleared his throat and then said rather hoarsely, 'I found him!'

'You did!' Maria cried. 'Where?'

'Well, I — I reckon you said something about some more dough if I — '

'But of course you shall have it!' Maria

dived her hand in her bag. 'Here is the money I promised you. You will receive even more when I am satisfied you know everything I expect you to know.'

Pulp nodded. 'Right. Let's go! See you again, Three-Shot.'

'Is it far?' Maria questioned anxiously, as they came out into the street. 'I'm beginning to feel rather tired . . . '

'Only about half a mile, and I know the short cuts. Stick by me.'

Though she was anything but a nervous woman, Maria felt uneasy as the route took them through dimly-lit streets mantled in growing dark. Here and there from open windows came sounds of raucous music. The elevateds clanged and rattled as before; somewhere eastwards ships in the harbour hooted viciously. It seemed to Maria that the streets were all alike — drab, grey, becoming more squalid as they progressed, until at last they came into a section of boarded-up, disused granaries and warehouses.

Pulp came to a stop, eyed Maria under the street lamp. 'I got the lowdown from one of Bald Charley's boys,' he confided.

'News travels fast with the guys I mixes with. The feller I'm tellin' you about saw where this con went to — but naturally we ain't squealed on him. We got our pride and sense of honour — 'sides, cops ain't none too welcome around here . . . He's in the top of this granary. Dame's visited him quite a few times, it seems.'

'She has, eh?' Maria reflected. 'Well, I've got to see him. You had better direct me.'

'O.K. But remember, no cops!'

She hung on to the tail of his coat as he stole cautiously round to the back of the granary. She had some difficulty in squeezing through the narrow gap of fencing he indicated, but finally she managed it and followed him across a flagged yard to a lower window filthy with dirt. He raised it gently.

'See?' he whispered. 'Left like this so the dame can get in when she wants . . . ' He scrambled through and looked back. 'You manage?'

'Well, I — ' Maria got no further. To her amazement she found herself suddenly hauled through, sunshade included.

Breathing hard in the dark and her nostrils full of dust she stood waiting.

'Take it easy,' Pulp warned, as she sniffed. 'Don't start to sneeze for the love o' Pete! Here — leave this to me. We don't want a sound . . . I'm a touch-an'-toe artist, see . . . '

She found out what he meant by that when, in the dark, he located a strong wooden ladder that led up to the upper floor of the granary. With difficulty she followed his example, using fingers and feet to guide her. They emerged on a pitchy-dark upper landing with a gaping hole where a skylight should have been.

'Swell hide-out,' Pulp breathed admiringly. 'But look, we're in a bit of a spot. If this guy packs a rod he'll shoot: if I speak he'll think I'm a cop. You're safe enough from a slug where you're standing so start talking. Go on!'

Maria assimilated the avalanche of slang and then cleared her throat.

'Hello there! Mr. Salter, can you hear me? Hello!'

There was no response.

'Mr. Salter, where are you? I have

important news from Patricia. I am her aunt . . . '

The silence remained.

'Hmm! So much for your information, Mr. Martin!'

He gave a snort. 'He's got to be here, I tell you! Bald Charley's boys never slip up when they put the finger on a guy — Hey, there!' he bawled. 'Open up!' He strode forward to encounter a door solidly locked. 'Open up, you mug, or I'll break the door down!'

There was no reply from beyond the door but there certainly was a faint sound. Pulp struck a match and in the momentary flare he noted just where the door was. Stepping back a pace he hurled his mighty shoulder against it. Breathing hard he crashed into it again — and again, until the lock snapped and precipitated him inwards in a sudden rush. Maria followed up just in time to see the dim silhouette of a window and hear the click of jaws as they bit together. A thud followed . . .

Pulp came back to her, breathing hard.

'I socked him — socked somebody,

anyway,' he said. 'He'd perhaps have gotten me first if I hadn't. Pulled my punch, though. His jaw'll be okay . . . I hope.'

Maria stumbled a little in the gloom: she was ankle deep in grain and meal. The street light outside cast a faint diffused glow into the place. It was rather like the loft of a hayrick. Finally Maria looked down at the man on the floor as Pulp hauled him to his feet, slapped his face sharply with the flat of his hand.

'Doesn't pack a rod, anyway,' he said briefly, after a quick examination. 'Not my idea of a con on the run,' he added in regret. 'You can't get far these days without a rod — Ah, it looks like he's snapping out of it!'

The man recovered consciousness suddenly and rubbed his jaw. He was shortish, broad-shouldered, with dark hair. That was all Maria could discern. He stood looking at the two dim figures.

'You Arthur Salter?' Maria demanded.

'Yes . . . ' His voice was quiet, unexpectedly refined.

'You'd have saved yourself a lot of

trouble if you had opened the door in the first place.'

'Maybe,' he replied bitterly. 'The police get up to all kinds of tricks. I couldn't believe that remark of yours about you being Pat's aunt: I thought it might be a trick. So I took no chances. But you got me just the same. Okay, let's get it over with.'

'If you are under the impression the police are around here, Mr. Salter, you are mistaken,' Maria observed.

'No police? Then — then who's he?'

'My bodyguard — Mr. Martin.'

'Bodyguard, eh? And plenty of dynamite in that fist, too — ! You say Pat sent you? You don't mean that something has happened to her? She isn't — '

'So far as I am aware Patricia is at home and in quite good health. Nor did she send me, though I found your abode through her activities. You see, I am . . . an investigator.'

'Pat referred to you as a nosy old dragon,' Salter murmured.

'Perhaps,' Maria murmured, 'she had reason. However, to get down to cases: I want some information from you. Upon that relies your chance of continued safety here, and my not summoning the police.'

'What do you want to know?'

'You and Patricia were married on April 29th, you using the false name of Archer Slater. Correct?'

'Yes,' Salter admitted. 'But how on earth did you find that out? Pat wouldn't tell you, surely — ?'

'Patricia has not told me anything. I found it out by deduction. But I'm wondering why you used the alias. You could not have done it then to prevent the police tracing Patricia's connection with you because at that time you had not been arrested.'

'I did it because Pat's father objected to our marriage. In case he kept an eye on registry records we decided it was best to put my name as 'Archer Slater.' True, he might suspect the truth, but he would have no proof. Later it turned out to be providential because when I got arrested it apparently liberated Pat from all connection with me.'

'Hmm. Tell me more.'

'I can tell you this: Ralph Black was a narrow-minded, grasping bigot. He saw nothing but his own advancement, to the exclusion of all and everything else. None of his children or so-called friends, had the least regard for him. I have certainly no reason to regret the day he died, believe me.'

'Is it not rather significant — at least the law would consider it so, maybe — that you escaped from that prison farm on the same date as my brother met his death?' Maria asked grimly.

'I didn't know anything about his death until days afterwards when Pat told me all about it. Sure the dates were the same. I broke free in the afternoon and he died in the evening. So what? At the time he must have shot himself Pat was driving me hell for leather somewhere between here and Jamestown — '

'But if it came to a point of law you would not admit that fact? You would not involve Patricia, I presume?'

'You bet I wouldn't!'

'Then where would you say you were?

You could not say you were hiding because it wouldn't prove anything — '

'Wait a minute!' Salter snapped. 'Are you trying to prove that I could have murdered Ralph Black?'

'The police could prove it if I told them a few things — and you could not defend yourself without involving Patricia,' Maria smiled.

'But who said he was murdered, anyway? It was suicide!'

'Murder! Murder most foul!' Maria retorted. 'However, you can calm your uneasiness, young man. I have no intention of telling any tales to the police. I merely show you that I have a stranglehold on the situation . . . Tell me, how could you possibly have been taken in Patricia's car? How did she ever get through the police dragnet with you beside her?'

'It was all planned. I worked out the details and got the news to her through my lawyer when he visited me. The sports car she first whipped me away in was a hired one. We ditched that in a marsh after the first ten miles. At that point her own sports car was ready — and it was prepared. If you've seen it you will know it has a small back seat portion as well as the two front seats. She had a cradle fixed under the leather seating at the back. All I had to do was get into it and lie quiet. The cops didn't go far enough to examine the entire car — but even if they had have done they would not have been likely to find me. Under the seat was an apparent wood base, while under my cradle was the car's main chassis. I was sort of sandwiched between the two. Pat got away with it because her car was not the one that had originally whisked me off. She posed as a commercial traveller, wore thick-lensed glasses to disguise her eyes — which are pretty distinctive — and a black wig. Altogether the set-up was perfect, though I was bruised all over when she landed me in this dump by night.'

'Very well planned,' Maria mused.

'It had to be — relied on split-second timing.'

'Then what happened?'

'Well, once I was here Pat got me an

old suit of clothes from a junk store — these things I've got on. She's seen to it that I've had food and all the rest of it. She is the grandest wife a guy ever had! Right now she is busy trying to clear the charge over my head.'

'Wouldn't it have been better for her to do that with you still in prison? Why did you have to take this desperate chance anyway?'

'Because I couldn't help her properly by her occasional trips on visitors' day. I had to be right on hand, as I am here, to give her information at any moment when she might need it. She is playing a tough game, and it can only succeed by her knowing every trick beforehand — which she does know, if I can manage it anyway.'

'I gather,' Maria said, 'that you were falsely accused?'

'I was *framed*!' Salter retorted. 'I was railroaded under the orders of the one and only Ralph Black himself!'

'Really?' Maria waited in grim attention.

'After Black had refused his consent for me to marry Pat — because of the social gulf between us, I imagine it was — he decided to make doubly sure she remained an untouchable by getting me out of the way, by sending me to prison on a charge of misappropriating company funds. He did not know we had married in spite of him — or if he did it made no difference — and neither Pat nor I let the secret out. We'd decided to wait for an opportune time to make things clear. I used to be a clerk in the Onzi Financial Trust, and plenty of money flowed through my hands. I was framed — fiendishly, cleverly — and could do nothing to save myself. That was Black's doing!'

'Just why was it?' Maria asked, thinking.

'Because the chief of the Financial Trust was one of Black's big business cohorts — and a slimier scoundrel never walked this city. He's got a finger in every underhand racket in town: his methods go right back to the rip-snorting 1920's. Gangsterism has been pretty well stamped out, but this one remains — a clever schemer and organizer always just outside the law. His real name is Ransome — Hugo

Ransome, and his headquarters are not in the Onzi Building, as one would expect, but in a dive in the town outskirts. Maxie's Dance Hall to be exact . . . Onzi is of course only one of many aliases.'

'Maxie's Dance Hall!'

'That's right — but I don't suppose you'll know of it.'

'But I do,' Maria said gravely. 'And I also see lots of other things I did not see before. I have tried in vain to contact the controller of Onzi's and get the name of the manager of the Dance Hall. I failed on both counts — for obvious reasons. The two boil down to one Hugo Ransome . . . But go on.'

'Maxie's Dance Hall is only a cover-up. All the secrets Ransome has are in a safe back of the hall — about the safest place on earth since it's the last place the police would ever look — even if they could, which legally they can't. Waiters in the dance hall are well paid to be strong-arm men for Ransome and keep his business quiet, guard his identity, and so forth . . . But to revert to myself: Ralph Black advised Ransome that he wanted me to be framed — that would be easy enough between them and a simple matter to Ransome since I was employed, quite legitimately too, in his business. I was trapped; so presumably Black was well satisfied.

'When I was accused Pat believed in my innocence, and knowing Ransome and her father had business associations — a fact she had learned easily enough from occasional casual family conversation — she strongly suspected a plot on the part of her father, knowing his antagonism for me and his brutal disregard of anything which blocked what he thought was right. Once I was imprisoned she resolved to try and get some information on Ransome and hold it at his head in return for a confession of the real facts concerning me. If it meant a scandal in the family she was not worried: she avers she loved me far more than her family name anyway. To get past Ransome's thugs in the dance hall was a difficult job — '

'Which she overcame by becoming a paid partner to dancers, and wearing a dark wig,' Maria finished. 'Ransome not knowing her in any case — and if he did, probably only from photographs which would show her as a blonde — she got away with it. She even let him make love to her in an effort to win his confidence . . . '

'Investigator is right!' Salter whistled. 'You know plenty! But what worries me is the danger Pat's in! If she makes one slip, despite my efforts to direct her every move, she'll just — disappear! Ransome has enormous power.'

'So I imagine,' Maria nodded. 'Tell me, if Patricia suspected her father had hatched a plot against you why didn't she speak of it at the trial?'

'Because cross-questioning would have produced the truth about our marriage, would have cast a blight on her father's business activity, and, even if I had been released through it, would still have left me open to her father's attacks upon me. Somehow, somewhere, he would have got me in the end — and probably Pat too for her defiance of his wishes. She was mortally afraid of him.'

'Few seem to have been endeared to him,' Maria sighed: then she brisked again, 'This Ransome person: is he a big man with thick, greasy black hair and a cherubic face?'

'Right! Looks as though he oozes perpetual innocence . . . So you've seen him, too?'

'Yes, but I wasn't then aware of his identity . . . ' Maria reflected for a moment. 'Then on the night of my brother's death you were somewhere between here and Jamestown, with Patricia?'

'Correct,' Salter said quietly. 'And I assure you I did not kill Ralph Black, though he deserved it. I wouldn't be crazy enough to do it with the police on my tail, anyway. Ask Pat for yourself! She'll tell you.'

'Perhaps . . . Patricia has little regard for me, young man.'

'Only because she is scared to death for my safety and her own,' Salter insisted. 'She was afraid when you turned up and started poking about that you'd find out about me and — Well, I guess she was right at that. You *have* found out! If you choose you can turn her in along with me; naturally she is an accessory after the fact. I really promise you, though, that all she is trying to do is clear me. And she's got to work fast. The police are already closing in around me; so the paper said this morning. Pat dashed over to tell me. I may have to move on.'

'You definitely believe,' Maria mused, 'that if we could somehow get a stranglehold on this Ransome person he could be forced into confessing you were — er — framed?'

'Definitely. He'd get some stooge to take a dive.'

'I beg your pardon?'

'He means,' Pulp explained, 'that this Ransome guy would find some other mug in need of money, and would then pay him off enough sugar to make it worth his while to say he framed the crime. He'd get a stretch, but it would pay him.'

'Amazing!' Maria exclaimed. Then, 'I think Patricia has been very short-sighted to keep all this to herself, though I quite see her point of view. I shall look into this for myself, young man. I have been waiting to get this Ransome person where I could nail him and I can perhaps do it . . . Don't you worry: I shan't give you away. But I shall seek Patricia's confidence.'

'That's fine of you! Honestly, I — '

'I will see to it that you get some news as we progress — probably through Mr. Martin here,' Maria went on. 'And now we must be getting along. You'll have to lock this door as best you can. I'm afraid Mr. Martin was a trifle forcible.'

Salter moved with them to the dim opening.

'I think you're a swell relation, Aunt Maria,' he murmured, grasping her hand. 'If you get Pat and me out of this fix we'll never forget you for it.'

'I shall bear it in mind,' Maria smiled. 'Come, Mr. Martin . . . '

They descended the ladder once more and retraced the course they had taken back into the street again. For a long time they walked side by side in silence under the dim lights, then Pulp began to scratch his head.

'Frankly, Black Maria, I don't get the

hang of this set-up at all!' he confessed worriedly. 'All that stuff you and that guy spilled is so much bunk to me. I thought you was a crook — a master mind. Now I find you mixed up in a murder rap.'

'I am solving one, Mr. Martin. I am not a criminal, but a crime investigator. Now I know you better I can admit it. I am Black Maria, England's greatest woman criminologist!'

'Yeah? Well, blow me down!'

Maria revelled in her white lie for a moment, then said seriously, 'My brother was murdered, and I am at work discovering who did it.'

'Whaddaya know!' Pulp whistled.

'Not half as much as I'd like,' Maria sighed. 'There are so many suspects, and every one has a motive. But the trouble is that each one has also a perfect alibi. Yet somebody murdered my brother, and with such fiendish ingenuity it was passed as suicide. I can only find the culprit by gradual elimination of suspects. That I am accomplishing, little by little — and in the course of dealing with others I expect to have more work for you.'

'Swell!' Pulp rubbed his hands. 'Say the word!'

'Listen carefully then . . . ' Maria stopped under a lamp. 'You heard Salter mention Maxie's Dance Hall? Do you know it?'

'Nope — but I can soon find it if you've work for me to do there.'

'Excellent! Yes, I have work for you. I shall, for instance, need the services of a safe-breaker. One who is an extremely fast technician.'

Pulp did not even hesitate. 'I know the guy you want — 'Fingers' Watson. But his rates are high. Depends on the size of the safe.'

'I don't know its size,' Maria said, frowning. 'What I want is to have this man Ransome's safe rifled and all its papers removed. I reason that he will not call in the law because that might reveal what the papers contain. You know where the safe is — in the back of Maxie's Dance Hall, presumably in a sort of office. What size of a safe do you expect it will be?'

'Wall safe probably, usually hidden behind books, flowers, or a pitcher. Guess a job like that has a risk — cost you a coupla thousand bucks at least. You'll get good work from Fingers, though, take it from me.'

'I haven't the money now, but you have my assurance that it will be paid on the nail tomorrow. You can trust me.'

'Sure I can!' Pulp nodded. 'What's the layout when I get hold of Fingers?'

'I flatter myself my plan is distinctly ingenious,' Maria mused. 'Ransome's safe could be robbed at night, but it is more than likely that he will have men on night guard. Therefore the time for such a robbery is undoubtedly when the place is in full swing and packed with dancers and diners. At that time any guard there will be at its laxest. Then, while a specially staged riot is in progress — which will, so to speak, draw Ransome's fire in an effort to quell it — Fingers will reach the office by any means he chooses and do the job. Do I make myself clear, Mr. Martin?'

'It's a natural!' Pulp breathed in awe. 'An' of course you want me to start the riot?'

'Exactly! I shall be present in the dance hall: the waiter knows me by now. I shall be on the balcony to give signals where necessary. My niece Patricia will be there too — at least, I expect so. She is the wife of the man Salter we've just been talking to. You will see that no harm comes to her once I've pointed her out to you.'

'Okay. I'll dig up some of the boys to make the riot look extra good. For my own part I'll work for half pay; I get plenty of pleasure out of a fight. The boys will want a hundred smackers apiece though. Three of 'em should be enough. Reckon me at fifty smackers and we're all set.'

Maria calculated quickly. 'Altogether, with Fingers, a total of two thousand, three hundred and fifty dollars. Splendid! It will be given to you without fail tomorrow night. You will meet me on the opposite side of the street to Maxie's Dance Hall at exactly midnight. Keep your colleagues out of sight. Understand?'

Pulp nodded.

'Then I'll say good night,' Maria smiled. 'Here is further payment for your trouble and extra valuable aid.'

He took the money, then caught her arm. 'I'm sort of forgettin' my manners,' he said briefly. 'A long time since I had to use them, I guess. You'll want a 'bus back home. Bit of a twisty way back to Three-Shot's street. Let's go.'

Holding her protectively he marched her through the frowning abysses of dark streets. She was glad that he did: they passed more than one unsavoury individual on the way . . . And so they returned to the bright lights of the main street. The last Maria saw of her mighty henchman as she looked back from the 'bus was his big paw waving to her energetically.

5

Weary from her excursions Maria dragged herself up the steps of the Black residence. It was just ten minutes to midnight when Walters admitted her. He looked at her rather doubtfully, but made no comment: then later when she saw herself in the hall mirror she realized what had made his wavering eyes jump. She was covered in dirt and dust, must have been seated in the 'bus with her face streaked in cobwebs. At least it had been fairly dim and mainly deserted. That was one consolation.

'Has the mistress retired, Walters?' she asked briefly, as she crossed the hall.

'Yes, madam. Miss Janet and Miss Patricia have also retired. The mistress said I was to wait up for your return. Supper was placed in your room a little while ago.'

'Thank you . . . Mr. Richard is out, I presume?'

'At his cabaret, madam . . . Will that be all?'

'I think so. Good night, Walters.'

Maria turned her weary feet to the stairs and went up slowly. She had spoken to Walters without turning, ashamed of her dirty appearance. That he was curious was obvious, only — Maria gave herself a little shake of impatience. No use thinking things about him again: she was too tired for it anyway. In spite of it, however, she kept herself alert enough to enter up her notes —

'*Patricia and Arthur Salter (under name of Archer Slater) are married. Salter was sent to prison on a false charge arranged by Hugo Ransome (otherwise Onzi) at the instigation of Ralph. Patricia is trying to clear up charge on her husband, in which effort her Maxie's Dance Hall excursion is explained. Shall endeavor to aid her.*

'*Janet has complicated matters. I found her tonight walking through an East Side park with her (so she says) fiancé, one Peter Wade, former big composer now*

149

suffering hard times.

'Peter Wade and Arthur Salter both have had excellent motives for wishing Ralph dead. For that matter I am much appalled by the gradual revelation of Ralph's cruelty and personal domination.

'Have contacted an excellent 'stooge' in the person of one Mr. Martin.

'I have the feeling that instead of solving this problem I am only adding more names to the list of possible murderers. However, I shall not give in.

'The time is exactly — 12.32 a.m.'

Maria read her notes through to date while she ate her supper . . . She had put the book away and was preparing for bed when she heard a faint sound on the landing outside her door. A grim smile touched her lips. She waited a moment or two, switched off the lights, then opened her bedroom window and peered into the night. She was just in time to see Patricia's light-coated form disappearing along the quiet vista.

'No wonder you spend so much time trying to recover sleep, my dear,' Maria sighed. 'But you have courage — fine courage. For that there must finally be a reward.'

She yawned, closed the window, and literally fell into bed. Her next conscious thought was of hearing a woman's voice crying desperately for help! Blinking, she sat up. It was still dark. With a frown she strained her ears and caught brief sentences, high-pitched with hysteria.

'I don't care! You can't do this thing to me! You can't, I tell you — !'

'Shut up, damn you!' snapped the voice of a man; and there followed a sound not unlike a slap in the face. After that the talking stopped suddenly.

Maria sat waiting, her head bent towards the wall from which the sounds seemed to have come. Next to her room was Dick's. Maria was a woman of action. She jumped out of bed into slippers, bundled on her dressing gown and made for the door. In a moment she had stalked along the corridor to Dick's room and knocked sharply.

'Richard! Richard, what is the matter in there? Richard!'

A click followed a moment later as a

key was turned. The door swung wide and Dick stood there. He was fully dressed, cigarette smouldering at the corner of his mouth, his hair tousled, a light silk gown over his shirt and trousers.

'Why, Aunt! Whatever's wrong?' He looked at her in concern.

'There is nothing wrong with me, Richard — but there does seem to be something wrong in here! I heard voices — a man's and a woman's. The man's voice was undoubtedly yours!'

'Huh?' He stared at her, then momentarily his face hardened. It was the same bitter expression she had once seen him register in the library when he had referred to his father's refusal to finance his cabaret enterprises. It went just as quickly too and with a rather crooked smile he asked, 'Just what kind of a guy do you think I am?'

'I don't know, Richard.' Maria's lips tightened. 'But I know I heard you and a woman arguing in here!'

'I guess you must have been dreaming. Come in — convince yourself.'

He stood aside and Maria walked in

slowly. All the lights were on and there was certainly no sign of disturbance. Nor was there any place where anybody could possibly hide — except the wardrobe. But this was open, as it happened, all parts of it with clothes included. There was nothing there.

'Well?' Dick asked quietly, crushing out his cigarette in a tray.

'I'm afraid it looks as though I have been making myself very absurd, Richard . . . ' Maria looked towards the window. The curtains were only partly drawn but it was enough to show her that there was no balcony outside on which anybody could have hidden.

'Very absurd,' she repeated, turning to face him. 'Yet I could have sworn . . . '

'You dreamed it,' he said, with a rather fixed smile. 'You know, dreams do the oddest things to people sometimes. And anyway, even assuming for one moment there were grounds for your belief, why should you be the only one to hear? Pat's room is next to this one and she's a very light sleeper. She'd have been in here like a shot . . . Yet she isn't.'

'No, she isn't.' Maria compressed her lips. Her non-appearance was hardly surprising. 'I'm sorry, Richard: forgive a fanciful middle-aged lady, will you?'

He put an arm about her shoulder as she reached the door.

'I don't want my favourite aunt to start having nightmares,' he said seriously. 'First sign of illness, remember, and that will never do! Tell you what! I'll leave my door open tonight and if you cry out or anything I'll have mother come and see you. How's that?'

Maria gave him a rather anxious look. 'It really isn't necessary, Richard. You'll be in a draught — '

'I'm used to draughts: stages are full of them. You leave it to me,' he smiled, urging her gently into the corridor.

She returned to her own room. One fact was uppermost in her mind at the moment: when Patricia returned it was almost inevitable that Dick would hear her, even see her pass his open doorway. And then —

'Matters might get even more complicated than they are,' Maria muttered to herself. 'If the enemy close in, follow their methods — so says Desmond in his *Outshooting the Shooters*. Right!'

She opened her own door slightly, drew up a chair to it, and sat down to wait, thinking. She was still by no means convinced that the voices she had heard were the products of a nightmare. Quite the contrary, in fact. Then she abandoned speculations for the moment, as there came a faint sound from the cavern of the hall. It was followed by a soft creak, from the stairs, coming ever nearer to the corridor. Maria rose, flung the door wide, and permitted a fan of light to shine on the dumbfounded Patricia. For a moment she was paralyzed. She had on her white coat and hat, black wig, and was carrying her shoes in one hand. Her green eyes stared in obvious horror at the sight of Maria's forbidding figure in its dressing gown.

Before the girl could cry out Maria raised a finger warningly, then motioned her inside the room, closed and locked the door behind her.

'Well?' Patricia asked coldly. 'I always

thought you were a confounded old snooper and now I'm sure of it!'

'Put your shoes on, Patricia, before you catch cold,' Maria replied calmly; then as the girl impatiently did so she went on, 'I had intended delaying this little talk, but it seems as opportune now as at any time. You might as well know that the door of Richard's room is wide open. He'd probably have seen you pass.'

'So what? I could deal with him.'

'No doubt, but why waste time in doing that when the truth is so much simpler? You see, Patricia, I know just what you are up to and where you've been tonight.'

The green eyes smouldered. 'That isn't possible!'

'Oh, yes it is, Maisie Gray!'

Patricia pulled off her hat and wig, shook free her blonde hair. 'Who told you that?' she asked, her lips set.

'I found it out,' Maria shrugged. 'And the time has come, Patricia, when you are going to listen to what I have to say. Sit down!'

'Who are you to tell me to — '

'Sit down!' Maria pushed the girl forcibly into the armchair, stood in front of her and gave a grim smile. 'You shall not stand there and talk to me, young lady. For a change you will listen! I've been dealing with girls all my life and I can certainly deal with you.'

Patricia sat back, her eyes contemptuous. 'Say what you've got to say and get it over with.'

'And you would be well advised to lower your voice!' Maria snapped. 'Don't forget Richard is only in the next room . . . Now' — she pulled up another chair and seated herself resolutely — 'the nosy old dragon is going to belch fire, my dear.'

'Nosy old — ' Pat sat up sharply. 'I never called you that! I only said it to — You've found Arthur! You've found him! Turned him over to the police! By heaven, aunt, I'll — '

'Quiet!' Maria insisted. 'I haven't turned in Arthur . . . yet. But I have seen him and learned quite a good deal . . . ' And she went into a detailed account of her exploit in the granary.

When it was over Pat sat with a vaguely

157

shamefaced expression on her sensitive features.

'I — I suppose you're thinking I'm pretty much of a heel, aren't you?' she asked at last, uncomfortably. 'I mean to say — after the things I've said and done to you. But I was scared — scared to death!' Her eyes misted with sudden tears. 'Can you understand that?'

'Yes . . . I can.' Maria smiled a little, patted the slender hand resting on the chair arm. 'Don't cry, my dear. I know just what you are going through, and how much you have already done. You are young, quite young, and I know that a girl like you, naturally refined and sensitive, has deliberately scourged herself to do the things you have. I know too that a girl like you takes shelter behind a façade of cynicism to hide her real emotions. You never were very convincing, you know — at least not to me. A headmistress has to be a first-class psychologist, you see. You are a girl of great courage, Patricia — and I like courage.'

Patricia gave a wan smile, dabbed her eyes with a wisp of silk.

'Th-thanks, Aunt . . . But now you do know where does it get us? Arthur's still in an awful spot. I begin to wish he'd never staged that prison farm break — ''

'He was wrong in doing that, certainly — However, I am going to help you.'

'But what on earth can you do?'

'Enough, I think, to secure a stranglehold over this Ransome person — just as you want to do. Tomorrow night I shall launch an offensive against him.'

Maria explained her plan in detail.

'But, Aunt, you don't know what you're getting into!' Pat gasped. 'You're planning to rob the biggest racketeer in town! Do you realize what will happen to you if you're found out — if we're both found out?'

'I can imagine,' Maria said.

'The last two who crossed Ransome were women,' Patricia muttered. 'The police found their bodies horribly mutilated. Everybody knows who did it but nobody can prove it. That can happen to us if we slip up. I was prepared to take a chance because as Arthur's wife I have the right to get into danger on his account. But it's my worry when all is said and done. There's no need for you to jeopardize yourself.'

'I am not trying to attack Ransome solely on your behalf — but also as a means to a final end of my own. The point is: are you willing to co-operate with me in my little war tomorrow night? Or rather tonight since it is already early morning.'

'Willing! I wish I'd thought of it myself . . . Believe me, the only thing I want is to clear Arthur from this whole beastly business. I loathe the job I'm doing; I'm revolted every time that greasy hog paws me: I take a risk every time I come in the house in case I'm seen and have to lie my way out — The whole thing's awful! But it has to be! So far I haven't been caught in the house — but I guess I might have been tonight but for you. It would have meant plenty of barefaced lying to throw Dick off the scent, just as you said . . . '
Pat paused for a moment and looked up sharply.

'You spoke of a final end of your own? Do you mean you are still on the hunt to

160

try and prove if dad was murdered?'

'He *was* murdered, Patricia; I know that now. Ransome is on my list of suspects . . . I might say many suspects,' Maria sighed.

'You do not think,' Patricia said quietly, 'that I had anything to do with dad's death? Honestly, I always understood it was suicide.'

Maria smiled. 'Unofficially, I consider you are entirely innocent, but I have to bear in mind the warning expounded by Allison in his *Summing Up the Crime* — namely, guilty and innocent look alike until proven otherwise — But forget all this for the time being. You must be tired. You must stay here for the rest of the night and slip out in the morning when it is safe to pass Richard's room. Come along: I will loan you some night attire.'

Pat stood up, tugged off her overcoat wearily. 'The more you do for me,' she said, stifling a yawn, 'the more I realize what a hellcat you must have thought me at first.'

Maria smiled, turned to the dressing table. 'And yet, had I ever possessed a

161

daughter, I would have asked for one with your courage and looks. Queer, isn't it?'

★   ★   ★

Patricia escaped to her own room before the maid arrived with Maria's morning tea, and Maria only saw her again at breakfast. She gave a tight little smile and winked solemnly — but to the rest of the family her change in manner towards Maria was more than noticeable.

'Decided to be civil at last, eh?' Dick asked shortly. 'What brought about the miracle?'

Pat calmly went on with her meal without satisfying his curiosity.

'Maria, dear, just what time did you get in last night?' Alice asked presently. 'I retired at eleven-thirty and you hadn't come in then.'

'I was in for midnight, Alice,' Maria replied. 'Altogether I had an excellent day. I saw the city, the outlying districts, the parks' — Maria's cold eyes wandered to Janet's rather tense features — 'and so finally came home again, only to be awakened by a nightmare the moment I had got to sleep.'

'Nightmare? How extraordinary!' Alice exclaimed. 'You don't strike me as being the kind of woman to have nightmares, my dear.'

'I have never had a nightmare in my life before,' Maria stated calmly. 'Nor am I too sure I had one last night.'

Dick lowered his grapefruit spoon and gazed steadily across the table, but Maria went on eating undisturbed.

'What was it about, Aunt?' Janet asked.

'I thought I heard Richard striking a woman, and she yelled for help.'

'Say, was that a dream!' Patricia cried amazedly.

'Of course I was wrong,' Maria smiled, gazing round. 'Richard very soon convinced me of that — but it really is surprising what a figment of the imagination can do sometimes.'

'Yes . . . Isn't it?' breathed Patricia, pondering. Then she looked across at Dick as he sat grim-faced and silent. 'Not that I'd put it past him,' she added dryly. 'I'm glad I'm only his sister instead of his girlfriend.'

'Meaning what?' Dick snapped, his jaws tightening. 'Aunt had a dream: she admits it! Why try and make something of it?'

'Why indeed?' Maria shrugged. 'In fact, Richard, nobody is making anything of it except you!'

He looked at her sharply, then Janet's cool voice broke in. 'Like Pat, I wouldn't put it past him. He's got twenty-two blondes and three redheads in that downtown leg show of his. If he can rule all those and get the best out of them he *must* be a woman beater. Just plain common sense, eh, Dick?'

'Oh — nuts!' He went on defiantly with his breakfast; but once or twice he looked up to find Maria's eyes fixed upon him steadily. It was the inscrutable stare that had put more than one Roseway young lady on the spot.

'For myself,' Alice said after a while, as though feeling it was incumbent on her to say something, 'I slept perfectly last night. Or did I? No!' She thought and frowned. 'No, now I recall it I woke up early in the morning under the impression I heard voices.'

164

'This is getting catching,' Janet observed. 'Don't tell us that you too heard Dick putting on a Simon Legree act!'

'No, nothing like that. As a matter of fact I thought I heard you, Maria — and the other voice sounded like Pat's. I must have been wrong, of course. I was half asleep anyway.'

'You must have been,' Maria said dryly, noting Pat's face had gone rather tense. 'Possibly this tendency for us to hear voices has some explanation — psychologically, I mean. You must read Freud's treatise on dreams some time, Alice.'

Having disposed of the immediate danger Maria glanced at Patricia significantly — Then everybody's attention was directed towards Cresty the parrot as he went off into a fit of chattering.

'Oi! I saw you! I saw you do it!'

'I just wonder who did teach him that line?' Dick mused. 'He saw who do what?'

'Wouldn't you like to know?' Patricia asked sweetly. 'I taught him that line, if you must know — but you don't know what it was he saw!'

'If anything,' Janet said indifferently.

'If he didn't see anything why did I teach it him?' Patricia challenged; and Janet shrugged.

'Search me — but I wouldn't put it past you to teach him that just to watch all our faces.'

'That's why,' Pat said innocently. 'You guessed it . . . '

The rest of the family looked at each other, except Maria, who was looking at the bird. Then Dick got up and excused himself.

'I'll have to be on my way, folks. See you later.'

'Not me you won't,' Janet sighed. 'I start singing at the Criterion Theatre tonight, remember. Rehearsal this afternoon,' she added to the others. 'Which reminds me I'd better go and test a few top notes. I've an idea my voice is a bit rusty from lack of use these last few days.'

She left the terrace, humming softly to herself. Within a few minutes the clear, mellow tones of the grand piano and her own exquisite voice were floating out from the room next to the lounge. Alice lay back in her chair, listening, giving little admiring twists to her head over and again.

'Superb!' she breathed. 'Positively superb!'

'Just what is she singing?' Maria asked, attentive.

'Nothing particular — just a ballad song,' Pat said briefly. 'No high notes in it, therefore I'm not much interested. But there may be in a while in some other song. When Jan hits the high C she is tops — '

She broke off and winced as the parrot gave a piercing whistle.

'Walters!' Alice cried. 'Walters, for goodness sake take Cresty into the lounge! He's drowning everything.'

'Very good, madam.'

He picked the bird up on its stand and transported it out of sight. But that didn't stop Cresty. The girl's voice had started him off on one of his singing imitations — and very clear notes he rendered too, utterly drowning the girl's voice at the greater distance.

'Sounds as though Cresty is trying Mozart's 'Alleluia in F Major' again — the one with the high C in it,' Patricia murmured. 'He has a passion for that one. Jan always uses it as her encore aria. It was dad's favourite song, too. She sang it during the last tour — There! Listen to that top note! A perfect imitation of Jan!'

All three sat in silence for a moment, impressed by the bird's clear purity of tone — then with a chortle at its own ability it finished with a guttural command to 'Go cook a hamburger!'

Maria smiled. 'Funny how parrots like to imitate singers,' she mused. 'One Luisa Tetrazzini had a parrot which could not only equal her superb top notes but could even beat them! The famous soprano admitted that the bird was her one dangerous rival . . . '

'Yes,' Alice said, in a rather queer tone, 'I seem to remember having read of that somewhere.'

'Well,' Maria rose to her feet, 'engrossing though this is I have to get some work done. I keep putting it off — but it just won't wait any longer.'

'Work?' Alice asked in surprise. 'You're on a vacation.'

'I still have those instructions to send to the estimable Miss Tanby.'

'They won't get there until after your college has closed, will they?' Patricia asked, puzzling.

'The college may be closed for education, Patricia, but Miss Tanby remains,' Maria smiled. 'Therefore, I have got to get a typewriter from somewhere. And incidentally I had Walters bring yours to me in the fond hope that I might be able to fix it. But — no!'

'Hopeless. I know,' Pat shrugged. 'Sorry I'm of so little help.'

'I recall Richard mentioning he has one at his town office,' Maria pondered. 'I think I might do worse than go down and see if I can borrow it. He can have it sent up since it is one of the heavy variety. If that fails I'll try Janet.'

'Why not do it now and save yourself the trouble of walking to town?' Pat asked. 'Or why not go in the car? I can tell Smithson to — '

'Why all the fuss?' Maria smiled. 'If I must be frank, I am finding a reason for taking a walk. I believe in exercise — yes, even at my age. But I don't like pointless ambling . . . So, into town I go.'

With that she strolled from the terrace and into the lounge. Janet was still practicing, testing an occasional top note now — but Maria was not listening very attentively. She was busy with her own thoughts, but even so her eyes glanced briefly around the lounge. She had an inborn necessity to see everything was in order . . . And almost immediately she saw something wrong. There was a flaw on the sideboard.

She frowned and went quickly over to it. A wineglass was there with half of its bowl sliced off as cleanly as though with a diamond cutter. The remaining section, a glass bracelet as it were, lay nearby.

'Walters!' she called sharply, and he came in from busying about the terrace. His puzzled eyes regarded the glass.

'What is the meaning of this?' Maria asked shortly. 'Do you not realize how dangerous that glass is like that? How did the top half come to be broken off?'

Walters turned and pressed the bell-push. Lucy, the parlour maid, arrived on the scene hurriedly.

'What is the explanation for this?' Walters asked coldly, motioning to the sideboard.

Lucy stared in obvious amazement. 'Why, I — er — I don't know, sir. It was not like that when I dusted this morning — '

'Really? You could not possibly miss a glass in that dangerous condition if you had done your work properly!'

'Honestly, Mr. Walters, without meaning any disrespect, there was nothing wrong when I dusted this morning.'

'Do you suggest it broke itself?' Walters asked acidly.

'It isn't the first time it has happened, sir,' Lucy said urgently.

'What do you mean?' asked Maria sharply.

'Well, I remember some time ago that I found a glass on here broken rather like this one, only much lower down, just as though somebody had cut it off with a razor. It was during the time the master was alive. I just took it away, replaced it, and said no more about it.'

'And was there any explanation for the

occurrence?' Maria asked.

'No, m'm. It must just have sort of happened, I guess.'

'Hmm, most extraordinary. Very well, Lucy, clear it away. Thank you, Walters, that will be all.'

He nodded, gave the girl a glance which threatened cyclones in the kitchen, then returned to the terrace. Lucy picked up the glass remains carefully.

Janet came out of the neighbouring room. 'Anything wrong, Aunt?'

'No — nothing.' Maria started out of her preoccupation. 'Just a wineglass smashed in the oddest fashion without anybody apparently being near it.'

'How very extraordinary!' Janet exclaimed, watching the maid. Then she shrugged. 'Probably Dick. He often takes a brandy and soda as he leaves. In a particular hurry he might have banged the glass down and a flaw in it caused it to break off.'

'Wineglass for brandy and soda?' Maria raised her eyebrows, shook her head, then went out with stately calm, ascended to her room and began to dress for her town journey. Her mind was completely occupied by the odd mystery of the smashed glass, but she could find no plausible solution for it as she sat on the 'bus which took her to Dick's cabaret headquarters. She remembered it clearly enough from his pointing it out to her on the day of her arrival.

Once she arrived she found herself wandering through a maze of upturned tables, humming vacuum cleaners, cleaning women, men in shirtsleeves, and slapping mops. One of the men — who was probably an opulent commissionaire by night — directed her to Dick's office, or at least to the little room he occupied for business during the run of his show . . . She had her knuckles ready to rap on the panels when voices from inside the room came to her through the open fanlight above. Involuntarily she paused and listened.

' . . . she can think what she likes!' Dick was saying. 'I know it looks odd, but I might have spoiled everything by revealing the truth. I don't trust a soul, not even the best of them, and if the news got to the public before the actual time we'd be sunk.'

'Quite so, but I think you're carrying it too far,' came a girl's voice, and Maria tensed a little as she heard it. It was the voice of the girl she had heard in the night in Dick's room.

'Too far or otherwise I'm keeping it hidden.'

'Maybe I made it sound too good! You ought to have seen that the thing didn't go off too loudly . . . '

'It happened and it's done,' Dick said grimly; then he went on earnestly, 'After all, Jean, we can't afford to take chances. We agreed on that, didn't we?'

'Of course . . . Well, I must be going!' There was a pause and a sound like a kiss.

Maria backed away hastily at the click of the door-latch, flattened herself by the corner wall near a massive dried tree. She watched intently as a slender blonde girl in neat attire hurried swiftly away towards the exit . . . Maria waited for a moment or two, then emerged and knocked lightly on Dick's door.

'Come right in!' he sang out; then he looked vaguely surprised as Maria came into view.

'Well, my favourite Aunt!' He seemed rather relieved — possibly because Jean had departed just in time, Maria reflected. Then he went on, 'What's wrong, Aunt? Want to look around? I'll be glad to show you — .'

'Some other time, Richard,' Maria broke in. 'As a matter of fact I came to borrow your typewriter. You said you had one, and I just have to get my letters done. So I took a little walk and came along. You don't mind?'

'Of course not, only — Well, fact is, it isn't here. I've loaned it out to friend of mine.'

'Oh!' Maria raised her eyebrows. 'Don't you find it a big hindrance in doing your own correspondence?'

He shrugged. 'I don't have very much and I can borrow it back when I want it. Yes,' he continued, elaborating a little, 'I lent it to a friend of mine so she can get some important work typed. Sorry, Aunt! If I'd known — '

'I should have acted before when I first mentioned it,' Maria said. 'I must say, though, that it seems odd for you to have to share a typewriter, and such a heavy one, with somebody else. With your money and interests why don't you simply get another?'

'Well, there's a reason. We are doing a job together which needs the same machine to finish it. Can't use two styles of typewriter. Every machine has a characteristic difference, you know . . . '

'I am quite aware of that.' Maria eyed him steadily.

'So there it is,' he shrugged. 'Why not borrow Janet's? She has a portable you know — better than my heavy thing, any time. She's singing at the Criterion tonight, so that means that her dressing-room — and presumably her typewriter — will be all set at the theatre. Her maid Mary will be there this morning for certain. The Criterion's only about two hundred yards further into town down this street.'

'Yes, maybe I'll try there,' Maria nodded, reflecting. 'I'm sorry if I bothered you, Richard,' she added, rather dryly.

'Bother? Forget it! Only too sorry I can't accommodate you . . . I'm afraid I haven't time to come along with you, but you'll find it easily enough.'

Maria nodded, turned away and wandered to the exit to digest his decidedly vague remarks.

'The lady friend is presumably Jean,' she muttered. 'She has the typewriter. One machine between two seems to suggest a manuscript on which both are engaged. Was she in the house last night, or not? Most extraordinary!'

She turned it over to herself as she walked along the hot street, finally entered the Criterion stage door.

'Anybody particular you want to see, lady?' the doorman asked.

'Definitely, my man. I have a message for Miss Janet Black, the singer. I'm a relative of hers.'

'Miss Black ain't here right now — '

'I understand her maid is.'

'Yeah . . . that's right. O.K., second door on your left.'

Maria marched in and rapped the panels of the door in question. A tall girl with dark hair, sallow complexion, and rather sad brown eyes opened the door and looked out questioningly.

'I am Miss Black's Aunt,' Maria said gravely. 'Your mistress is not here yet, I understand?'

'No, madam, not yet . . . Is there a message I can give her?'

For answer Maria walked calmly into the dressing room and stood gazing round. The maid waited, her mouth setting a little.

'Your mistress said I could borrow her portable typewriter, so I have come for it.'

'Typewriter!' Mary looked astonished for a moment; then she changed to an obvious uneasiness. 'I'm sorry, madam, but I can't take that responsibility on myself. I must have Miss Black's permission first.'

'Then ring her up,' Maria shrugged. 'I'll sit here and wait.'

The girl hesitated then picked up the telephone and dialled the residence number. First Walters, then Janet herself squawked in the receiver. Maria sat listening to Mary's remarks.

'There's a lady here, Miss Black — your aunt, she says. She wants to borrow your typewriter . . . Yes, that's right . . . Oh, you'll be over yourself in a few minutes . . . ? Yes, very well, Miss Black.'

The girl put the receiver back and Maria eyed her questioningly.

'Miss Black asks if you'll wait, madam. She'll be along herself in a few minutes.'

Maria shrugged, settled herself more comfortably, watched as Mary busied herself with the dressing table and various cosmetics.

'How long have you been with your mistress, Mary?'

'About a year, madam.'

'My niece speaks very highly of you.'

'I'm glad of that. I do my best, m'm.'

The girl was not given to talking much, that was evident. As she sat on, Maria's gaze moved to different parts of the dressing room, but she failed to discern the machine for which she had come, unless it was concealed behind the curtains of the hanging wardrobe.

Then suddenly the door opened and

Janet came in quickly, pulling off her gloves.

'Morning, Miss Black,' Mary said, glancing up.

'Hello, Mary — good morning. Hello there, Aunt! Hope you haven't minded waiting for me?'

'Not at all, Janet — only I fail to see the reason. You surely did not expect somebody was impersonating me for the purpose of borrowing your typewriter?'

Janet laughed. 'Heavens, no! It was just that I wanted to have a few words with you and it was pretty well a providential chance that you decided to get in touch with home. Tell you about it in a moment . . . Get the typewriter, Mary, will you?'

The girl turned and searched behind the curtains of the hanging wardrobe. She rummaged about for a few minutes, then withdrew.

'I've just remembered, Miss Black — You sent it to be cleaned and overhauled. Don't you recall that you told me to take it when we were finishing the last run . . . ? I'd forgotten all about it until now.'

Janet gave a start. 'So I did!' She looked

at Maria apologetically. 'Tell you what you do, Mary: go along and get it, will you? Don't bring it here — have it sent up to the house. Come back here afterwards.'

'Yes, Miss Black.' The girl hurried into hat and coat and then departed.

'Silly of me,' Janet smiled. 'I'd quite forgotten.'

'We all forget things sometimes,' Maria replied ambiguously. 'Tell me, Janet, what did you wish to talk to me about?'

'It's about Pat.' Janet's face became suddenly serious. 'Something happened this morning just after you left. I still do not properly understand it. Two men called and insisted on seeing Pat privately. They wouldn't state their business to anybody but Pat, and they were with her for quite a little time. Result was she left the house with them and said that she wouldn't be long. She looked frightened, Aunt, as I saw her departing. What makes it worse is that Walters tells us the men were from police headquarters.'

'Police headquarters!' Maria gave a start. 'If that be true where would they take her?'

'Well, the precinct station for our

neighbourhood is two blocks away. It would be there, I expect. But Aunt, what on earth could they want to — '

'Obviously the whole thing must be a mistake,' Maria said. 'I shall look into it personally.'

'I'll come with you — '

'Frankly, Janet, I would rather you didn't.'

'But why not?' Janet asked in wonder. 'I'm her sister, am I not? If she is in trouble I want to help.'

'You cannot help unless you know the nature of the trouble,' Maria said steadily. 'It so happens that I do.'

'You do! What's she done? Tell me!'

'You would not expect me to break a confidence, Janet — any more than you would expect me to divulge the secret of your association with Peter Wade.'

'Oh,' Janet said slowly, 'I think I see your meaning.'

Maria nodded and turned to the door. Then she looked back thoughtfully. 'Janet, there is one thing I would like you to make sure of. You have already told me that your maid knows of your association with Peter Wade

— but what makes you so sure you can trust her?'

'Because I'm satisfied as to her honesty. You see, I know the family she comes from — everything. Her mother and father ran a store in Columbus, Ohio, which dad bought in to add to his chain stores. So, in a way, I felt it was in the family. Mary's parents died just after dad had bought their place over and when I was in Columbus Mary came and asked me for a job, hearing through my former maid — who left me to get married — that there was such a position waiting. So I gave it to her. With her parents dead and the business sold Mary had to look for a fresh living.'

'I see,' Maria reflected. 'And you say the girl's mother and father died just after your father had bought their place over? A bit odd, isn't it? I don't imagine they could have been very old.'

'I didn't inquire into it,' Janet shrugged.

'Well, it's your own responsibility anyway,' Maria said. 'I do not think, for myself, that one's servants should be so conversant with private matters . . . I'll see you later, Janet.'

Janet nodded, frowning over some of Maria's remarks . . . Then the door closed softly.

6

On her way to police headquarters, Maria stopped at her temporary bank to withdraw enough money to pay off Pulp and his boys in the evening. Then she set off again, was finally shown by the sergeant in charge into the office of Inspector Davis.

The chief of the neighbourhood precinct station was a massive, bull-necked individual with immaculate fair hair and piercing grey eyes. He rose from his desk as Maria entered and drew up a chair.

'Well, Miss Black?' He glanced down at the card she had handed in.

'Am I right in assuming, Inspector, that you had my niece, Patricia Black, picked up this morning?'

'I am afraid so,' he said quietly. 'I rather expected some member of the family to come along soon.'

'What is the charge against her?' Maria demanded.

Davis resumed his desk. 'She is being held in connection with the escape of a prisoner from a penal farm, and on a charge of impeding the path of justice in effecting his recapture. That's all I can tell you, I'm afraid.'

'Is there anything to prevent me seeing her?'

'I guess not. We are keeping her here until her lawyer arrives: she has that right, of course ... ' Davis pressed a button, gave brief instructions to the man who came in. A moment or two elapsed and then Patricia appeared, a granite-faced woman immediately behind her.

'Aunt!' Patricia cried, racing forward. 'Aunt! Thank Heaven you came along! But — but how did you know of all this? Who told you?'

'You have Janet to thank ... Now, what is it all about?'

'The Inspector says I'm being held because I spirited Arthur away in my car! Says he has witnesses who can prove it! What's more, they want me to tell them where Arthur is. But you won't get anything out of me!' she finished bitterly, swinging round to the desk. 'You hear me? He's innocent, and you shall not take him back — '

'I understand you've sent for your lawyer?' Maria asked.

'Yes — for Mr. Johnson. He'll handle everything and I'll be out of here in no time.'

Maria was silent for a moment, thinking. Then she got up and led the girl gently to a chair. Rather puzzled she sat and waited — then Maria turned to the Inspector.

'In other words, Inspector, it has been discovered that Miss Black here was the woman who aided Arthur Salter to escape from the prison farm?'

'We've enough evidence to prove it,' he assented grimly. 'And it's a pretty serious offence too!' He swung to the girl suddenly. 'Young lady, do you realize what sort of a mess you are in?' he demanded. 'The more you try and impede us the worse it will be for you. Why not come out into the open and tell us everything you know?'

'I'm doing nothing and saying nothing

without my lawyer,' Patricia retorted, and folded her arms adamantly.

'I think perhaps I can explain,' Maria stated quietly.

'You mean — ' The Inspector broke off as the door opened again and Johnson was ushered in. He glanced round through his pince-nez and nodded affably.

'Good morning, Miss Black — Now, Miss Patricia, what's all this about?' He crossed over to her.

'They say I helped a convict to escape — '

'The convict is her husband,' said the Inspector briefly.

'Her husband!' Johnson exclaimed. 'That — that isn't possible! Miss Patricia — '

'There is little to be gained by wasting time, Mr. Johnson,' Maria cut in. 'Suppose I tell the truth?'

'If you don't mind, Miss Black, I would prefer to handle this matter in the proper legal manner. I have reasons for thinking that — '

'Such reasons don't interest me, Mr.

Johnson,' Maria retorted. 'I do not intend to have my niece's already precarious position made worse by a lot of legal chicanery. I have a statement to make, Inspector, and I want it recorded.'

'Very well.' He pressed another button and a clerk arrived with writing pad and pencil, sat down and waited.

'Miss Black, can't I urge you — ' Johnson implored.

'Yes, Aunt, what are you going to say?' Patricia burst out, jumping to her feet.

Maria smiled faintly. 'I am sorry. Patricia: I have my own way of doing things . . . Inspector, my niece here did assist Arthur Salter to escape from the prison farm. She took him first in a borrowed car and then in her own, which was specially prepared to conceal him — '

'So we found out,' Davis nodded. 'Right now we're most interested in trying to find where Salter is hidden. We've gotten pretty close, but to be sure would save a load of hard work.'

'I can tell you — exactly.'

'Aunt!' Patricia screamed. 'You're throwing him back into their hands — !'

Maria ignored her outburst and turned to the massive wall map, studied it for a moment, then put her finger on a particular spot.

'This is where you will find him,' she said calmly. 'My niece told me all this last night.'

'If that be so why did you not come sooner and reveal all you knew, instead of waiting to be forced into it?' Davis demanded.

'For the obvious reason that my niece might have found out about it and so warned Salter to move. As it is, you will be able to catch him.'

'I see ... Well, Miss Black, your statement coincides exactly with what we already know. I'll have some men on Salter's trail right away.' Davis turned and gave brief instructions.

'To think I trusted you!' Pat breathed venomously, her eyes flashing. 'To think I was mug enough to believe you wanted to help me! All you have done is smash everything for which I was working! One day, Aunt, I'm going to make you pay for this — to the full!' She swung to the inspector. 'Listen to me, you! I helped my husband out of that prison farm so he could direct me in operations to prove his innocence. He is not guilty, I tell you! He's — Oh, what's the use?'

Before the inspector's calm, unmoved gaze she sat down in her chair again, ran a worried hand through her hair.

'Don't worry, Miss Patricia,' Johnson said gently, patting her shoulder. 'I'll get you out. It can be done, you know — '

'Until such time, take her out,' Davis instructed; then when the door had closed behind her Johnson moved to the desk.

'Now, Inspector, suppose we — '

'I have not finished yet, Mr. Johnson,' Maria broke in, then as he looked at her in amazement she turned again to Davis. 'Listen, Inspector, I told you the whole truth in regard to this matter because it was the wisest thing to do . . . But I also know — in fact I am quite convinced — that my niece is right in declaring her husband to be innocent.'

'I'm afraid that doesn't concern me, Miss Black,' Davis shrugged. 'I was instructed to go to work on Miss Patricia Black. Judge and jury convicted Arthur Salter. In the eyes of the law, therefore, he is an escaped convict.'

'Suppose,' Maria said quietly, 'his innocence were proven to the hilt by facts which might still come to light?'

'If there were facts enough to show that Salter was wrongfully convicted the District Attorney would use his discretion concerning a re-opening of the trial. If he went that far you could take it as pretty well sure that Salter would be acquitted . . . But the evidence would have to be extremely convincing, I promise you that.'

'This morning,' Maria said rather bitterly, looking at the two men in turn, 'I have had to perform a most unpleasant task. I deliberately betrayed the confidence of my niece in order to save her. Mr. Johnson, I do not wish you to press for her release. I want her kept in custody — and her husband too.'

'He will be,' Davis said grimly. 'If you've gotten the facts rightly we'll have him under lock and key in an hour. If not, then I'm afraid I shall have to ask you some more questions.'

'It's right enough,' Maria said; then she thought for a moment. 'Once he is returned here, what happens?'

'He'll be sent back to the Jamestown prison farm under guard.'

'When?'

'By tomorrow at the latest — once I've made out my report to the proper quarter.'

'And in the event of fresh vital evidence being in your hands before he is sent back, what then?'

'In that case it might be considered expedient to hold him here in case a retrial should be decided upon.'

'There will be a retrial with the evidence I intend to get!' Maria stated firmly. Then as Johnson and the inspector looked at her rather doubtingly, she went on, 'I want my niece and her husband kept under lock and key so that they may be kept safe from the possible conse-quences of my future actions. I know the real causes behind Arthur Salter's arrest, and I know he is innocent — but the finding of the right evidence might endanger the lives of both my niece and her husband. Now you know why I had to break confidence with the girl.'

'Just what are you proposing to do?' Johnson asked ominously.

'I'm afraid that will have to remain my secret, Mr. Johnson.' Maria looked at him levelly for a moment, then turned to Davis again. 'Well, Inspector, I have co-operated with you. Now you co-operate with me by holding Salter until at least noon tomorrow.'

'O.K. — that can't make much difference — But that's the deadline! And I hope you fully realize what you're doing,' he added bluntly.

'Completely, Inspector . . . You have nothing further to ask of me, have you?'

'Not right now. I know where to find you, if I do.'

Maria turned to the lawyer. 'You had better come with me, Mr. Johnson. I'd like a word with you.'

Out in the corridor he looked at her in mystification. 'Just what are you driving at, Miss Black?'

'I'm hunting a murderer, and — '

'Yes, yes, I know that — but how did

Miss Patricia get into this mess?'

'That's a long story, and does not really signify. What does matter is that I believe I can now take a short cut to the possible murderer. The evidence I need, as I see it at present, is in the hands of one Hugo Ransome, otherwise known as Onzi, the financier. Ah! You begin to see! By the plan I have devised I can clear Arthur Salter and Patricia and get a stranglehold on Ransome at the same time.'

'So Ransome is Onzi!' Johnson breathed; then he shook his head gravely. 'I don't like it, Miss Black. Ransome is very dangerous! The police have tried practically everything to get some evidence to convict him, but they've never managed it. They know he's guilty of countless crimes, murder included, but there's never any proof. He always has plenty of shyster lawyers to help him, too.'

'Even they could not twist the right kind of evidence,' Maria said firmly.

'But think of the danger to yourself — '

'I have a most trustworthy bodyguard, believe me. But I shall need your help, on the legal side. You will know at a glance whether the evidence I intend to get is worthwhile or not. So be at home tonight. I shall probably call on you somewhere after midnight. You might let me have your home address.'

He handed over his card, studied her through his glasses. 'I begin to understand now why your brother so often referred to you as a very remarkable woman,' he sighed.

She smiled, shook the hand he held out, then on the building steps she left him and caught the 'bus for home. Alice was the first person she encountered as she entered the hall.

'Maria dear, have you seen Pat?' she asked anxiously. 'Two men called and asked her to go with them. I've been on tenterhooks ever since. Walters says they were policemen — '

Maria led her into the lounge, and closed the door. Then she motioned to a chair.

'You'd better take this sitting down, Alice . . . Remember me saying that Patricia might have helped the convict to escape from the prison farm at Jamestown?'

'Arthur Salter? Yes, of course — '

'She did,' Maria stated. 'And what is more, Salter and Patricia have been married for some time, since just before Ralph died, in fact.'

'Married!' Alice shrieked, jumping up. 'She would never do a thing like that! She — What have the police done to her?' she snapped.

'They have arrested her in connection with young Salter's escape. Don't look so overwhelmed, Alice. This is only the beginning. I could have let Johnson bail Patricia out, but I preferred that she be left in custody. For vital reasons . . . '

Maria detailed them, leaving out only such facts as she deemed necessary. When she had finished Alice waved her hands hopelessly in the air.

'My daughter posing as an unknown in a cheap dance hall in order to get evidence! Prostituting her divine adagio artistry as a professional partner! My son-in-law an escaped convict! My sister-in-law crossing swords with the biggest gangster in town — ! Lord, Maria, what sort of a woman are you?'

'Just a determined one,' Maria smiled.

'And I know exactly what I'm doing.'

'So I should hope! If you fail you may lose your life. And think of the scandal! The Black name smeared right across the front pages!'

'It has happened before — when Ralph committed suicide,' Maria reminded her. 'One scandal is no worse than another . . . However, you may safely leave everything in my hands. Now I must go and tidy up for lunch.'

Maria went off resolutely and at the bottom of the staircase found Walters intercepting her.

'Begging your pardon, madam, but a typewriter has been sent for you. I had it sent up to your room.'

'Oh, yes . . . ' Maria had almost forgotten. 'Thank you, Walters.'

Hurrying upstairs, she locked her room door, then whipped the lid off the portable machine. It was not a new typewriter, but it had been so thoroughly cleaned and overhauled it could nearly have passed for one. Certainly it was not what she had expected to see.

Sitting down, she picked it up and

tipped it about in various directions, studying it minutely, and examined the springs. There was nothing the matter with it, apparently. Certainly it was impossible to tell if any springs had been replaced. They were all oiled alike.

At last she put the machine down. Then she got out her book and wrote steadily:

'Patricia is in the hands of the police for aiding her husband, Arthur Salter, in a prison farm escape.

'Tonight I shall launch my plan for saving the pair of them and getting possible further evidence that may lead me to the murderer of Ralph.

'This morning I found a wineglass smashed (in a most unique fashion) without any apparent reason . . . Last night I distinctly heard a woman arguing with Richard in his room, and this morning I think I know who the woman was. Her name is Jean (Christian name). I have yet to tie up the bedroom incident. I have also to find out why Richard keeps his typewriter out of my way. Is he afraid of something?

'Have seen Janet's maid. Drab, uninteresting girl — but I am prepared to suspect anybody and will consider her carefully. Janet's typewriter has been overhauled, destroying all clues there might have been.

'Points to solve: smashed wineglass; bedroom mystery; and above all what was it that was used in the library as well as a spring, to cause the thinner scratch on the lower X nails?

'Cannot understand Janet's manner: seems to be cooling a little towards me. Patricia believes I have betrayed her. Alice is devastated by events ... Has 'Cresty' the parrot any possible connection with this puzzle? Perhaps — because he is a first-class imitator of voices and of Janet's singing voice in particular.

'Re Janet's maid: The girl's parents died and made it necessary for her to find work. She found it with Janet. Why did they die? They could not have been very old judging from Mary, and their business (hardware) was not exacting. Seems odd to me that it happened after Ralph had bought over their business.

*This is well worth an investigation
. . . The time is 12.43 p.m.*

'Altogether, a web with numberless strands,' Maria sighed, putting the book away. 'Either the creator of this murder scheme had great intelligence or else it was planned by more than one person . . .'

★   ★   ★

During lunch, which Alice and Maria had alone since Dick and Janet remained absent, very little conversation was exchanged. Alice was clearly moody, worried, ate but little . . . Altogether Maria was glad when the meal was over and she could excuse herself on the pretext of at last typing out her letters. She had borrowed a machine for the intended purpose of doing correspondence: it was the first law in Nathan's *Deluding the Suspect*, therefore, that she must corroborate her original motive, deflecting possible suspicion of an ulterior reason.

So, once in her room, she spent most of the afternoon typing — but not letters. Instead she compiled a typed dossier of her discoveries to date.

Once during the work she heard Alice walk along the corridor; that quick, light tread was unmistakable. It was certain she must have heard the machine. Then Dick returned home for his afternoon rest before turning out again in the evening. He too must have heard the machine. Maria smiled grimly and went on clicking industriously . . . There were no signs of Janet: presumably she was hard at work on rehearsals.

'Anyway,' Maria mused to herself, when at last she had the sheets clipped together, 'it might serve to convince them that my aim was letters and not a search for a spring . . . '

She read through her notes thoughtfully.

'That wineglass . . . ?' She tugged her watch-chain. 'I am convinced there is something there — a pivot on which the whole issue can turn.'

She did not flog her brain to try and grasp a solution, however. Instead she put her notes away and, knowing what the night had ahead of her, calmly went to bed. It was late evening when she awoke. She found she had missed dinner — a fact that satisfied her because she was in no mood for talking. When she reached the lounge she found Alice there alone, listening to the radio.

Alice switched the radio off as she saw Maria regarding her watch.

'So you are going to do this thing, Maria?' she asked grimly. 'You are really going to launch this hopeless crusade against Hugo Ransome?'

'Definitely! The time is now just ten forty-five, therefore I must be on my way. I have to meet my associate, Mr. Martin, at midnight.'

'I've learned by this time that it is useless to try and stop you when your mind is made up,' Alice sighed. 'When will you be back?'

'I have not the least idea. Probably in the early hours — and the less that is known of my activities the better ... I refer to Janet and Richard.'

'I shan't even see them,' Alice said quietly. 'Dick will not be home until early morning and Janet said she would be very late. Tonight is first night, of course, and it means a lot of people to see after the concert.'

Maria asked, 'When does she broadcast again?'

'Tomorrow night. First nights are not broadcast until it is seen how the show goes over. If it hits the mark it is put on the air at the beginning and the end of the run. That was how Ralph was able to judge Janet's voice.'

'Yes, I remember Janet telling me about that . . . Well, my dear, I must be off.'

Maria departed, made her way leisurely towards the bright lights of town and stopped at a restaurant for a late supper. Then, fortified for action, she made for the spot opposite Maxie's Dance Hall. It was exactly midnight when she arrived there and she had hardly gained a shop doorway before a familiar figure in loud checks and a pork-pie hat loomed in view.

'Hi'ya, Black Maria! Are we all set to go to town? I got the boys, and Fingers. You got the money?'

'Yes.' Maria handed him a sealed envelope. 'You'll find it all here. Divide it between you later on. I take it you know where your 'boys' are stationed?'

'Yeah — sure. One whistle from me and they'll be right with us. I figured we might go in twos at intervals, and when we're all in — barring Fingers that is, who says it's a back window job — we'll start the fight.'

'Excellent,' Maria agreed, as he pushed the money in his coat pocket. 'I'll go on ahead and take up my balcony position.'

'O.K . . . Oh, wait a minute! What about the dame you said you wanted us to protect?'

'She won't be here,' Maria replied. 'As far as I am concerned, Mr. Martin you don't need to — er — pull your punches with anybody. Just — sock 'em!'

Pulp rubbed his hands. 'Now you're talking my language, Maria! Now look, about those papers you want: I'd better just explain the set-up before you go in. When Fingers has got 'em he's going to slip out and hand 'em to Joey, see? He's a taxi-driver; he'll be right outside the dance hall, or at least doing a gutter crawl. All you've got to do when you get my all-clear signal from the hall is dash outside and jump in the taxi. Leave the rest to Joey. He'll drive you to a safe spot until the heat's off. You get it?'

'You have done excellently, Mr. Martin,' Maria beamed. 'Now I'll get moving.'

She crossed the road and entered the dance hall for the second time. This time she was more familiar with it. Deliberately she spent a moment or two discussing irrelevances with the gum-chewing maiden in the box-office, then she passed through the stuffy foyer and nodded to the commissionaire. He nodded back and gave a rather clumsy salute accompanied by a leer . . .

Maria went on to the balcony and found it practically deserted. Taking the same table as on her previous visit she waited.

The unhelpful waiter came forward and gave a reminiscent nod. 'Yeah, I know! Lemonade!'

Maria watched him go off with slovenly strides, noted with some misgivings that there was a suspicious bulge in the region of his shoulder — obviously a revolver.

Then she turned and looked below as the familiar giant figure of Pulp came into view with two very doubtful-looking henchmen. Their heads were shaven close to baldness. From the blue jerseys and baggy pants they wore Maria placed them as seamen. It was odd, but Pulp, obvious thug though he was, looked the most refined of the trio.

His technique, Maria decided, was promising. He started off by bumping with apparent mischance into a waiter; then he sat down at a table on the edge of the dance floor and thumped violently for attention. Once he glanced up slyly and gave a slow nod of his head; then he turned to watch the few couples drifting about the floor to the squawking of the orchestra. Most of the dancers seemed to have repaired to the tables for supper.

'Anything else?'

Maria glanced up to see the waiter with the lemonade. He sucked his teeth and took the money she handed him.

'Yes, there is. You remember that girl I asked you about? Maisie Gray? Where is she tonight?'

'Taken a powder, I guess. Never know with dames, I always say. They come and go — just like that!'

'Pity — I liked her dancing . . . ' Maria mused for a moment, then, 'I suppose she hasn't eloped with that gentleman with whom she was so obviously enamoured?'

'Huh?' The waiter stared. '*What* gentleman?'

'I don't know his name. He was very attentive to her last time I was here — a biggish man with thick black hair and a pale face.'

The waiter hesitated, then he nodded his head to the identical man in immaculate evening dress standing near the orchestra, a smouldering cigar between his teeth and his gaze fixed on the dancers.

'Mean him?' the waiter asked bluntly.

'Why, yes . . . ' Maria affected surprise. 'Who is he?'

'I wouldn't know,' the waiter retorted. 'Maybe he got fresh with Maisie; happens around here sometimes. So she just beat it.'

Maria smiled enigmatically and turned

to her lemonade. The waiter eyed her suspiciously for a moment and then went away.

'In other words, the one and only Hugo Ransome,' Maria muttered. 'Here, Maria, is where you go into action . . . '

She pulled a leaf out of her notebook and wrote hastily — 'Ransome has the cigar. Standing by the orchestra. Get him in the fight. Destroy this note. B.M.'

She waited for Pulp to catch her eye, then she rolled the missive in her palm and tossed it down. He read it, gave a brief nod, then burned it casually to light a cigarette. For a while afterwards there was an ominous calm.

At intervals other men drifted in and took different tables, most of them bull-necked individuals in jerseys or worn coats and baggy pants — all of them with unlovely faces. One of them had a scar running from ear to lip as though he had been slashed somewhere with a butcher's cleaver . . .

Then all of a sudden Pulp was on his feet. He swung aside the table at which he and his companion sat.

'Blast you to hell, you did that on purpose!'

His roar was heard all over the hall. 'I'll show you whether you can throw beer over Pulp Martin!'

His fist shot out, the punch deliberately pulled, and his ally went whizzing backwards to a beautifully simulated fall. He collapsed against the next table, overturned the crockery and the man and woman seated there, finished up with a threshing mixture of arms and legs . . .

That started it. A waiter came tearing forward with clenched fist, but hardly had he arrived before Pulp's right shot out like a piston and struck him clean in the jaw. He tottered on his heels; his teeth slammed together under a second punch. With a howl of pain he toppled backwards into the demoralized diners.

Maria watched intently. She saw Ransome throw down his cigar, step on it, then plunge into the fray. The balcony waiter deserted his job too and raced downstairs. The place was suddenly a bedlam of yells and slogging impacts. But there was no gunplay. To start shooting was to ask for trouble from the law — even if attackers and defenders could be distinguished, which was now next to impossible.

Maria found herself close to cheering when she saw Pulp's red head rise from the melee. He singled out Ransome for special attention. He caught the man by the lapel of his immaculate coat, whirled him round, then planted his fist clean in the middle of the pasty face. Ransome fell helplessly across an overturned table, found himself punched again and again — then a blinding uppercut sent him spinning backwards into the midst of the struggling orchestra. He finished up amidst the splintered wood of a bass fiddle.

The dance floor by this time looked like a dye-cauldron on the boil. Varicolored dresses and heads swam about violently: men and women were fighting like alley cats, apparently settling old scores. Maria stood up now in impartial calm, a lone observer, keeping her eye on Pulp's carroty head as he pounded and hammered his way along. Clearly he was working to a plan for he moved slowly but surely along in the direction of the office door. If a man blocked his path he simply removed him by a sledgehammer blow under the jaw: or if it was a woman he caught her beneath the arms and whirled her to the safety area beyond the circumscribed limits of the onslaught. Curious, Maria reflected, what a streak of chivalry the man had.

And so at last he reached the vantage point where he could slide out of sight into the office. He reappeared in a moment or two and signalled briefly. Maria hurried off down the stairs. The foyer was deserted: obviously the commissionaire had joined the onslaught. Outside Maria looked round anxiously. To her ears came the wail of an approaching police siren.

'Here, lady!' a man bawled, and she saw a taxi halt under a lamp from round a neighbouring side street. She raced for it, jumped in, fell into the back as it raced away from the kerb. It turned down the side street immediately, pursued an erratic course through various back alleys before it finally came to a halt.

The driver pushed back the glass partition and grinned. He was a little-faced man with a big, hooked nose, beady eyes, and a cleft chin.

'Well, Black Maria, we made it! Glad to know you. I'm Joey.'

'So I gathered,' Maria nodded.

'Here's the dope,' he went on, handing over a bundle of documents with a rubber band around them. 'Fingers worked dead to time.'

Maria took the bundle and surveyed it anxiously. 'You are sure we are safe here, Joey?'

'Trust me! I know this city backwards and inside out.' He grinned. 'Rather cute of Pulp to think of asking me to send for the police, wasn't it?'

'The police!' Maria exclaimed. 'But why?'

'Pulp sure knows how to organise a riot. He knows just how long it takes a squad car to get to a joint when there's a raid. Quite legitimate for a passer-by to hear the racket in the dance hall and call the riot squad . . . So, I was the passer-by.

You can bet your eyelashes that Pulp and his boys will be in the clear long before the cops arrive. They got things timed. See?'

Maria gave a nod. 'I knew I picked the right man in Mr. Martin . . . But what will happen to the other diners, and Ransome himself?'

'They'll be picked up, of course, and will have to account for themselves. They'll be let out by morning, I expect. But in any case, even figuring Ransome gets out again tonight it will be too late by then for him and his boys to chase you, even if they suspect anything. You can bet that Ransome won't call the police even if he does discover the theft: too much in those papers for the police to see . . . But his boys can get you, and I'm warning you, Black Maria, to keep your eyes peeled when we're not with you.'

'I'm prepared for that,' Maria smiled grimly. 'For the moment I want you to take me to this address . . . ' and she read out lawyer Johnson's card.

'O.K.,' Joey assented, and started the taxi off again. Ten minutes later he drew up outside Johnson's home and Maria alighted to the pavement.

'You'd better wait for me, Joey. I'll want you to take me home afterwards.'

'I'll be here . . . '

It was Johnson himself who opened the door in response to Maria's ring.

'Well, I'm relieved you're still in one piece, Miss Black,' he said seriously, leading the way through to his comfortable library.

'You had little need to worry over me,' Maria replied calmly, taking the armchair he drew forward for her.

He looked at her quizzically, then turned to the sideboard. 'You'll want some refreshment after this?'

'Port, if you please . . . ' Then she slowly drank it down as he turned to the documents she had tossed on the desk. For close on ten minutes he was preoccupied, then at last he looked up with eyes gleaming behind his glasses.

'It's incredible!' he breathed. 'The police have tried times without number to get evidence enough to break Hugo Ransome, and failed — and yet a determined woman and a band of hired thugs accomplish it in one night?'

She smiled faintly. 'Perhaps because I used simplicity. One cannot blame the law: they cannot go in and rob a citizen — but another citizen can! You believe the evidence is sufficient for me to get a stranglehold over Ransome? Sufficient for him to be anxious to get these documents back at any cost?'

'I still think you don't realize what you have done, Miss Black,' Johnson said seriously. 'These documents here, used in the right quarter, could indict Ransome on numberless crimes — including grand larceny and murder.'

'In that case I shall revise my plan. I think I should not be helping the law and order of this community if I let Ransome have those papers back . . . Let me see — Yes, I think I have it. I shall first get his confession to clear young Arthur Salter, then I shall keep my promise and in return for the confession give the papers back to him.'

'But you just said — '

'Newspapers,' Maria smiled. 'These documents must stay in your possession tonight, Mr. Johnson. Tomorrow at noon I want you to meet me at police headquarters. We will tackle Inspector Davis together . . . ' Then as Johnson digested her instructions she got up, bundled the papers together and studied them. 'Hmm, nine inches long, three wide, and four thick. That is all I need to know . . . Well, you will do as I suggest?'

'Certainly!'

He accompanied her back to the front door, shook hands and renewed his promise. Back in her taxi she talked to Joey as she was swiftly driven home.

'I have some instructions for you to send on to Mr. Martin. First you will thank him for his excellent work; then you will tell him to be at the same place opposite the dance hall at eleven tomorrow morning. I am going to visit Ransome, and shall probably require a bodyguard. After I have seen Ransome I shall want you to take me to police headquarters . . . probably at high speed.'

Joey grinned. 'I get it. Rely on me. I'll fix it.'

'Splendid — Stop here! Here we are.'

Maria climbed out, paid Joey his fare double, then crept silently into the house. Almost instantly the lights came up in the hall and Alice stood there, fully dressed, her face anxious.

'Maria, thank heaven you're safe! Tell me what happened . . . '

Maria drew off her gloves unconcernedly. 'Naturally, Alice, I succeeded in my mission. With Mr. Johnson's legal knowledge and my own — er — shall we say, impromptu methods, I have managed to get enough evidence to indict Ransome and free Patricia and Arthur Salter. I understand there will now be a reopening of the trial. Tomorrow I shall know for certain — or rather today.'

Alice led the way into the lounge, motioned to the sandwiches she had prepared. Maria started on them gratefully.

'And what makes you think Hugo Ransome will let you get away with this?' Alice demanded in agitation. 'He has ruthless men everywhere — They may kill you!'

Maria shrugged. 'I have survived this

far, and I shall continue to do so.'

Alice made a helpless movement. 'Tell me, Maria, is there nothing that can frighten you? Don't you ever get nervous?'

'One schooled in control of oneself never shows either fear or — guilt.' Maria started on another sandwich complacently. 'Notice how most people used to being in the public eye control themselves at times — such as lecturers, actors and actresses, headmistresses . . . But perhaps you're not interested, Alice?'

Alice said nothing, but her face seemed to have gone grimmer. She waited until Maria was finished then got to her feet.

'You must be tired, Alice, waiting up — '

'How could I think of being tired when your activities are tied up with Pat's release from jail?'

Maria asked a question. 'You haven't told the others anything?'

'No. Dick didn't press matters — but Janet wanted to know everything you intended doing. I gave nothing away and maybe you can deal with her yourself later on.'

'Strange she should wish to know so much,' Maria mused. 'She knows detectives took Patricia away.'

'But she doesn't know why! And you're so mysterious, Maria.'

'If it were only I . . . ' Maria shrugged. 'Well — to bed, Alice. I think we both need it.'

7

To avoid the family and answering a barrage of questions before she had every fact marshalled, Maria had breakfast sent up to her room the following morning, and at the same time instructed the maid to find her a batch of old newspapers. Lucy was obviously mystified, but promptly obeyed the request.

Her breakfast over, Maria spent time wrapping the news-sheets in brown paper from her luggage, thereafter putting them in different-sized envelopes which she had brought with her against possible need. When she had finished she had a fair-sized parcel heavily sealed and stringed.

She smiled as she surveyed it; then she dressed in her severest attire and endeavoured to escape the house without being noticed. But Alice caught her in the hall. She had the morning paper in her hand.

'Maria, dear — look!' Her voice was obviously distressed. 'All over most of the front page . . . '

The main headline was HEIRESS AIDS CON IN GETAWAY; and a smaller column was headed RIOT AT MAXIE'S: POLICE CLEAN UP.

As she read first one report and then the other Maria gave a grim smile.

'You can't stifle facts from the Press, Alice. It may even be for the best. When the exoneration comes the family prestige will be immensely heightened and it is possible the scandal created by Ralph's death will be offset.'

Alice reflected. 'I never thought of it that way, Maria.'

'As to the dance hall incident, it tells me just what I want to know,' Maria said. 'Those seized by the police last night included the manager — whose name is suppressed, you notice — but all of them were released this morning, just as my associate Mr. Martin believed they would be. It is all a matter of judgment, Alice. And it means that Ransome will be present this morning to receive — this!'

She indicated the parcel she was carrying.

'Maria, please be careful!'

'Of course!' Maria smiled and departed, but once out in the street her face became hard and determined. She marched resolutely, sunshade gripped in one hand and the parcel in the other. As she began to near Maxie's Dance Hall, the figure of Pulp emerged suddenly from a store doorway opposite.

'Hi-ya!' His paw moved in a cordial semicircle. 'How's tricks after last night?'

'I am in excellent health, Mr. Martin. You escaped the police?'

'Nothing to it! Pretty smart idea for me to send for 'em, eh?'

'Very.' Maria glanced down the street as a taxi drew up against the kerb. 'That's Joey, I take it?'

'Yeah — ready and waiting. I saw Ransome go into the Hall a bit back — and was his puss sour! It may be a while before he finds out those papers of his have been frisked. Fingers tells me he shut the safe after him . . . Those them?' Pulp glanced at the parcel.

'So Ransome will think,' Maria said

dryly. 'They are newspapers, wrapped in several envelopes and sheets of brown paper. It will take him at least three minutes to get through all the wrappings and in that time you and I will have got away in Joey's taxi.'

'I got to hand it to you, Black Maria, you sure know all the answers,' Pulp breathed admiringly. 'Right now I suppose you want me to go in with you to see Ransome?'

'Just in case,' she acknowledged gravely.

'Don't worry!' He patted his hip pocket reassuringly. 'I've packed a rod this time. Ready?'

They marched through the foyer together. The place was deserted and in a state of hopeless disorder. Tables were overturned, broken bottles were lying about in all directions.

Pulp gave a grin. 'Looks like we messed the place up plenty! And it seems as though Ransome's the only one to get here so far: if so we're in the clear . . . Come on!'

He tugged his gun out of his pocket and walked to the office door, flung it open.

Hugo Ransome looked round in surprise from his filing cabinet. His lips tightened about his cigar as he saw the automatic levelled at him. Gradually his dark snake-like eyes moved up to Pulp's grim face.

'What the hell do you want? And put that gun down!' Ransome's eyes narrowed. 'Say, you're the guy who started the row out in front last night. You've got your nerve coming here and — '

'Are you Hugo Ransome?' Maria asked, coming from behind, and taking a seat.

'Supposing I am?'

At close quarters Ransome was not quite so repulsive as Maria had imagined. He was neatly dressed, had thick, coarse hands with needless numbers of rings on the fingers. His face was puffy and flabby-jowled, probably from almost interminable confinement in a smoky atmosphere.

'One or two things you might as well understand, big shot,' Pulp said affably, kicking the door shut. 'This lady's with me, see? One pass at her will make my trigger finger jump.'

Ransome moved slowly to his desk, turned to face Maria.

'Well, what is this? A stick-up, or what?'

'Have you looked through your safe this morning, Mr. Ransome?' Maria asked calmly.

'My safe?' He looked mystified for a moment; then he gave a start and swung aside to a picture on the wall. It moved aside and revealed a safe door. In a moment he had it open, dived his hand into the empty interior — Suddenly he swung round, so suddenly Pulp levelled his automatic with even more accuracy.

'Take it easy, Ransome. Remember what I told you!'

'Just what do you know about this?' Ransome breathed. 'Somebody's cleaned out my safe and there isn't anybody living who can do that to me and get away with it!'

'Your safe was emptied last night during the riot,' Maria said, unmoved. 'The documents taken will remain in my possession until you give me certain information.'

'In your possession!' Ransome stared at

her in speechless amazement for a moment; then his emotions exploded. 'Who in hell do you think you are? Do you realize — '

'You're talking to Black Maria, Ransome. Better use the soft pedal,' Pulp advised.

'Black Maria!' Ransome blazed. 'Never heard of you!'

'You have now,' Maria murmured.

'She's got more dope on you, big shot, than the police ever even sniffed at! She pulled a straight clean job while your back was turned. Your safe emptied — just like that!'

'Nobody can do this to me,' Ransome repeated, breathing hard. 'Nobody, I tell you — '

'On the contrary, Ransome, it has been done,' Maria interrupted him curtly. 'I'm not here to sit listening to your blustering threats. I am here for business: you, as a man of business — in fact many businesses — should appreciate the point. Sit down and listen to what I have to say.'

Ransome obeyed slowly, his black brows scowling. 'I suppose you realize that for the theft of my documents I can have the police pick you up?'

'I realize it — but maybe you can tell what will happen if the police get the documents first? There is plenty in those papers that could make your position very — well, difficult.'

'Is that my stuff in that parcel?' Ransome snapped; and Maria's hand closed over it more tightly.

'Yes — but don't forget a revolver is covering you,' she replied. 'I am prepared to do business with you, Ransome, for my chief aim is not so much to expose you as to get a confession from you — or a statement, whichever you care to call it . . . I am referring to Arthur Salter.'

Ransome smiled crookedly. 'Well, what about him? He is back in the hands of the law, isn't he? What's that to do with me? He was convicted of converting company funds to his own use — '

'He was convicted, Ransome, because you arranged it. And unless you are prepared to admit the fact and bring the whole thing into the open your parcel of documents will find its way to the quarter where it can do the most good for decent society. You can take your choice.'

'Do you think for one moment I'd let you hand over that stuff to the police?' Ransome blazed. 'You don't know just how much power I have got, Black Maria.'

'True,' Maria shrugged, 'but I do know how much power *I* have got! You were not clever enough to prevent me getting the incriminating documents I needed, and you certainly will not be clever enough to prevent the rest of my plans coming to a head.'

'If you know what's good for you you'll hand those papers over!' Ransome shouted. 'You can't get — '

'Get wise to yourself, Ransome!' Pulp snapped. 'Get it through your thick skull that Black Maria's got you taped! And if it comes to that get it through your skull that I wouldn't mind drilling you. You're a pretty low-down sort of heel anyway and by rubbing you out I'd probably be doin' lots of guys a favour. I know enough to fix the rap for your murder on somebody else, don't you forget it. I haven't dealt with your kind of scum all my life for nothing . . . So start talking to the lady, and talk fast!'

Ransome shrugged. 'I guess it seems as though our carrot-headed friend has all the advantage,' he commented bitterly. 'Okay, what about Arthur Salter? What do you want me to do?'

'You will write a statement to the effect that his arrest was a — a frame-up, and you will state explicitly upon whose orders you acted. You had no particular reason for wanting Salter out of the way, but another man — Ralph Black — had.'

Ransome looked vaguely surprised, then he gave a reluctant nod.

'You're right — But look here, this 'Black' business is getting catching. Ralph Black — Black Maria . . . ' His dark eyes took on a glint. 'I get it! You're his sister! He told me about you once . . . '

'Indeed!' Maria froze completely. 'Then you may understand why I am interested in this business . . . My brother told you to fix up some charge against Arthur Salter to get him out of the way because he wished to marry Patricia Black — '

'Right,' Ransome assented grimly. 'I'll

230

tell you how it happened if that's what you want — but only on the understanding I get that parcel when we're through . . . '

Maria nodded gravely. 'You have my assurance. Go on.'

'Ralph Black and me did plenty of business deals together, and one deal involved a pretty large amount of money. Now I'm a guy that can't afford to stand out of money for long; too big an overhead. So I wrote Black that I'd do plenty if he didn't come across with the payment, see? He handed me a lot of boloney about being embarrassed or something. Maybe he was; I wouldn't know — but I did know I'd got to have my money . . . '

'Which in the first place, as I understand it, was borrowed not by my brother himself but by one of his underlings?' Maria put in.

'Yes, that's so. As a matter of fact it was one of his chain store managers, but it still made Black responsible for the whole return. I have no truck with underlings when it comes to repayments. Well, I wrote Black letters, but they had no effect; I tried to see him, and failed. Then at last I got him by telephone. He told me he couldn't lay his hands on the actual cash at that time but that he had an investment bond he'd transfer to me if I liked. Now the bond was worth double the money he owed me. He asked me if I was prepared to do a simple extra job to make the thing quits. I said I was.'

'Which was to fix Arthur Salter?' Maria snapped.

'Right! I fixed up a nice job and Black sent me the bond. It's amongst those papers you've got, as a matter of fact.'

Maria mused for a moment. 'Then that virtually brought to an end any real need to threaten Ralph Black for the money he owed you?'

'Sure it did. A week later your brother committed suicide, so I guess I only got what was owing to me just in time.'

'You've been very explanatory,' Maria observed. 'Now you will write a statement to the effect that you were ordered to do the job at the behest of my brother and — '

'Nothing doing!' Ransome shook his sleek head. 'Just what kind of a mug do you think I am? If I were to sign a statement like that I'd have the police poking their noses into all my activities and that's a chance I can't take.'

'You can take it or let the police have these papers,' Maria stated flatly.

Ransome thought for a moment, then he looked up eagerly.

'Listen, there may be other ways! I can pay off a guy called 'Bristles' who'd be willing to take the rap in Salter's place — Besides, think of the scandal it's going to make for the Black family if it's known your late brother deliberately had a man framed.'

'Your concern for the family doesn't interest me, Ransome. I have also heard about paying off other men to take the blame but that is of no use to me. I want a statement of fact and I mean to get it — an exact report of your orders, the investment bond you received, everything!'

Ransome thumped his fist on the desk. 'Supposing I do as you ask: do you think the police would accept the statement as given by me to you, and so to them? Like hell! I'd say you intimidated me into writing it. No, it won't work: I promise you that.'

'You are getting very irksome, Ransome,' Maria said wearily. 'I've told you what I want, and unless I get it I shall ask Mr. Martin to give his trigger finger some exercise.'

'Right!' Pulp agreed, his brows lowering. 'Get busy, Ransome, and start curling yourself around some notepaper!'

Ransome compressed his lips and turned savagely to the typewriter on the side desk. He fingered it with obvious unfamiliarity.

'Guess you'll have to wait a bit,' he growled. 'I'm no fast typer and my secretary's away — '

'I'll do it for you.' Maria got to her feet, motioned Pulp to keep her covered. 'I know better than you do what I want said, Ransome. Give me one of your memo sheets, a sheet of plain paper, and a carbon.'

'I've got no memos here — '

Pulp whipped open the desk drawer with his free hand and pulled out the requirements. The memo had the 'Onzi Financial Trust' heading.

'This is no surprise to me, Ransome,' Maria said dryly, seeing his bitter look as she screwed the interleafed papers into the roller. 'I've known for a long time you are at the back of Onzi's. Maybe the police would like to know it, too.'

'Someday,' Ransome breathed, 'I'll catch up on you for this!'

'Over my dead body,' Pulp said affably.

Maria started to click away industriously. At the end of her first line of type she slapped the roller lever then frowned as the roller failed to move. Grasping the knob she turned up two spaces and eyed the lever at the same time. The spring was missing so that the lever flapped loosely back and forth.

'Forgotten what to put?' Ransome asked sourly, as he saw she was lost in thought.

She recovered abruptly and went on typing. Finally she pulled the papers free, plonked down original and carbon and snatched up a pen.

'Sign!' she ordered.

Ransome studied the original and frowned. 'Say, what in heck is this? It reads like a receipt — 'In consideration of Investment Bond number blank, I am prepared to undertake the necessary steps for involving my employee, Arthur Salter, on a charge of embezzlement — ' Good God, what do you call this?'

'A statement of fact,' Maria replied. 'You notice that I have dated the receipt a week in precedence to my brother's death, which was the time you got his instructions — or so you have intimated.'

'Right — but what is the carbon copy for?'

'I am taking the carbon, and the original will be placed among my late brother's effects for discovery by the police at the time I shall decide. You neglected to confirm your telephone arrangement with my brother; you neglected to send a receipt for the Investment Loan. Now you are going to remedy the omission and prove the innocence of Arthur Salter at the same time. Your smart lawyers can figure out how to save you. Sign — and hurry up!'

Ransome looked at the still levelled automatic, snatched up the pen and scribbled his signature on both sheets.

'You'll have to hand over those documents before I can fill in the number of the Bond,' he said grimly.

Maria smiled, folded the papers up and put them in her bag.

'That won't be necessary, Ransome. I have been through your documents and taken notes and numbers of everything. For the moment I have all that I need from you. I will fill in the blanks for myself. And here — is your parcel.'

He snatched it from her and glared. 'Don't think you're getting away with this! I'll settle the account before either of us are much older.'

Maria made no reply, turned to the door as Pulp opened it for her. They hurried through the empty disorder of the dance hall and out to the taxi at the front. Instantly Joey jammed in the clutch and shot away from the kerb into the stream of traffic.

'Police headquarters,' Maria instructed;

then she relaxed and looked at Pulp triumphantly. 'Well, Mr. Martin?'

'You got me,' he muttered. 'Probably I'm dumb, but I don't get the hang of this letter-receipt business. I can see it shows the rap can be pinned on your dead brother, and I can see it makes Ransome a kind of catspaw — But you've slipped up,' he went on anxiously. 'If you give that statement to the police you'll have Ransome saying you forced him to write it at the point of a rod — which you did.'

'And suppose,' Maria said, 'the carbon copy of the receipt-letter were to be found among the documents I intend handing to the police?'

'Oh, well, in that case you'd be in the clear. It would look like the copy of a letter Ransome had sent out to — Holy cats!' Pulp sat up sharply, his eyes bright. 'I get it! You wouldn't be involved at all! And the original letter is among your brother's stuff, just like he'd received it on that date, huh?'

'Exactly.' Maria looked troubled for a moment. 'The police may wonder why it was they never found the original before when they tackled the matter of my brother's suicide. However, no doubt I can get over that by revealing some new and unexpected spot where my brother kept his papers — or even the ruse of the receipt sticking at the back of the drawer is not to be discounted . . . Quite a small point, which I shall master. I fancy, Mr. Martin, that we have written finis to Ransome's career — Ah, here we are,' she finished, as Joey drew in to the pavement.

'If you don't mind I'll hang around,' Pulp said uncomfortably. 'Cops and me don't sorta mix . . . '

Maria nodded and found Johnson in the station outer office as she entered. He got to his feet immediately, brief case in hand.

'Well?' he asked eagerly.

Maria did not reply immediately. She took the documents he gave her from the brief case — filled in the Investment Bond number on copy and original letter-receipt, then handed them back and started to explain. Johnson smiled and nodded grimly as he thrust the carbon receipt amidst the wad of documents.

'I fancy that takes care of everything, Miss Black,' he murmured, heading for the private inner door. 'Let's go.'

Inspector Davis was as grimly polite as usual as he drew up chairs, then he stood watching in some surprise as Johnson unloaded the documents from his case on to the desk.

'What's this?' His sharp grey eyes looked from Johnson to Maria.

'The evidence you need,' she replied. 'You will find among these documents many different reasons for arresting Hugo Ransome. And you will also find direct evidence of the fact that Arthur Salter was wrongfully convicted of embezzlement because of the machinations of my late brother.'

'This . . . for instance,' Johnson said quietly, and handed over the newly-added carbon letter.

Davis read it through, his lips tight. 'If there is an original of this letter among the effects of your late brother, Miss Black, it might do plenty towards exonerating Salter — '

'It *would* exonerate Salter,' Johnson

stated. 'I'd stake my reputation on it. At a retrial no jury could do anything else but acquit him — even less so when those other papers reveal the true extent of Ransome's activities.'

Davis gave a faint smile. 'Naturally we all know he is a crook. He's been a thorn in the side of the law for long enough — but we could never prove it. This time I think we have managed it ... ' He frowned as he went through the papers and pulled forth the investment bond. 'So he traded a man's liberty and honour for this, did he? Now I know he is several kinds of a rat — And to be frank, Miss Black, your brother doesn't seem to have been over-scrupulous.'

'I'm aware of that,' she nodded. 'But he is dead, and Ransome is not ... The point is that we've got enough evidence here to acquit young Salter.'

'Yes ... I'll see that the District Attorney has everything, believe me.' Davis stopped and looked at Maria thoughtfully. 'Speaking unofficially, Miss Black, I feel bound to tell you one or two things. This evidence will undoubtedly convict Ransome, but during the trial you will inevitably be cross-questioned about the statements of Salter and his wife — your niece. That is all right: you will be able to answer everything satisfactorily. But you will also have to explain where and how you got this evidence against Ransome. God knows, we're glad enough to get it, but the law is a tricky business and you might get into difficulty with Ransome's lawyer explaining how you got all this stuff. Naturally — again unofficially — it was stolen from Ransome?'

'Naturally,' Maria agreed calmly.

'That is where it is going to be tough on you,' Davis growled.

'But *I* didn't steal them,' Maria added. 'I spent yesterday evening in Maxie's Dance Hall, just as a sightseer. I talked to one or two people, and they talked to me. One waiter in particular can verify that. Then the riot broke out. I left in rather a hurry, as you can imagine. I was hurrying along the street outside when I came across a bundle of papers that had obviously been dropped. At that hour in the morning there were few people about and I was quite clearly the first person to find them. I picked them up, and knowing nothing of their value decided that the best person to handle them was my lawyer, Mr. Johnson. For that purpose I called on him early this morning.'

'Correct,' Johnson nodded.

'Then?' Davis questioned.

'Then I went home,' Maria shrugged. 'Mr. Johnson considered the documents were best in the hands of the police, so here they are.'

'You can prove what time you arrived home?'

'Easily. My sister-in-law was waiting up for me as it happened.'

Davis gave a grim smile. 'Just a case of a thief, completely unknown, dropping his booty after a getaway from the Dance Hall, eh? And quite by chance you happened on that booty?'

'As far as the law can prove otherwise, yes,' Maria said, and waited complacently.

'And I will verify that story,' Johnson stated.

Davis gave a reluctant sigh. 'Well, I've got to admit that it hangs together — and you've certainly been a darned sight smarter than any of my men. That of course is because you had no red tape to hold you back . . . As to Ransome, we'll have him before the day's out. The probability is that he'll try and skip town when he finds how you've tricked him — but I'll clap a warrant on him before he can get far . . . But you'd better watch out for yourself, Miss Black. Getting Ransome doesn't include his numerous boys, and they'll probably have orders to get you.'

'One is harder to get at than three,' Maria smiled. 'With my niece and her husband out of the way I feel much more comfortable: at least they are out of the firing line. As to myself — well, I am not an easy target. I take it that Salter and my niece will remain in custody?'

'Until the reopening of the trial, yes. From now on the matter will be in the hands of the District Attorney. But I'm sure the outcome of all this is not for a moment in doubt, Miss Black. It's you I'm still worrying about. If you want it you can have police protection.'

Maria rose and shook her head. 'No,

thank you, Inspector. I have many things to do yet, and I have my own way of safeguarding myself. I presume I am free until I am needed as a witness?'

'Certainly — but please remain within the city limits.'

'I will . . . Now about the original of this carbon-receipt letter. You are going to come and search for it?'

Davis nodded. 'It strikes me as odd we didn't discover it when a complete examination was made of your late brother's papers. However, we all make mistakes.' He gave a grave smile. 'I shall probably come myself and make a search in about an hour.'

Maria smiled too. Then she turned to the door.

'I'll stay, Miss Black,' Johnson said, as he held the door open. 'I've one or two things to talk over with the Inspector.'

Maria found Pulp waiting for her anxiously as she emerged on to the pavement.

'Well? How'd it go?' he asked eagerly.

'Everything is what you might call — jake,' Maria replied. 'I rather fancy the admirable Inspector is co-operating with me to put Ransome where he belongs — and now I have to hurry home to put the original letter-receipt among my brother's papers. And I have further work for you, Mr. Martin . . . From now on, until further orders, I want either you or somebody you can implicitly trust to keep a constant watch on my movements. Even though Ransome may be picked up that will not prevent his men from operating in reprisal. You see?'

'Leave it to me,' Pulp nodded. 'It'll cost you though — ' He named a sum, and looked at her apologetically.

'You shall have whatever is needed. Money is no object in achieving my end, to catch the person who murdered my brother . . . So far I have done pretty well, but I have not got what I want. My continued efforts may take me far afield — hence the need for constant protection.'

'While I'm around you're safe,' Pulp said calmly. 'Never, night or day, will you be left unobserved. I'll fix it. You may not see the watching eye but it'll be there. Rely on it!'

Maria opened her bag. 'Here is a week's money in advance. I know you will do the rest . . . When I want you again I'll contact you somehow.'

'All you'll need to do will be to signal with your hand. I will be there.'

Pulp helped her into the back seat of the taxi and slammed the door. She sat thinking as Joey drove swiftly through the streets back to the residence. Uppermost in her mind at the moment was the broken spring on the roller lever of Ransome's typewriter. It had come as a complete surprise to her and in a way conflicted with certain other notions. She had been pretty sure that the letters of 'Onzi' had constituted a possible threat to her brother's life unless prompt payment had been made. Ransome himself had exploded all that by revealing that payment *had* been made, thereby dispensing with any apparent reason for requiring Black's elimination.

Yes, it dispensed with the possible motive on the one hand — but on the other was the matter of the spring, and

Maria was convinced that somehow, somewhere, the spring played a decisive part.

As she entered the house there was nobody about. Quietly she slipped into the library, and parted with the original letter-receipt among the papers in the desk. Then she went upstairs and stayed only long enough to tidy herself before coming down for lunch. Alice, Janet, and Dick were present, halfway through the meal. As Maria seated herself, a bombardment of questions began immediately.

Maria went into the details as she proceeded with her lunch. 'So there it is,' she concluded. 'It will all be in the papers anyway when the trial is reopened, so there is no harm in you knowing the facts beforehand.'

Dick and Janet looked at each other, then at their mother. Alice was silent, toying with her serviette.

'Good for Pat!' Janet exclaimed at last, with an admiring shake of her dark head. 'I always knew she'd got plenty of nerve — And good for you, Aunt, for finding out so much! You have rather a weakness for looking into things, haven't you?'

'I do more than look into them, Janet,' Maria answered her calmly: then Dick said:

'Just how did you happen on to all this? I mean, did you deliberately interest yourself in the matter or was it just a chance?'

'I found it, Richard, in the course of my investigations in another direction . . . You might as well know something else now, too. Your father — your husband, Alice — did not commit suicide. He was murdered!'

'How can you be so sure of it?' Janet asked quietly.

'Mr. Johnson has given me a letter, written by your father, in which he says that if his death happened in any way contrary to natural causes it could certainly be assumed as murder. I have also gathered enough by now to know there was little reason for suicide. Your father left me twenty thousand dollars for expenses that I might incur in finding his killer. I am engaged on that work now.

Should I find the murderer — and believe me, I shall — I shall then claim my full bequest.'

'Which explains much,' Janet mused. 'We all thought it was a paltry sum for dad to leave you: now we can see there was a string attached to it . . . Whom did father say he thought might kill him?'

'He gave no clue.'

'Then who do you think did it?' Dick asked bluntly.

'I don't know yet, Richard,' Maria shrugged. 'And incidentally, was your reason for suspecting murder created by those letters among your father's effects?'

He seemed to hesitate momentarily. 'Yeah — sure. What other reason would I have?'

'I don't know; but it struck me as a flimsy basis for your belief.'

Dick shrugged, glanced at Janet and his mother sharply, then went on, 'Well, anyway, it was the only visible reason I had for suspecting it was murder. Of course I have lots of other theories — and one in particular . . . But there's no proof — '

'I'd like to hear some of those other theories,' Maria said grimly.

'O.K. Suppose, then — ' Dick broke off and looked up in irritation. 'Well, Walters, what is it?'

Walters looked at Alice. 'There are two gentlemen here, madam, from police headquarters — an Inspector Davis and — '

'I'll see them, Walters.' Maria rose hurriedly. 'This is my field, Alice,' she added. 'I can handle it better than you, I think.'

Annoyed at the interruption she swept into the hall and found Davis and his colleague waiting.

'Oh, good afternoon, Miss Black,' Davis said. 'I have the authority to — '

'To conduct a search once more through my late brother's papers? Follow me.'

Maria led the way to the library and waited while the desk drawers were examined. At last Davis had singled out the letter he needed, together with all other technical details relating to the investment bond that had passed to Hugo Ransome.

'I guess we missed this last time we searched,' he observed calmly, putting the drawers back. 'Thanks, Miss Black: this is all we need.'

At the front door she retained Davis for a moment. 'About Ransome, Inspector . . . Did you get him?'

'Yes, we got him. As I had expected he tried to skip town but we nabbed him at Pennsylvania Railroad Station. Right now he's where we want him. I also contacted the District Attorney and am awaiting his final okay concerning a reopening of the Salter trial. But I'd still advise you to be careful, Miss Black. From what I hear several of Ransome's boys are around looking for you. We can't do anything about that: we've got to have proof. So unless you'll take police escort it is still your own responsibility.'

Maria smiled. 'Thank you, Inspector, but the answer is still the same.'

He shook hands and departed. Maria returned quickly to the dining room but to her irritation Dick had gone.

'Where did Richard go?' she demanded of Alice.

'Why — upstairs.' She looked surprised for a moment, then she asked earnestly, 'Maria dear, what did those men want? Tell us!'

'All they wanted was some more evidence for convicting Ransome and freeing Patricia and Arthur Salter,' Maria replied hurriedly. 'Now you must excuse me. I have to speak to Richard . . . '

She hastened upstairs, to find Dick just leaving his room. 'Anything wrong, Aunt?' he asked, as Maria confronted him.

'I thought,' she said, 'you had come up for your usual rest. I wanted to catch you before you got settled — '

'No rest this afternoon,' he smiled. 'And anyway I don't always take one. Depends on how I feel. Today I've plenty else on my mind. I've special work to get done in town. See you later . . . '

'Just a minute, Richard. What were you going to say to me at lunch when I was called away? About your suspicions regarding the murder of your father . . . '

He glanced at his watch. 'Listen, Aunt, I just haven't the time to go into it now.

I'm late as it is. Tell you what: we'll get together later, eh? Right?'

Without giving her time to answer he hurried on his way downstairs. Maria was standing lost in thought when Janet came up to the corridor.

'Dick seemed to be in a hurry,' she commented. 'What happened to his usual rest?'

'For some reason, by no means clear to me, he has decided to forgo it,' Maria shrugged; then she looked at Janet's placid features. 'I am glad we have a moment together, Janet. I'd like to have a little private chat with you.'

'Surely. I've only come up to rest, anyway. Come along into my room.'

She led the way in and motioned to the armchair.

'I don't want you to take offence at some of the things I am going to ask, Janet,' Maria said quietly, sitting back and interlocking her fingers. 'Believe me, I have good reason . . . Firstly, about your young composer friend — Mr. Wade. You say you are in love with him and are trying to keep it from Montagu, your producer or manager, or whatever he is, in case he might make things awkward for you if he found out . . . '

'Right,' Janet assented quietly.

'Your father — with the one exception of your maid — was the one person who knew of your affection for this young man?'

'Right again.'

'Your father,' Maria persisted, 'was a man of ruthless purpose. If he saw anything likely to eclipse or even cast a shadow over the family standing, if he had reason to suspect the least lowering in the social prestige he had set, he was likely to be prompted to sudden and unscrupulous action . . . ?'

'Yes . . . ' Janet nodded moodily. 'His merciless exactitude was the one thing which always went against the grain.'

'Assume — only assume, mark you — that he had decided to do something to drive a wedge between you and Mr. Wade,' Maria proceeded. 'Since he knew you were associating together he might quite easily have thought of something on the lines of Arthur Salter's affair to separate you and Wade. Suppose he had

had such a plan and Wade had found out about it?'

'Are you daring to suggest that Peter — But you can't be! The thing's too ridiculous!'

'Listen to me, Janet,' Maria snapped. 'From what I have discovered I have every reason for thinking that whoever murdered your father arranged the 'suicide' on the same day that your father met his death.'

'What of it?' Janet asked coldly. 'You can't mean you think Peter would do such a thing. How do you imagine — even granting there was a plan laid by father to separate Peter and me — how do you imagine Peter could ever have found out about it?'

'I don't know . . . unless you knew of it and told him.'

'Really, Aunt, this is puerile!'

Maria shrugged. 'It is easily settled. Where was Mr. Wade on the day your father died?'

'I don't know.' Janet's face set in adamant lines. 'On the day father died it was the last night of my concert run and I was at the theatre from about five in the afternoon until the early hours of the following morning. I didn't see Peter all that day.'

'And what did you do during the afternoon?' Maria asked.

'I attended to correspondence. I was in the lounge all the afternoon with Mary. Dad came home about twenty minutes to five and promised to listen to my concert over the radio. Not that it signifies. Everybody knew he was going to listen to it, anyway.'

'Including Mr. Wade?'

'Yes; I believe I told him about it.'

'I'm sorry if I offended you, Janet — but I did warn you, you know. You've been a great help, if that is any consolation.'

Janet relaxed a little. 'Sorry I blew up, only I'm afraid you touched a sore spot. Just what do you hope to get out of all this? Peter would never have done the thing you suggest, I'm convinced of it. One might as well say that I did it.'

'That possibility had occurred to me,' Maria reflected.

'What!'

'Only because your alibi is so perfect,' Maria beamed. 'You were at the theatre singing when your father died. That is an established fact.'

'Am I supposed to have killed my father by remote control, or something?'

'Somebody did,' Maria answered, with conviction. 'Some device or other killed your father after he entered the library for the evening to do his work and listen to your singing. The device was arranged between the time when the maid Lucy tidied the library in the morning and the time your father went into it in the evening. Had it been otherwise the maid would in all probability have seen the device.'

'What device?' Janet demanded, puzzled.

'I don't know yet — but something diabolically clever which fired your father's own gun and dropped it beside him afterwards.'

'Well, anyway, that discounts Peter,' Janet said, thinking. 'How could he have got into the house during the daytime to fix a — a device in the library?'

'Many things are possible to a resolute person, Janet. The grounds are devoid of clues at the back of the house, where the library abuts — that I know, but then, as Anstruther has pointed out in his treatise, *Murder Without Clue*, there are twelve different methods that can be employed by a criminal to avoid leaving either footprints or marks of tampering on the window . . . I do not suggest that Mr. Wade knows any of these methods: I am merely passing comment. Another thing I know — the murderer was well acquainted with your father's movements.'

'Which puts Peter further away than ever from your unjust suspicions!' Janet retorted. 'How could he know father's movements.'

'Only from you, my dear . . . ' Then as Janet stood grimly silent Maria turned to the door. She looked back thoughtfully. 'Remember, Janet, that if an outside agency was not responsible it leaves only those in the house!'

With that she left, made for her room, and began to tabulate her notes while matters were still fresh in her mind.

'I believe I have trapped Hugo Ransome, thereby clearing Patricia and Arthur Salter. Ransome's letters to Ralph are no longer a threat and motive for murder. But against this there is a missing spring on Ransome's typewriter, which could correspond to the one I found in the library. But something goes with the spring to complete the contrivance and I still do not know what it is.

'In other matters I have used more open tactics in order to judge reactions. Alice is guarded and has lost all her early manner of inanity: I begin to suspect a shrewd, grim side to her nature. Janet is cold, but inwardly agitated. Richard hints at new theories that led him to suspect murder — and the moment I came into the open it seemed to lead him to the decision to visit town suddenly. I cannot agree that it was purely coincidence and shall therefore look into it.

'Where was Peter Wade on the day of Ralph's death? What smashed a wine-glass? These two points I must clear up.

'Janet says she spent the fatal afternoon doing correspondence with her maid

Mary. This must be checked.

'*Richard's typewriter must be found and the puzzling incident in his bedroom fully cleared up.*'

Maria locked the book away, dressed for further outside excursions, then went downstairs. In the hall she summoned Walters.

'Walters, I want you to think very carefully. What exactly happened here on the day your master — er — died? Can you recall the events which took place?'

'Very easily, madam. Pardon me . . . ' He dived a hand into his coat and produced a small, thick diary, thumbed the gold-edged leaves swiftly and looked apologetic meanwhile. 'I hope, madam, that you will forgive this little indulgence but it is a habit of mine to record all matters of the household — for efficiency, you understand . . . '

'A very excellent system,' Maria acknowledged, beaming — and wondered why on earth she had not questioned him ere this.

'June the fourth,' he said presently. 'In

the morning until after lunch, everybody was at home — the mistress, Mr. Richard, Miss Patricia, and Miss Janet. By 'everybody' I am excepting the master, of course. He left the house as usual at precisely eight-forty-three. After lunch Miss Patricia left the house and departed in her sports car. Mr. Richard went up to his room for his usual rest. Miss Janet's maid Mary arrived and she and Miss Janet spent the afternoon in the lounge attending to correspondence . . . '

'Go on!' Maria exclaimed, making notes of her own.

'The mistress spent most of the afternoon on the terrace, reading. There was only one caller beside the usual tradesmen — '

'Whom?' Maria looked up sharply.

'A young lady, madam. She had an urgent message for Mr. Richard. I took it up to his room and awaited his answer. He had to write it down, so I presume it was private.'

'Then he didn't come down and see this young lady for himself?'

'No, madam.'

'Hmmm . . . While you were upstairs, where was she?'

'I asked her to be seated in the hall here — in the chair over there.'

'She gave no name?'

'I'm afraid not.' Walters reflected; then, 'I imagine it was an important message because Mr. Richard asked me to get a book out of the library — Dunsant's *Electrical Reactions* I believe it was. Then he seemed to change his mind for he cancelled the request before I had even reached the door of his room. He said he would get it for himself later on.'

'And did he?' Maria asked.

'I think he did, madam, yes . . . ' Walters paused, his wavering eyes back on his diary. 'There are more notes if you would care — '

'In a moment, Walters. Tell me, what did this young lady look like?'

'She was blonde; straight-featured, good-looking. A little over five feet tall and maybe twenty-four years of age.'

Maria smiled pensively. 'Did you ever

consider entering the field of criminology, Walters? You have an amazing mind for detail . . . '

He gave one of his rare smiles. 'You are too generous, madam. The well-trained servant knows every detail, otherwise he is not well-trained. I have long prided myself on having an eye for events . . . But to revert to my diary — The master came home at five-forty-one precisely. He went to his library at six fifteen. Only the mistress was at home otherwise and she had retired to her room . . . At nine-ten precisely the master rang for his wine. I took it to the library and you know what happened then, madam.'

'He rang at nine-ten for his wine?' Maria repeated, thinking. 'Was that not rather an early hour for it?'

'He varied the time to suit his requirements, madam. But it was nine-ten: I noted it by the kitchen clock when he rang.'

'Hmmm. Naturally you gave these details to the police?'

'Yes, madam.'

'Then you broke into the library, found

my brother lying dead in the armchair with the revolver near to him, and the radio going full volume?'

Walters nodded. 'I switched it off and called the police.'

'Can you recall what the radio was playing?'

'Er — yes. It was operatic music, obviously relayed from the concert in which Miss Janet was singing.'

Maria nodded and made a note. 'What time exactly did you break into the library after realizing tragedy had happened?'

'It would be about ten minutes after the master had rung for his wine. I became alarmed at the lack of answer from the library, called the mistress down, and — It would be approximately nine-twenty,' Walters concluded.

Maria put her notebook away and smiled. 'An excellent record of events, Walters.'

'Thank you, madam.' He put his diary back in his pocket.

'One other thing, Walters. During the afternoon did you hear any strange sounds from the library, observe anybody go in or out of it? Did anybody in the family, for example, ask you for a pair of stepladders?'

'Why — no!' Walters looked astonished.

'Thank you — that will be all.' Then as he turned away Maria added, 'Please tell the mistress I shall be home during the evening sometime.'

8

Maria left the Black residence with Dick's headquarters as her goal. As she went she thought a good deal about what Walters had told her — and of other recollections, particularly the broken wineglass. She was still thinking about it when she arrived at the cabaret building. Dick was absent and his little office was closed. Maria compressed her lips as she recalled that he had merely referred to 'business in town . . . ' That might mean anywhere.

She returned to the doorman. 'Where is Mr. Black this afternoon, my man? He isn't in his office.'

The doorman reflected, then: 'I know where he might be, if it's really urgent. Depends if it is a business matter.'

'It is most definitely urgent,' Maria retorted.

'Ah! Then you can reach him no doubt at Hanray Apartments in Times Square. His associate, Miss Conway, lives there.

Any important messages for him can be left with her — see? I wouldn't have told you had it not been urgent.'

Maria gave a nod of thanks and went on her way. In ten minutes she had reached Hanray Apartments and stood in the imposing doorway surveying the copperplate list of tenants. Finally she took the lift to the fifth floor, stepped out and walked along the richly carpeted corridor. Everything appeared very opulent. There seemed little doubt that the finances of Miss Conway were extensive . . .

At the door of 409 Maria paused, eyeing the neat copperplate under the bell push —

Miss Jean Conway
Sound Engineer

'So — the science of sound,' Maria reflected. 'And she is probably the young lady I saw leaving Richard's office . . . '

She paused with her knuckles an inch from the door panel as a voice made itself heard. It was a girl's voice, quite distinct.

'I think you're a rat! A two-timing rat! And I don't care who knows it!'

'Oh, you do!' Dick's voice snapped back, cold and hard. 'Then get this, you damned little gold-digger! For two cents I'd — '

He stopped suddenly and muttered something. Maria took advantage of the lull and knocked sharply. In a moment the door opened and Dick stood there in shirtsleeves, a pencil behind his ear, his face hot and harassed.

'Aunt! How on earth did you find me?'

'The doorman at the cabaret — '

'Won't you come in?' asked a girl's voice, and from round the angle of the door there appeared the slender blonde girl Maria had seen leaving Dick's office the previous day. She was holding a wad of clipped typescript in one hand and a blue pencil in the other.

'This is — is Jean Conway, a close friend of mine,' Dick said, essaying a smile.

'Why, of course, Miss Black!' Jean said impulsively. 'Dick has mentioned you so often.' She tossed aside her pencil and held out her hand. 'Do come in, please!'

Maria shook hands, took the chair Jean indicated, and sat down. She glanced about her. The room was well furnished and yet looked untidy. By the window was a desk upon which reposed endless sheets of quarto, a dictaphone, a telephone, and a typewriter. Apart from this office-like quality the room was clearly intended to be a lounge. There was a grand piano, bookcase, bureau . . .

'Well, Aunt, has something important happened?' Dick asked briefly.

'It was important, yes, but — ' Maria broke off and frowned. 'Am I right in thinking that you two were quarrelling a moment ago? I distinctly heard — '

'Oh, that!' The girl laughed. 'It was the dictaphone . . . ' She nodded her fair head towards it. 'Our play,' she said proudly. 'We were doing a bit of rehearsal. Naturally Dick has told you all about it?'

Dick looked uncomfortable. 'No, I haven't told anybody anything,' he growled. 'We said we would keep it a secret and I've done so. That was what we planned, wasn't it?'

'Yes, but — ' Jean looked at Maria

solemnly. 'I do believe I have put my foot in it!'

'So,' Maria said slowly, 'this dictaphone was the 'woman' in your room the other night, Richard?'

'The — the what?' Jean exclaimed; then when Maria had explained to her she went off into a fit of merriment.

'Yes, it's right enough,' Dick growled. 'You see, Aunt, Jean and I are working together on a play, but the plot is so original — at least we think it is — that we don't want it to leak out before we're ready to launch the thing properly. In my profession a chance word might give the business away. So we tried — at least I tried — to keep the whole thing a secret. We even play the parts ourselves in the preliminary stages so that nobody else can be in on it until we're ready for casting. We speak our parts into the dictaphone and then play them back and judge results. The other night I was not sure of one section and took the dicta-phone home with me. I had the thing on full volume without realizing it — Well, I guess it woke you up. Rather than give

271

anything away I tried to convince you that you had had a nightmare.'

'And why should I have given anything away?' Maria asked calmly.

'No reason: only you might have — We all let things slip out accidentally sometimes. I couldn't take the chance. Plenty of smart aleck writers could beat me to it with this plot because we don't get much spare time in which to work on it.'

'In other words, Miss Black, a play plotted in camera,' Jean smiled. 'And is it giving us a headache! Dick has to spend half his time with his cabaret and that means I have the typing to do. Then when he gets time off I'm usually out somewheres doing professional work, and he types instead. Only on very rare occasions do we both get time off together as it is today.'

'Which, Richard, is why you did not have your usual rest today?' Maria asked. relaxing.

'That's right,' he nodded. 'I'm so sorry, Aunt, if I led you up the garden . . . By the way, Jean and I are engaged only nobody knows just yet. It might stop me getting the best work out of some of my lovelies,' he grinned.

Maria looked at them both in turn — his warm and anxious face; the girl's keen and bright . . . Then she gave one of her rare chuckles.

'I was just thinking of some of the things I had thought of to explain the presence of a woman in your room in the early hours. And it wasn't improved by your sisters' talk of woman-beating propensities, either!'

'Just gas,' Dick grunted. 'You know what sisters are.'

'Suppose,' Jean said, 'I fix up some tea? Suppose too, Miss Black, that I call you 'Aunt'? So much more informal. I'll go and fix it . . . ' and she departed to other regions.

Maria rose, moved leisurely to the typewriter and studied it. Dick watched her in complete silence.

'Bit of an old crock,' he said. 'Only we manage to work it between us. We started off with it, doing the manuscript I mean, and there was no point then in getting a

273

new machine and doing all that retyping. Two sets of type in one script puts a producer off his stroke. I know!'

Maria went on studying the machine. It was perfectly intact even though it was an archaic model. At length she turned.

'This play of yours should be remarkably original, Richard, to need so much secrecy . . . '

'We think so. Matter of fact the original plot was conceived by Jean. She got it together as the natural outcome of her profession. Maybe you've noticed the plate outside the door? She is employed by a firm who control sound apparatus in cinemas. Her job is to service the apparatus, correct faults in an emergency, and so forth. Highly technical work . . . ' Dick broke off and smiled ruefully. 'I suppose it's really rather odd — both of us with plenty of money yet no time to get together . . . Now, what did you want to see me about?'

'I was going to ask you to elaborate your views on why you thought your father was murdered.'

'Yes . . . Well, I have one very good

274

theory of how the murder might have been done, as I told you. But I have nobody whom I suspect — only the method. You see, I — '

'Now, Aunt, here we are!'

Jean returned from the domestic regions, wheeling a tea wagon in front of her on which tea was prepared.

'How's that for efficiency?' she asked, smiling. 'And I'm hanged if we won't have tea as well this time, eh, Dick? In honour of Aunt's visit!'

'Yes — sure we will . . . ' He looked at Maria and shrugged his shoulders at this second interruption in his efforts to explain.

'Rather a disturbing business about Patricia, isn't it?' Jean asked seriously, pouring out the tea. 'Dick was telling me how you — '

'I'd rather forget the whole business for a while, Miss Conway — '

'Oh, please call me Jean.'

'Very well — Jean.' Maria took the cup of tea. 'Tell me, what sort of a plot are you working out? Or is it still too much of a secret to divulge? Richard tells me that it was your idea . . . '

'Yes, it was. A completely new way of killing somebody without being near them . . . ' Jean smiled reflectively. 'Sounds a diabolical way for a bright girl to spend her spare time, doesn't it?'

'It might prove of ultimate benefit,' Maria said gravely.

Just for an instant the girl's grey eyes were full of sharp inquiry; then again she was her smiling self.

'I think Dick is too cautious,' Jean went on, stirring her tea. 'When we planned secrecy it was hardly intended to include relations — at least not responsible ones like you. Why, you might be able to make some suggestions! You see, it is the story of a man — a nasty piece of work — who is murdered while the real murderer is far away. The solution is — a locomotive whistle! What do you think of that?'

'A locomotive whistle?' Maria repeated, puzzled.

'Well, that is how it is at present. For that matter any strident whistle would suffice . . . You see I happen to know almost all there is to know about sound.

In our story the villain is a crystal gazer, a quack astrologer, but that's a blind for his real motives. He is found dead with his face all cut up as it lies in his broken crystal. It looks like heart failure . . . only it isn't. It's murder.'

'Very interesting.' Maria sipped her tea. 'And just how is it done?'

'The murderer switches globes. He takes away the real crystal and substitutes one filled with lethal gas: At a chosen time — which we haven't yet fixed — an engine whistle or a factory siren goes off. The crystal gazer is looking into the 'crystal' at that moment: all that has been planned, of course.'

'And then?'

Jean put down her cup. 'The whistle smashes the globe and the gas floods the villain's face, killing him instantly. The gas evaporates and leaves no clue. The murderer is far away at the time and can prove it.'

'Hmm . . . ' Maria said, and pondered. 'Isn't it just a bit unconvincing?'

'Lord, no! It's entirely logical. Ask any expert in sound — a singer, a piano tuner, a teacher of the deaf . . . It is a proven fact that a sound wave, a vibration in the air, will smash a hollow glass globe in pieces — a Humboldt globe as it is called — providing the sound is high enough in pitch, sustained enough, and intense enough.'

'You really mean it?' Maria asked earnestly.

'I'll prove it to you . . . Watch this!' Jean got to her feet, picked up a thin tumbler from the sideboard and put it on the table by the window.

Opening the lid of the grand piano Jean depressed the loud pedal and began to gently tap a single note high on the keyboard. After a second or two it merged into a continuous steady flow of sound — then abruptly the glass on the table split clean in half and fell apart in two semi-circles.

'Voila!' the girl exclaimed, laughing.

'That wineglass . . . ' Maria muttered.

'The what?' Dick asked, surprised.

'I — I was referring to the glass,' she said, recovering her composure abruptly. 'That was a very remarkable demonstration, Jean. Would any note on the piano do it?'

'It is all a matter of pitch and direction. Piano and table are in a straight line, as you see — which is the way a sound wave travels. If the glass had been out of the straight line it would have needed a horn or architectural device in the room itself to bring the sound into focus . . . As for the pitch any note around high C will do the trick.'

Maria gripped her watch-chain and meditated.

'So you see, Aunt,' Jean resumed, 'the idea is sound enough . . . In more senses than one! Don't you recall that Caruso used to smash a wineglass many a time with the higher notes of his voice? It has to be an empty glass, mind you, or an empty globe as in our play — then the glass will break at the part in 'sympathy' with the sound wave. Sometimes the top falls off, sometimes a diamond shape, sometimes the thing splits in twain, as happened just now. As for the globe in our play, a globe full of gas is empty for all practical purposes. So our plot isn't at all bad.'

'I'm inclined to agree with you,' Maria

said. 'Tell me something, Jean — Is it only glass which will break under these special vibrations?'

'Not necessarily. Any brittle object will: even a complete mirror can crack up its entire length. A sheet of thin metal, a thin layer of ice, a taut skin like a drum top, or a length of thin wire under great tension . . . ' Jean stopped and gave a little shrug. 'You are not thinking of writing up the idea yourself, are you?' she asked, in mock gravity.

'I'm afraid my interests go deeper than play writing, Jean.' Maria thought for a moment, then: 'Did you ever meet Richard's father?'

'Once or twice,' the girl said quietly. 'It was mainly through him that I met Dick. You see, Mr. Black's business was concerned a great deal in buying up all kinds of small firms for the purpose of conversion into his network of ever-expanding stores. He paid the minimum compensation allowed by the law — and a pitiably small amount it was in many cases. My brother Alfred was one of the victims. When his business was appropriated and the money for compensation was worse than useless, he just went to the dogs. I went to see Mr. Black and had a showdown with him. I as good as told him he was a commercial dictator who didn't give two buttons whom he trampled on so long as he gained his ends . . . '

'And what was his reaction to that?'

'He laughed in my face! I admit quite frankly that my one aim thereafter was to injure him, ruin him if I could, just as he had ruined my brother. With that object in mind I decided to strike at him through Dick. I arranged it that I met Dick. But . . . well, I couldn't go through with it. I'm afraid I fell in love instead. And when Alfred happened to get a good position far away in England — which he still holds — my ideas of revenge faded. But of course Dick and I kept our romance secret from his father because he hated me like poison — and now we don't tell anybody for different reasons — mainly Dick's chorines.'

'So your brother got a position in my country after all,' Maria smiled. 'I wonder if I know the firm?'

'Perhaps . . . Edward Layton and Associates, the big steel people.'

'No, I don't know of them.'

'The more I hear of things generally the more I wonder how many lives father did wreck,' Dick said moodily.

Maria got to her feet decisively. 'I'm afraid I must leave. I have one or two matters to attend to. I only came to ask Richard a question and he answered it for me while you were preparing this excellent tea . . . So I won't keep you two young people from your work any longer. I know time is precious for you.'

'You'll come again, of course?' Jean urged, holding out her hand as she opened the door.

'I shall see you again without doubt,' Maria responded, with a rather ambiguous smile. 'See you later, Richard.'

She went off down the corridor, but at the lift Dick caught up with her, detained her before she could press the bell-push.

'I made the excuse to Jean that I had forgotten to tell you something,' he said quickly. 'Partly true, for that matter . . . I wanted to tell you that it is Jean's plot outline that I think might account for father's murder! That's what I've been trying to tell you. Since she has come out into the open I might as well tell you the truth. I was going to outline the same theory without admitting it was the plot for a play.'

'I see.' Maria looked at him levelly. He seemed to be in earnest. 'As a matter of fact, Richard, the same idea occurred to me the moment I heard the plot . . . But how do you suggest it might apply to your father's death?'

'It can only apply to his death if somehow the plot has leaked out. Jean may unwittingly have let something slip to one of father's many enemies. Now you see what I mean . . . why I said I suspected murder. If anybody got hold of the idea they would have the perfect setup for murder.'

'Hmm maybe. Have you ever had any drafts of this idea knocking about the house? Ever mentioned it to anybody yourself?'

'No. I've done plenty of typing of the play at home, of course, but I've always taken care never to let anything get about.' Dick's face became serious. 'You see, the murderer, granting he or she got hold of this idea, even has the means of doing the trick . . . I mean Janet. She is a singer and can hit high C and above. Of course I know it's crazy to cast any reflections on her but — '

'As I see it,' Maria said, 'there is reflection cast on another person besides Janet . . . I mean Jean. She alone would understand the mechanics involved.'

'I know that, but — Honestly, Aunt, that's beyond the pale.'

'No more so than suspecting Janet; less so, in fact. Jean admits she devised the plot, admits she had no liking for your father despite her final decision to abandon her desire for revenge. It would not even be necessary in her case for her to find a copy of the plot . . . ' Maria paused and frowned. 'The trouble is that I personally like the girl. She's charming, and most intelligent — but I can't let that influence me. Incidentally, Richard, Janet knows by now that I have discovered that whoever arranged the 'suicide' did it on the day of the murder, probably in the afternoon. You might as well know that, too.'

'Well, that settles a lot,' Dick smiled. 'On that afternoon I was in my room trying to get some rest; Jan and her maid were somewhere or other, and I think mother was reading. Pat had gone out. Come to think of it, she must have gone to Jamestown to — '

'Quite,' Maria interrupted. 'But you have missed something.'

'I have?' Dick thought, then a startled look came into his eyes. 'Good lord, Jean! On that day . . . '

Maria gave a grim smile. 'On that day a blonde young lady called — during the afternoon — with a message for you. She was left alone in the hall for ten minutes . . . '

'Yes, it was I,' Jean said frankly, suddenly appearing. She was looking concerned. 'I came along to find what was keeping Dick. I — I couldn't help overhearing what you were saying. You don't have to hide anything, you know. I know Mr. Black was murdered. Dick told me he suspected it long ago and he also told me how you had proved the fact beyond doubt . . . '

'Why did you call on Richard that afternoon?' Maria asked quietly.

'I had a section of the draft play I wanted Dick to check. It was not feasible to ring him up about it; besides, it needed information from one of the technical books in his father's library. I knew he rested in the afternoon so rather than bother him I sent up Walters with a note. He rewrote the section I wanted and said he'd let me have the library book later on.'

'And you waited in the hall?'

'Yes. I didn't give my name in case Mr. Black happened to be about. I knew it was unlikely but I was taking no chances. He'd have had the door slammed in my face and would probably have made things unbearable for Dick, too . . . '

'I suppose,' Maria mused, 'nobody saw you as you sat in the hall?'

'No. I heard a typewriter clicking away noisily in the lounge but I didn't see anybody.'

286

'Well, Jean, thank you for being so frank. I don't doubt it will all straighten out finally ... Now I really must be going.'

She entered the lift and descended to the street level again. She was smiling grimly to herself as she started off back for home. She had spent a most profitable afternoon ...

★   ★   ★

Walters intercepted her as she entered the house. 'There has been a telephone call for you, madam, from police headquarters. An Inspector Davis would like you to call him.'

'Get the number for me, Walters. I'll 'phone from my room.'

She hurried on upstairs and by then the call was through. Davis's clipped voice came over the wire.

'Hallo, Miss Black ... I've just had word through from the District Attorney's office saying that he will reopen the Salter trial seven days from today. Thought I'd better tell you so you can make your arrangements to stand by as a witness. You'll probably be needed.'

'I will, yes,' Maria said. 'Did the District Attorney give any hint as to the possible outcome of the trial?'

'He could hardly do that, Miss Black. But unofficially you can take it for granted that Salter and his wife are as good as free right now . . . Good-bye.'

'Thanks . . . good-bye.' Maria hung up. 'Seven days. Once the trial starts it might last any length of time and I'd lose all the ground I have covered. I have got to finish this job in seven days come what may. And I think I can . . .'

She brought her diary to light, compared her notes with the typewritten dossier, then started to write steadily —

'*Have met Jean Conway, Richard's fiancée — a very likeable girl and extremely intelligent, I should imagine. She is a sound (acoustic) engineer. I am concerned that she has outlined a perfect plot for murder — presumably intended for a play. It could have been used to kill Ralph, and Jean Conway alone (at least* so far as I have found up to now) had the time, the motive, and the necessary knowledge. I am wondering if she realizes that she gave me a clue. She referred to 'taut wire under immense strain — ' Is that the other necessity which matches the spring? I believe I might find out from the book 'Electrical Reactions.'

'Did Jean Conway sit quietly in the hall for the ten minutes that she was alone? She says she heard the typewriter clicking in the lounge, which seems to check up. Investigate further.

'The time is exactly — 4.45 p.m.

'P.S. — She says her brother is employed by Edward Layton & Associates of England. Why 'Associates'? This either is a deliberately false statement or else a quite natural mistake due to her being an American. Check same.'

Maria put her diary away then hurried downstairs to the library. A search through the card index soon gave her the position of the book she required. She took down Dunsant's *Electrical Reactions*, moved to the desk with it and began to browse through the pages. Half an hour . . . an hour, before she was through. Closing the book, she got up and rang for Walters.

'Madam?'

'Walters, I want you to obtain for me a length of single-gauge wire — about six feet length will do. It must be steel, not copper, and its width must not exceed one hundredth of an inch. Its tension must be capable of standing a strain of two pounds under full load.'

Walters made notes. 'In a steel wire, madam, that is going to be very brittle,' he remarked.

'Yes, I know.' She studied him keenly as he waited, then she went on, 'I want that wire at the earliest moment.'

'I'll have it obtained from the electrical stores within fifteen minutes.'

'Thank you, Walters. I'll wait here for it — Oh, Walters!' He turned at the door and waited.

'Walters, have you ever had a similar request from anybody?'

'No, madam — never.' And as Maria

nodded he went out silently. She thought for a moment then hurried upstairs to her room and took the typewriter spring from her box. By the time she had returned to the library Walters was just re-crossing the hall. He came in behind her and laid a length of hair-thin wire on the blotting pad.

'Is that correct, madam?'

'I think so, yes.' Maria pulled the wire gently in her fingers. 'I shall now require a pair of stepladders, if you please.'

He swallowed something and retired majestically. The ladders were duly brought, then when she was alone again Maria locked the door and stood the ladders in front of the crossed antique guns nearest to the chair where her brother had died.

Wire in hand she mounted up, made a loop in the wire and put the loop on the nail that supported the barrel of the downwardly-pointing gun. Her eyes gleamed at what she saw. The faint scratch in the rust was exactly of the same infinitesimal width as the wire itself.

'So, Maria, you were right,' she muttered. 'A wire similar to this was looped round this nail — and the spring loop was round the other nail which supports the gun butt. Now let us see . . . '

She stepped down and recovered the .38 automatic. Ascending the ladder again she laid the automatic over the antique gun, using the central nail as support through the trigger guard. It struck her as being more than coincidence that the .38 was almost exactly the same size as the antique gun. The nails, if anything too large for the antique, projected just far enough to also support the .38.

'Now let me see . . . ' she mused. 'This automatic could not hold up like this. But if the spring were fastened to the trigger and drawn back to the butt-nail — so; and the wire were fastened at just sufficient tension to prevent the trigger being pulled — being looped round the barrel nail, so — we have the gun secure. Then what? Obviously the snapping of the wire would allow the spring to pull back and fire the revolver. The support would go at the same time and the gun would jump off the centre nail support to the floor . . . So! Splendid!'

She got down to the floor again, put her wire away carefully, and the gun back in the desk drawer. She had the stepladders removed again, then she made her way thoughtfully into the lounge where Alice was resting before dinner.

'I shan't ask you where you've been, Maria,' she said, rather hopelessly. 'Ever since you arrived you seem to have slipped in and out of the house like a phantom . . . '

'I may do so for quite a time yet,' Maria smiled, seating herself. 'Slowly but surely, Alice, I am getting to the root of the mystery surrounding Ralph's death, and of course nearer to the identity of the murderer.'

Alice raised her eyebrows and waited.

'Alice, on the afternoon preceding Ralph's death in the evening you were reading on the terrace, were you not?'

'Was I?' Alice reflected. 'Really, my dear, I don't remember. In any case, how you could know of it I can't imagine.'

'It so happens that you have a very

observant servant in Walters,' Maria replied calmly. 'He has a tabulated record of what happens in the house every day — and for June 4th, the fatal day, he has you sitting on the terrace all afternoon, reading.'

Alice looked irritated. 'Doesn't he know what I did in the morning?'

'You may be sure he does — but that is irrelevant. You see, whoever arranged the murder of Ralph did it apparently between lunch hour and the time Ralph came home at twenty to five.'

'Really!' A variety of expressions chased across Alice's face. 'So you are on a rampage of suspicion again, eh? You don't stop at anybody, do you? Not even me?'

'Not even you,' Maria admitted blandly. 'How much I suspect you Alice, depends on whether you can prove you were reading all through the afternoon.'

She shrugged. 'I'm afraid I can't prove it — nor for that matter do I see any particular reason why I should. You can ask Janet if you like, or Mary. Both of them were in the lounge next to the terrace, in this very room, typing letters all the afternoon. As I recall it was about half-past four when I moved in here.'

'Do you remember,' Maria asked, 'if either Janet or Mary moved out of here at all?'

'I don't know! They might have done. I believe I dozed part of the time . . . Why? Where do you suppose they might have gone?'

'Possibly to the library . . . '

'Dinner is served,' Walters announced gravely, appearing in the doorway.

Maria caught Alice's arm tightly as they walked across the lounge. 'Don't take this questioning of mine too much to heart, Alice,' she smiled. 'Maybe my investigative qualities are not very polished. I am simply testing a little plan of my own and I am bound to tread on people's toes in the doing.'

Conscious that her methods were perhaps too aggressive, Maria soft-pedalled her remarks during dinner, at which only she and Alice were present — but the moment it was over Maria began to open fire again as they went back into the lounge.

'Alice, I want you to realize that my suspicions do not rest directly on you. I have perhaps framed my questions badly. What I am trying to do is to eliminate wheat from chaff. That makes it that I have to include you whether you like it or not.'

'Now, Maria, you listen to me!' For once Alice's voice was firm and decisive. 'I told you once before — and I'm telling you again — that I consider your interferences pretty close to insulting! We know Ralph was murdered. Very well. You have dared to assume it might be somebody in the family who did it . . . We will presume for a moment that you are correct. But do you not think that if it was, say Janet, or Dick, or Patricia, I would not work heart and soul to cover their guilt? Of course I would! They are my children, Maria: something you seem unable to grasp. I know how Ralph balked each one of them, yes; I could even forgive them for wanting to be rid of him for some of the things he did . . . '

'I thought,' Maria remarked, sitting down, 'you were fond of Ralph, Alice?'

'I was. I am not referring to myself but to my children. I am telling you that I intend to protect them with all my power against your interfering probes. I would rather Ralph's death remained for ever as an apparent suicide than that any one of my children should take the blame for a fate he probably deserved.'

'Why should you fear so much for your children if they are innocent?'

'I am simply telling you my line of action!' Alice retorted.

'You have a rare gift of eloquence, Alice,' Maria smiled. 'You should have been an actress.'

'Maria, do you not realize what I'm saying? I'm telling you that I shall — '

'That you will protect your children,' Maria nodded. 'A noble sentiment, Alice. But whatever you say, and whomever it may be who is guilty, I shall still bring him or her to justice.'

'Wash your neck! Ho-ho, you're a bonny 'un!'

'Quiet, Cresty!' Alice snapped, swinging to him as he twirled about his cage.

'Aw, go cook a hamburger!'

'That reminds me . . . ' Maria said, watching the parrot's antics. 'Yesterday morning the bird imitated the aria which Janet sang during her last tour. You remember Patricia remarking on it?'

Alice shrugged. 'What of it? Janet sings that aria at most of her concerts, usually as an encore. You mean Mozart's *Alleluia in F Major* don't you?'

'Yes . . . Do you happen to have a record of that aria? I mean, has Janet ever made one of it?'

'As it happens, yes — and of lots of her other songs, too. But if you want to hear it,' Alice went on, 'you'd do much better to listen to the original. It is being broadcast tonight, don't forget. That is what I am waiting to hear. Be on any minute now. Janet told me she would include *Alleluia* as an encore tonight. If she does you can hear it. If not, I will get the record.'

Maria nodded, then asked another question.

'Tell me, Alice, were you listening to her in your room on the night Ralph died?'

'No. I had heard her recital on the earlier broadcast so I didn't bother on the second occasion . . . '

Alice got up and switched on the radio. At the moment it was only a swing band, but presently the announcer stated that they were going over to the Criterion Theatre for a musical recital, with Janet Black, soprano, and Dennis Raythorn, tenor . . .

Maria rose suddenly and went over to the sideboard. Alice watched her absently for a moment or two, then she gazed in surprise as Maria drew up a little table, stopped, and then studied the position of the radio. She edged the table round, nodded, and on top of the table placed an empty wineglass.

'What on earth — ?' Alice asked, staring.

'A little experiment in ultrasonics, my dear,' Maria smiled. 'And if you do not know the meaning of 'ultrasonics' I would recommend you to read Dunsant's *Electrical Reactions* in Ralph's library. Ultrasonics deals with the science of *unheard* sound. Sound either so high or low it escapes audibility and manifests itself instead as a vibration . . . '

Maria sat down again, folded her arms, and waited, Alice frowning beside her . . . The concert began. Janet's pure notes, first in solo then in duet with Dennis Raythorn, floated into the lounge, winding up in a storm of applause. By this time Alice had abandoned herself under the warmth of golden notes.

'Beautiful! Has she not a wonderful voice, Maria, dear?'

'Certainly a remarkable one,' Maria said ambiguously, her eyes half-closed; then she abruptly became all attention as the orchestra struck up for an encore.

'This is it!' Alice exclaimed, waving her fingers in the air. 'Mozart's *Alleluia* . . . '

'You know at which point the high C comes?' Maria asked.

'But of course! I know every note.'

'Good! When it comes watch this wine-glass . . . '

Maria got up, turned up the volume of the set a little, then stood watching the little table. Still puzzled, Alice sat listening as the girl's voice swept higher and higher up the scale towards the conclusion of the aria; then at last she reached high C and held it steadily. Alice opened her lips to make an enraptured utterance, only to close them again with a start as the wineglass in line with the radio suddenly parted with a piece of its bowl which fell in slivers of needle thin glass.

'What — what did that?' she gasped, noting Maria was nowhere near it.

'Ultrasonic wave from Janet's voice,' Maria said laconically. Then, as the aria came to an end, 'Do you mind if I switch off?'

'No, of course not. She has finished anyway . . . ' Alice got up and stared at the shards scattered on the table. 'But how could Janet's voice do this? It's — ridiculous!'

'No, it is amazingly logical. Listen while I explain . . . ' Almost word for word, Maria repeated what Jean Conway had told her.

'So you see,' she finished, 'a portion of the glass was in exact sympathy with the vibration from Janet's voice, and therefore it broke. The great singer Caruso used to do it.'

'But what does it all mean?'

'It may mean the answer to Ralph's death, Alice . . . Now, I am not accusing Janet: but I am rapidly becoming convinced that somebody knew her voice has just the right timbre for smashing glass when it reaches high C or above . . . and not only glass but any brittle object. This line of reasoning started yesterday morning when Cresty imitated Janet's voice and smashed a wineglass on the sideboard. It could not have been Janet yesterday because she was singing just an ordinary ballad — and she was in another room too. The maid said she had seen a wineglass smashed like that before. Probably Cresty did it on that other occasion too . . . It is possible, I daresay, that Janet is quite unaware that her voice is capable of doing such a thing.'

'But what has this to do with Ralph's death, Maria? How can a wineglass breaking — '

'Or any brittle object!' Maria repeated. 'It was not a wineglass which caused

Ralph's death — but a revolver, a spring, and a piece of brittle wire . . . For that matter this evening is as good a time as any to explain just what I mean. We are alone for a change. Where is that record of Janet's *Alleluia*?'

'It will be in the radiogram in the library. I'm not much interested in records myself, but Ralph was. He has a huge library of them — whole operas that play in sequence. It is an automatic radiogram, you know. The kind that puts on and takes off records for itself.'

Thoughtful again Maria led the way to the library, again asked the astonished Walters for stepladders. Alice began to watch in mystified silence as Maria once more took the .38 from the desk drawer and fixed it over the top of the antique revolver so that the barrel was pointing directly downward.

'You observe, Alice, that this gun almost covers the antique underneath it, thereby rendering it practically unnoticeable?'

'Ye — es,' Alice said, uneasily. 'What now?'

'This . . . ' Maria put the smaller loop

of the spring over the nail supporting the gun butt and fastened the larger spring loop round the trigger of the .38. She held it tightly, prevented the trigger from drawing back. With her free hand she looped the wire — joined end to end now in 'O' shape — also round the trigger and then to the nail holding the revolver barrel. A few adjustments followed, until at last the trigger was within an ace of being pulled back sharply by the spring, prevented only from so doing by the wire holding it in the opposite direction.

'There!' Maria got down from the ladder and flashed a glance at Alice. 'Now, if the wire were to snap what do you think would happen?'

'Obviously the spring would snap back and pull the trigger, and the bullet would fire . . . at the armchair!' Alice's voice trailed off. 'Oh, Maria, it's horrible!'

'Horrible — but brilliant,' Maria said grimly. 'I haven't finished yet, however. Where is that record of *Alleluia*?'

'In the radiogram there . . . '

Maria turned to it and raised the lid, looked at the score or so of records turned edgewise to her, put there with mechanical neatness. She went through them swiftly, then turned.

'No record of *Alleluia* here, Alice.'

'But there must be . . . ' Alice turned from her contemplation of the revolver and looked through the cabinet hastily. Then she smiled and lifted a record off the take-up arm.

'Here it is! I see now what happened. Ralph must have decided at some time to play through all Janet's records — Yes, look! Here on the feed-arm are six of her records. One had played — this one of *Alleluia* — and the second one had gone halfway. The rest were not played at all . . . ' Alice frowned. 'Queer! The record still has the needle resting in the middle of it. Unlike Ralph to do that . . . '

'I noticed that some time ago,' Maria commented, her eyes narrowed in thought. 'But in any case it does not signify at the moment. Put on the *Alleluia* . . . '

Alice put aside the record that was on the turntable — and Maria noted exactly where it went in the rack — and replaced it with *Alleluia*. She switched on, put the needle down gently.

'What happens now?' she asked, closing the lid.

'Everything . . . I hope,' Maria murmured, and stood in tense expectancy as Janet's voice flowed forth steadily. Gradually she climbed again to that high C, and as that pure note vibrated from the radiogram a variety of things happened.

The wire holding the revolver trigger snapped suddenly. The spring instantly pulled back the trigger and for a second or two — long enough at least for a bullet to be discharged in a straight line — the revolver was motionless. The spring, released, flew backwards off its nail and vanished. The loop of wire fell too. The .38 itself, no longer supported and jerked with the recoil, dropped off the central nail and thudded to the carpet perhaps eighteen inches from the heavy armchair.

'Heavens!' Alice whispered, wide-eyed. 'Maria, had there been a bullet in that gun; had somebody been sitting in that chair — '

'There would have been another 'suicide,'' Maria said grimly, switching the radiogram off. 'I have proved that my reasoning has been entirely justified. This alcove here collects the sound waves from the radiogram and directs them in just the right intensity to that out-jutting piece of wall. The brittle wire snapped instantly in sympathy with the right note. Automatic suicide, Alice! A devilish scheme! Somebody must have experimented quite a lot to perfect the idea. Somebody knew that Ralph invariably sat in that chair when listening to the radio: somebody knew the chair is too much of a fixture to be moved about very much. And somebody knew that Janet's voice would do the trick! Yes, on the night of the murder this device went off when Janet sang high C from the concert platform. I worked it all out from only one clue — a spring. Possibly the murderer tried to find that spring, and failed — whereas I was successful. It was lodging in a crevice.'

She turned and searched about until she had recovered it again. She also picked up the thin piece of snapped wire.

'Exhibits,' she announced. 'The police are going to be very interested in these before I'm finished.'

'I — I just don't know what to say,' Alice breathed, her face pale. 'But Maria, why didn't Ralph see the second gun? The automatic, I mean . . . '

'Very unlikely. He would be looking at the radiogram for one thing: it is surprising how one looks at a radio when very interested, as though expecting to see something. Again, the automatic exactly covered the antique. Had he looked carefully he would have seen two barrels pointing at him — but obviously he did not. Again, the murderer reckoned that Ralph would have no need to use the automatic from the desk: the belief was right. Therefore, you know now why I am sure the device was fixed between the time Lucy cleaned up and the time Ralph came home.'

'Yes . . . I see.' Alice looked up anxiously. 'But surely, Maria, you do not think that I could have planned such a brilliantly executed, not to say technical, suicide?'

'I know you didn't fix the device, Alice — and for a very good reason. You are only about five feet tall.'

'What has that to do with it?'

'Plenty. I am assured by Walters that on the fateful day nobody borrowed step-ladders — and yet to fix this device would demand them. The murderer would therefore have to rely on the furniture in the room itself. By using all the cushions and the chair — the only possible articles, you observe — I can then only just reach the crossed guns up there, and I am five feet four. So we are forced to the admission that the murderer is tallish — not under five foot seven, anyway.'

'That takes in many people,' Alice sighed. 'If we dare to think of the family, though I know that to be wrong, we can have Janet, who is five feet eight; Dick, who is six feet; Patricia, who just touches five feet seven . . . Walters is tall, too, and so is Janet's maid, Mary. Lucy is my height, so she's out of it.'

'Excluding any other people we have not mentioned whom I might yet encounter,' Maria mused, thinking of Jean Conway, whom she guessed at five foot seven. 'Patricia, I think, we can leave out. We know where she was.'

'Yes . . . we do. Well, Maria, all I have to say is that I shall stand by my children if it is proved that one of them did it. If that is the final solution at which you arrive, promise me that you will tell me first.'

'Murder is murder, Alice,' Maria answered inflexibly. 'No matter whom it hurts, no matter who is guilty, he or she shall pay to the full. Advance warning might give the opportunity to escape and I do not intend to allow that to happen.'

'And who are you to pass judgment in this fashion?' Alice demanded bitterly.

'For one thing I am Ralph's sister, entrusted with the mission of seeing that justice is done. I am bound to honour that. In the second place I am the only one above all suspicion because I was in England when the thing happened . . . '

'But look, surely you must have some idea by now who did it? Can't you give me a clue?'

'I can't, Alice. So far everybody who has come under suspicion seems to have had a perfectly logical reason for wanting to be rid of Ralph: I have to determine which one finally took the plunge ... '

She broke off and glanced at her watch. 'I have some work to finish off tonight, Alice. Think over all that I have told you, and if you recall anything likely to be helpful let me know.'

'Yes, of course,' Alice agreed quietly.

9

Maria's 'work to finish off' took her to the Criterion Theatre just as the concert was finishing. She made her way through the little group round the stage door, and the doorman recognizing her from her first visit nodded his permission for her to go through. Mary opened the door of Janet's dressing room in response to the knock.

'Good evening, Mary. Miss Black still out at the front?'

'She'll be in any minute, madam.'

The girl cleared a chair of odds and ends and Maria settled herself to wait. At length Janet appeared, disentangling herself from earnest reporters and critics crowded round the doorway.

'Later — later!' she promised, closing the door on them. Turning, she gave a faint start of surprise. 'Why, Aunt, this is unexpected! Come on, Mary — hurry, please!'

'I came,' Maria said calmly, 'to

compliment you on your voice. I heard it over the radio at home, came into town to have a look at the bright lights, and thought I might as well have a look in here as well . . . Your 'Alleluia' was particularly fine.'

'I'm so glad you liked it. It was dad's favourite aria too, you know.'

Janet seated herself and fussed with her hair before the mirror. Mary began to get busy with brush and comb.

There came a sudden knocking on the door and at Janet's call to enter a lean, hungry-faced man in evening clothes came in quickly. He paused and glanced at Maria then hurried over and caught Janet's right hand.

'Jan, you were really magnificent tonight! The critics are saying that you are even better than on the last occasion — '

'All right, all right,' Janet interrupted, rather irritably. 'I know — Oh, you haven't met my Aunt, Miss Black, have you? This is Mr. Montagu, Aunt, my manager . . . '

Montagu bowed stiffly and Maria gave him a level gaze. She did not like him: she instinctively knew it. There was something about him . . . Handsome, yes, in a synthetic sort of way. It was his obviously superficial warmth that was the least interesting thing about him. Perhaps he sensed Maria's impression for he turned back to Janet.

'Jan, you are not forgetting you are dining with me tonight?'

'Not tonight, Monty; I made no promise.' Janet surveyed her reflection in the mirror critically, then added, 'Tomorrow perhaps . . . Frankly, I'm tired. I want to get home early.'

'You're always going home early!' he objected. 'Hang it all, I have some right to be with you, haven't I? Unprofessionally?'

'Have you?' She gave him a cool smile, then went on with her coiffure.

He hesitated, then shrugged. 'Well, all right — but I shall not be so lenient tomorrow night. Don't forget that you have made a promise . . . ' He turned, bowed again to Maria, then went out and closed the door with unnecessary force.

'For a girl who is tired you look remarkably radiant, my dear,' Maria murmured, rising.

'You know the reason why I put him off, Aunt. I don't give two hoots for Montagu, though I guess I shall have to give him some sort of a break in case he gets sore. I'm going to see Peter tonight . . . You had the car brought round, Mary?'

'Waiting, Miss Black.'

'And my other clothes laid in it?'

'Everything is ready, yes.'

Janet looked up with a smile. 'You see, I am driven as far as the East Side, changing on the way, then by the time I arrive I am a different person entirely, outwardly that is . . . It is odd sometimes what length a woman in love will go to, isn't it?'

'I have become aware of that quite forcibly during my stay. But frankly, I don't blame you. But I would warn you to be careful in dealing with this Montagu person. I don't like him . . . And by the by, I'm nearly forgetting why I really came over here tonight. While listening to your voice over the radio this evening I was struck by a peculiarity in it when it reaches high C.'

'Oh? I never — ' Janet broke off with a cry of impatience. 'Mary, what is the matter with you? Pick the brush up and get on with my hair. I'll never be out tonight.'

'I'm sorry, Miss Black — I seem to be all thumbs . . . ' The girl dived for the brush, then went on with her task rather jerkily.

'You were saying?' Janet prompted, tugging off her flashing stage jewellery.

'Your voice,' Maria said, 'is very beautiful — but it is also very destructive. As an instance, you may like to know that you smashed some glassware at home tonight.'

'I did?' Janet stared; then she snatched the hairbrush from Mary, gave her a bitter glance, and went on with the job herself. 'My hair isn't a horse's tail!' she said hotly — then looking back at Maria, 'is this some sort of a game, Aunt? I've been here all the evening. How could I — ?'

'Your voice has not been limited to here, Janet. Do you remember that

316

yesterday morning a wineglass was found smashed on the sideboard and you made the rather lame suggestion that Richard might have done it?'

'Yes, yes, of course I remember . . . Put my costume out, will you, Mary? You don't mean, Aunt, that I broke the glass?'

'Not on that occasion. Cresty imitated your *Alleluia* and did it instead. But tonight your own voice smashed a wineglass when you reached high C. I thought it might interest you.'

Janet looked at Maria for a long moment. Then she shrugged and began to unhook her sequined gown.

'I am interested, yes, but it doesn't surprise me. It is a characteristic of many singing voices . . . I guess mother will be sending me in a bill for broken glassware next. What do you think of it, Mary? Almost creepy, isn't it?'

'Yes, Miss Black, it's certainly very queer.' The girl did not look up: she was busy laying out Janet's costume.

'You'll excuse me rushing, Aunt, won't you?' Janet went on quickly. 'I want to cram as much as possible into the spare time I have got — You've interested me quite a lot in your revelation about my voice. If I fall on hard times as a singer maybe I can get a job as a vocal freak or something.'

Maria gave a grave smile. 'Well, I will leave you to it. See you at home . . . Good night, Mary.'

''Night, madam.'

Maria elbowed her way through the Press crowd again and out into the street. She caught a glimpse of a figure dodging back into the shadows, but motioned to him just in time. In the little backwater of humanity she drew Pulp on one side.

'Still around, see!' he grinned. 'Watching you, just as you wanted. How's tricks?'

'I'm still hunting, Mr. Martin — still hunting. Tell me, would you know Janet Black's car if you saw it?'

'Not ordinarily I wouldn't — but I heard a girl come out and call for Miss Black's car . . . That's it!' He nodded to a slender limousine parked against the kerb. 'Why? What's the angle?'

'As soon as my niece — that is Janet

Black, of course — gets into that car I must follow it. I'll need a taxi.'

'Oke. Joey's round the corner just in case. He was going to pick up theatre people but you're more important. I'll be back . . . '

He departed and returned within three minutes, pacing beside Joey's taxi as it drew to the kerb. Joey waved his hand in the air as he saw Maria, and she nodded back to him.

All of a sudden there was a stir among the people outside the theatre's rear exit and Janet came hurrying out with Mary, the maid doing her best to keep the crowd aside. Pulp gave a sudden frown as he saw them under the bright lights.

'Say,' he breathed, as Maria hurried to her taxi, 'I've seen that dame some place before! Now she's in the light I seem to remember — '

'Probably in the newspapers,' Maria answered briefly, climbing into the taxi's rear seat.

'No, I don't mean — '

'I've no time for your memories now, Mr. Martin. Later . . . '

'Sure you don't want me to come with you?' he asked urgently.

'Yes, yes, I'll be all right. See you again.'

Janet's car started off, leaving Mary on the pavement looking after it. Maria sat back in the taxi cushions and watched intently as Joey's expert hands sent his vehicle flying through the midst of the night traffic in the wake of the limousine. It passed through the centre of the town and finally drew up on the outermost parts of dingy East Side. Joey drew up a few hundred yards away. Maria sat watching as Janet emerged, now in her former drab costume. She went away swiftly under the dim street lights.

'Wait for me, Joey,' Maria ordered, climbing out.

She dodged round a back street to avoid passing Janet's car and thereby contacting the chauffeur — probably the family one. That caused her to think a little too. Evidently the chauffeur was in on this as well, but if he was the right kind of chauffeur he would keep the girl's trust implicitly. And anyway, he probably did not know the real implications behind his mistress's behaviour.

Presently Maria picked up the girl's trail again as she walked swiftly towards the misty reaches of the harbour. Maria's main object in this pursuit, decided on the spur of the moment, was to discover for herself exactly where Peter Wade resided. After that she could contact him personally at a more convenient time without anybody being the wiser.

Janet's walk was so swift it took Maria all her time to keep up with her. The trail led past all manner of buildings, provender stores, through dark and dismal alleyways full of shadows, along a deserted wharf beneath which the waters of the harbour slapped with oily swell. Out in the mist ships lay at anchor, lights rocking to and fro — And so to a cheap lodging-house overlooking the harbour. Maria saw Janet vanish through the open front doorway and promptly followed.

She was in time to see the girl head up the dimly-lit staircase and finally stop at the second landing. Maria paused, watching from the concealment of the balustrade below. She saw a door open and Janet disappeared inside . . . Maria relaxed, taking stock of her surroundings for future reference. Satisfied, her breath recovered, she returned to the outside again and began to retrace her way along the harbour wharf.

She was perhaps halfway along it when she heard a sudden sound. She turned instantly, but in the dim light of the hidden moon could see nothing to account for it. She frowned, continued on her way at a quickened pace, darting glances about her as she went — Then the sound came again. She swung round, and at the identical moment something like a sack dropped over her head and shoulders. She felt herself receive a mighty push — then the wharf was no longer there and she was falling helplessly through space. She landed finally with a smack in the harbour waters, fighting desperately to clear the sack or whatever it was over her head. From sheer desperation she accomplished it, stared above as she threshed the water desperately.

For the briefest instant she caught a

glimpse of somebody looking down at her — then the figure vanished abruptly . . . Maria kicked and clawed frantically, weighted down by her clothes, her swimming days long over. She could feel herself slowly losing the battle as she was tugged by tremendous undercurrents — A wild shriek escaped her.

Then there was a resounding splash within a few yards of her. She worked her way round and glimpsed a mighty arm and shoulder. A bullet head followed it. Within a few seconds Pulp came up, striking out forcibly, and caught her as she began to sink again.

'Service!' he gulped, spitting out a mouthful of water. 'That's me, Black Maria! Okay, just hang on to me . . . '

Maria was gurgling so much she could not speak. She relaxed and felt herself swept through the water until they reached the massive teak pillars under the wharf. Pulp climbed out on to the low built platform, dragging her up beside him. Shaking in every limb she straightened up, wiping back her saturated hair.

'Thank — thank God you came, Mr. Martin! You saved — '

'Aw, to heck with that . . . ' He nodded to a flight of wooden steps leading upwards. 'Inspection ladder,' he said. 'One under every wharf. Up we go — Go on, I'm right behind you.'

She nodded and began to climb with trembling legs. The moment she reached the top she moved to the nearest capstan and leaned against it thankfully, wringing the water out of her cuffs. Pulp followed her a moment afterwards, retrieved his coat from further along the wharf and threw it about her shoulders.

'Can't stop here,' he said earnestly. 'You'll catch cold. We've got to step on it. Joey's waiting, and I know the quickest way to him. Come on!'

'Just how did you find me?' she asked, as they hurried along.

'Nothing to it. I know you said you'd be all right when you left the theatre, but I figured I'd better keep on your tail. I got on the carriage rack of Joey's cab: he's had it made kinda wide for that purpose. Good job I did. You might have drowned down there.'

'I would have drowned, Mr. Martin: that was the intention!' Maria's voice was hard. 'You didn't happen to see who did it, I suppose?'

'No. I shadowed you to that tenement dump, and then back along the wharf. I saw somebody dash out from the shadow with a sack or something and throw it over you. Before I could reach the guy — Or come to think of it, it could have been a dame — he saw me coming and ran for it. I figured it was you that needed help, so I dived — That's all there is to it. Seems to me it might have been one of Ransome's boys after you.'

'Perhaps,' Maria muttered.

'Who else then?' he asked grimly.

'I don't quite know for sure . . . but I have every reason to think that quite a few people are becoming uneasy about my activities — '

Maria broke off with a thankful sigh as the taxi came into view. In the distance Janet's limousine was still parked. Maria paused a moment, pondering, as Joey looked at her and Pulp in amazement.

'What in heck have you been doin'
— swimmin'?'

'Take Black Maria home, double
quick,' Pulp ordered, pushing her in the
back of the cab and slamming the door.
'Fast as you can, before she catches cold.'

'Remind me to give you a bonus for
this, Mr. Martin,' Maria smiled, handing
back his coat. 'You saved my life tonight.'

'Aw, forget it. And take care of them
lungs.'

Thereafter Joey stepped on it to good
effect, and whirled her home in record
time. She gave him double his normal
fare and hurried inside the house: the
door was unbolted as usual in readiness
for Dick's early-hour return. Ten minutes
after gaining her room, and without
anybody being the wiser, she was warm
and dry again. Wrapped in a dressing
gown she ate the supper that had been
left for her, then took up her diary
. . . After a moment or two of grim
reflection she began to write —

*'Without doubt Janet's voice fired the
gun which killed Ralph! Now I have*

absolute proof! Janet herself seems unmoved by my efforts to trap her into an unwary admission. Either she is indeed innocent, which seems improbable to me now, or else she is a consummate actress.

'Whoever worked out the details of Ralph's 'suicide' got most of the information from a book entitled 'Electrical Reactions.' Now anybody in the house could have obtained it — yet the two most obvious people to make use of it are Jean Conway and Richard. Janet also, if she really knows her voice is unique. These are the final points in the tangle:

'Ransome's typewriter spring is still unexplained.

'Tonight somebody tried to drown me. It could have been one of Ransome's men. If not, only three people are possible. Janet herself (who might have known I followed her to her fiancé's lodging-house and tracked me as I returned); her maid Mary, who might have seen me leave in Joey's taxi; and thirdly the chauffeur who might have seen me prowling, though am doubtful of this. Altogether quite a few *people are getting worried. But I am getting nearer — ever nearer.*

'*Shall see Peter Wade on my own account.*

'*Would remark some peculiarities about the radiogram which may stand checking. Why was the needle in middle of record?*

'*The time is exactly — 1.40 a.m.*'

Maria put her book and pen away, turned to the bed and was asleep almost instantly . . .

★　★　★

Daylight was just commencing to pale the windows when Maria awoke with a sudden start. Always a fairly light sleeper she had been subconsciously aware of something peculiar going on in her room for some time. Now she awakened abruptly and sat up, switched on the bed light and gazed round her. She opened her mouth to exclaim, closed it and snatched her bed-jacket.

In front of the dressing table stood Joey, a revolver in his hand, and opposite to him in a chair, scowling bitterly, the waiter she had encountered in her activities at Maxie's Dance Hall. For a moment Maria wondered if she were dreaming.

With an effort she got a grip on herself. 'Joey, what is the meaning of this?'

He shrugged. 'Pulp left me on night guard of the place while he went and dried off. Good job I was around because I saw this guy sneaking up to your window by the drainpipe. I followed him right up to the balcony outside your window here. He had his gun' — Joey raised it from the dressing-table complete with its silencer — 'and was obviously figuring on letting fly at you when I stuck my own rod in his back. No sense in disturbing you, so as the window was a bit open I thought we'd climb inside and wait until you woke up.'

Tight-lipped, Maria sat up and eyed the waiter fixedly.

'Well, what in hell are you starin' at?' he demanded. 'I didn't do nothin' to you, did I?'

'Thanks to Joey, no! But you can

explain this to the police, my friend — in detail.'

'Wait a minute, lady — ' The man got to his feet. 'I ain't got nothin' against you personal. Honest! I was only doin' what I'd been told to do, see?'

'Which was to kill me!' Maria snapped. 'Besides being a waiter and serving very indifferent lemonade at Maxie's, you are also a strong-arm man for Ransome. Right?'

'Yeah, that's right. When he was picked up he told me to find you since I'm the only guy who knows you by sight — '

'Sit down!' Maria ordered, and he obeyed at a wave from Joey's gun. 'And keep your voice low,' she added curtly. 'I don't want the whole household to hear us . . . Obviously then it was you who tried to finish me off earlier tonight on that East Side wharf?'

'Huh?' The man looked blank. 'What wharf?'

'You needn't profess innocence, young man — '

'Now wait a minute, lady! I ain't no amateur! I use a rod or nothin'! I ain't never been near no wharf. I don't know what you're talking about.'

'Hmm ... ' Maria felt for a watch-chain that was not there. Then: 'I am inclined to believe you, but — '

'Look, if you'll give me a break I'll never try again — Honest! I'll blow town. I'll do anything ... '

'The break, my friend, has conditions,' Maria added grimly. 'I want some information from you — and this time you will give it. Ransome has a typewriter in his office, hasn't he?'

'Why, sure ... ' The man looked his surprise.

'Have you ever typed on it?'

'I used to do a bit of one-finger work.' He gazed at her queerly. 'Haven't done any in a long whiles, though. I bust the roller lever about a week back and I guess it's too much trouble to turn it up every time — You ain't thinkin' of engagin' me as a typist?' he asked sardonically.

'You broke the roller lever?' Maria demanded, her eyes lighting.

'Yeah ... So what?'

331

Maria mused. 'You can tell me something more. Where was Hugo Ransome on the fourth of June?'

'June fourth? Hell, that's a long ways back. Any idea what day it was?'

'It was a Tuesday.'

'Tuesday . . . I can't remember what happened in the morning, but on the Tuesday afternoon he'd be at a Directors' Meeting at the Onzi Trust. Always goes on Tuesdays — did anyway, until he got pinched.'

'Thank you,' Maria said softly. 'Thank you very much, my friend. And now a final word of warning. I'm going to let you go now, but my bodyguard will have orders to turn you over to the police immediately if you dare threaten me again.'

'I won't. I promise you I won't.'

'Very well. Joey, take him out the way he came. And leave his gun: I may need it for evidence.'

'Okay, Maria. Go on you, get moving! Quick!'

Maria watched them climb over the balcony in the dawn light, then she got up and closed the window after them.

'So Ransome is eliminated,' she muttered, and for a long time stood thinking.

Finally she went back to bed, but she could not sleep after the interruption . . . She lay meditating, knitting together the threads of the web, taking out the strands no longer strong enough to stand the weight of suspicion.

She was glad when Lucy arrived with the morning cup of tea.

Maria was putting the finishing touches to her dressing when Janet knocked lightly on the door and entered. She gave a rather tired smile as Maria greeted her.

'Good morning, Aunt. Everything all right?'

'Is there any reason to expect otherwise?' Maria asked, screwing her hair into its famous bun.

'No, I suppose not . . . ' Janet hesitated, then went on in a quiet voice, 'I wanted to catch you before breakfast and save you some embarrassment in case you should say too much . . . You see, I know you followed me last night.'

Maria finished her hair in silence, then turned her cold blue eyes on the girl's troubled face.

'I think,' Janet added, 'that I'm entitled to some explanation. I saw a taxi hard on the trail of my car all the time we were heading for East Side. Besides, I caught sight of you twice as you followed me across the harbour wharf . . . You are not very good at shadowing, Aunt.'

Maria gave a bleak smile. 'Maybe I had better re-read Calfort's *A.B.C. of Tracking* . . . As for you knowing that I followed you, that would condemn you badly at a trial for attempted murder, my dear. Some unknown tried to drown me last night after I had left your beloved's lodging-house. I was pushed off the harbour wharf and left to drown. I would have drowned, too, had it not been for — a passer-by.'

'*Tried to kill you!*' Janet gazed in stunned amazement for a moment. 'But, Aunt, this is terrible! Who on earth — '

'By your own admission you know I followed you,' Maria said coldly. 'What was to prevent you tracking me back?

Nothing! Again, your opening words in this room a moment or two ago showed you were not best pleased that I had followed you — '

'Oh, why do you try and twist everything?' Janet's face had colored hotly and her voice was like a whiplash. 'Why do you always have to have a smart answer for everything everybody says? I didn't push you in the harbour, nor do I know who did.'

'Very well then,' Maria replied quietly. 'You have no need to raise your voice to me, Janet. My hearing is excellent. I always had the impression you were the kind of girl who remains calm under all circumstances . . . '

'I still want to know why you followed me!' she blazed. 'And I *am* annoyed about it! What business is it of yours where Peter lives?'

'I think it is my business to know where Mr. Wade was on the day your father was murdered. I intend to question him about it, hence I had to know where he lives. Otherwise your strange private romance does not interest me in the least. I could have given you away long ago had I wanted.'

Janet cooled a little, but her face was still angry.

'I don't know where he was, Aunt. I've told you so before.'

'I know. That is why I intend to ask him for myself.'

'I could have saved you a lot of trouble last night, if you had asked me for Peter's address in the first place.'

Maria smiled. 'I like to find things out for myself, Janet. And besides, I had no guarantee that you would have given me the address had I asked for it . . . So I took the initiative.' She paused and added quietly, 'Shall we go down to breakfast?'

'We might as well — Oh, wait,' Janet broke off. 'I came for something else, too. Have you finished with my typewriter yet?'

'Surely,' Maria nodded. 'There it is on the table. Runs very nicely, too.'

Janet went over to it and flung up the lid. 'Yes, they seem to have made quite a good job of it. I guess it would never have broken down at all if that reporter woman hadn't blundered in.'

'What reporter?' Maria paused at the door and turned. 'Tell me about it.'

'Are you off again?' Janet sighed, picking the machine up in its case. 'Well, it was the day before dad — died. I was at the theatre collecting my things following the run. I was alone; Mary had gone to fix up about returning some costumes or something. Anyway this reporter turned up and her card said she was Kathleen Melrose, of the *Stage Echo*. She wanted a quick reaction to the finish of my run. How did it feel when a recital had ended? And so on and so on. I said anything to oblige and shot her the works. She asked for the loan of my typewriter — it was on the dressing table — and then she began to type at a furious speed. Said she wanted to rush the copy right away to her rag . . . I thought nothing of it and when she left she had the interview all typed out. Only . . . ' Janet frowned as she and Maria reached the lounge. 'Only the article never appeared in the *Stage Echo*,' she finished slowly, putting her typewriter down. 'I suppose that's rather odd. I'd almost forgotten about it until now.'

'And afterwards your typewriter was damaged?' Maria asked.

'Well, it seemed pretty rocky. I couldn't be bothered to find out what was wrong with it so I told Mary to take it to be overhauled.'

'Hm! What did this reporter look like?'

Janet reflected. 'She had blonde hair, pale complexion — Oh, yes, and thick glasses. Very thick. They made her eyes look like little spots. It rather beat me how she could see what she was typing. I don't think her sight was too good for she blundered into the door as she went out . . .'

'Thick glasses . . .' Maria was tugging at her watch-chain.

'Uh-huh . . . But I don't suppose it matters, anyway. Come along to breakfast.'

Maria was silent as they went out on to the terrace for the usual morning meal. The conversation, mainly owing to Maria's continued muteness, stopped at commonplaces. When the meal was over Maria got to her feet and drew Janet on one side.

'Janet, where did you send your typewriter for repair?'

'Mason's, just off Times Square. Why?'

'I just wondered. I'm thinking of buying a typewriter for myself.'

'You can still use mine if you want,' Janet offered. 'I only have a couple of letters to do . . . Better still, if you are going to Mason's why not tell them to call and pick up Pat's machine? Then I can send my own back to the theatre where it really belongs.'

Maria looked surprised. 'You mean you don't keep it at home when you do your own correspondence?'

'Why, no! No sense in lugging it about when Pat has one. I used to do my correspondence on hers — or rather Mary used to do it for me at my dictation — when at home. Until the spring snapped, that is. It went in the middle of my last letter on that — that afternoon. Pity!' Janet gave a regretful shrug. 'Pat's is such a lovely machine, too, if only it were seen to — brand new really and completely noiseless. That's why I used to use it. Doesn't disturb mother if she's trying to doze in the lounge, or on the terrace.'

'Of course,' Maria said slowly, nodding. 'Of course.'

'Of course what?' Janet looked surprised.

'Of course it would save disturbing your mother,' Maria smiled. Then she went on, 'Well, I'll tell Mason's to call for it. I'm going anyway because I can't impose on your generosity any longer. And besides, you must have your own machine . . . Yes, I'll buy one.'

She went on her way through the lounge, her eyes gleaming. Up in her room she searched the 'phone directory and finally dialled the number of the *Stage Echo*.

'Managing editor, please,' she said briefly; and in a moment his deep voice came over the wire.

'Hallo? Yes, managing editor speaking . . . '

'I have an enquiry to make,' Maria said. 'Have you ever at any time had a reporter working for you by the name of Kathleen Melrose?'

'Never heard the name, madam. In any case our articles don't have a by-line. Our interviews are done through the mail as a rule — freelance stuff. Why? Has such a person tried to claim our publication as her source of authority? If so — '

'No — no, nothing like that,' Maria interrupted. 'I just wondered if you had a reporter of that name. I am trying to trace a — a friend.'

'Oh, I see . . . Sorry I can't be of more help, madam.'

Maria put the receiver back, sat in thought for a moment, then got up and put on her outdoor clothes. Leaving the house she took a bus for Times Square. This time walking did not appeal to her: it was more a case of speed being the necessity.

She found Mason's Typewriter Emporium without difficulty. A smartly-dressed individual emerged from a waste of gleaming stands, typewriters, duplicators, and dictaphones.

'Good morning, madam, good morning! What may I be privileged to show — '

'I think,' Maria interrupted, 'we can dispense with the sales talk. I would like some information, young man . . . A little while ago a typewriter was repaired by you for a Miss Black. I'd like a copy of the bill. It was paid, of course, and everything is quite in order — but I would like an itemized statement of the repairs that were made. Can you do that?'

'Certainly, madam. Be seated, won't you . . . '

Maria nodded and waited impatiently through a long interval while the salesman vanished to parts unknown. He returned with a billhead in his hand.

'Here we are, madam. Sorry to have kept you waiting.'

Maria glanced down it quickly. Then she said, 'Do you recall who brought the machine in?'

'Why, yes,' the man nodded. 'We get very few repairs, as a matter of fact: we are mainly suppliers. I saw the young lady myself . . . She said the machine wanted overhauling and a spring replacing on the carriage rack. There were more things that were wrong, however, as you can see from the bill. It needed a thorough rebuilding . . . ' The man stopped suddenly and looked devastated. 'Madam, can it be that our service has not given satisfaction?'

'On the contrary, your service is excellent,' Maria smiled, putting the bill in her handbag. 'Tell me, do you recall what this young lady looked like?'

'Not very clearly, I'm afraid. She was fairly tall — a little taller than you perhaps. I seem to remember she had on a brown coat and hat —Yes, and fair hair. I cannot recall anything else. My main surprise was — hm! — that a young lady should be so conversant with a typewriter's workings. So few ladies seem aware of mechanical intricacies, if you know what I mean.'

Maria smiled without warmth. 'Thank you, young man: you have been most explicit . . . ' She wrote down the address of the Black residence on the back of her personal card and handed it over. 'Send up to this address as soon as possible to collect a portable machine for repair, will you? Thank you . . . '

'It shall have my personal attention, madam.'

Maria went out into the sunshine again, lost in thought. Reading the bill again she found it a highly technical summary with frequent references to 'dogs' and 'claws.' What really signified however was the spring replacement.

'And the girl was obviously Mary, Janet's maid,' she mused, 'who knew the spring had gone, whereas Janet apparently did not. Hmm! A most interesting ramification — '

'Hey! Pssst!'

She turned at a faint cry and a hoarse whistle. Pulp was in a neighbouring doorway, trying to attract her attention. She moved to him.

'Why, Mr. Martin! You still at it?'

'Until you tells me to stop,' he said doggedly. Then with sudden anxiety on his face he asked, 'How's them lungs? You didn't catch cold?'

'No, Mr. Martin. I am in excellent health, thank you. And you?'

'Aw, forget all about me! A guy like me

doesn't know how to catch cold — But say, I wanted to tell you where I'd seen that dame before. Remember that I tried to tell you last night?'

'Oh, yes!' Maria recalled the incident. 'You mean about my niece, Janet Black? Well, it's quite possible you've seen her. She is a well known singer — '

'Not her!' Pulp insisted. 'The dame with her! The one who called her car at first — '

'Her maid?' Maria exclaimed, starting.

'Is that what she is? Yeah, I guess she will be . . . ' Pulp mused. 'I didn't see her clearly at first when she called the car; but I did the second time under the lights — But maybe you're not interested?' he asked doubtfully as Maria stood eyeing him fixedly.

'I am deeply interested, Mr. Martin. Where did you see this young woman before?'

'A year back I was doing a job over in Columbus, Ohio, see? I had to call in a store and find my way to a joint I had to get to. The dame in the store was the same dame who's now that maid. I'm sure of it. I never forget a face.'

'Columbus, eh?' Maria's eyes narrowed. 'Yes, that checks exactly. My niece was singing in Columbus when she employed this girl . . . What sort of a store was she in?'

'Hardware. Electric light globes, paraffin oil, screws and bolts . . . The dame didn't know the place I wanted so she called her ma and pa and asked them. They told me . . . ' Pulp gave a shrug. 'Nothing to it, I guess — but when I see a face I like to place it. Now I've done it I'm satisfied.'

Maria pondered, then at last she seemed to make up her mind.

'Mr. Martin, I have an important case for you. Find Joey and let him take your place as bodyguard — though I hardly think I need one now. Then' — she dived her hand in her bag — 'you will take this money and entrain for Columbus right away. Can you find that store again?'

'Yeah . . . sure.' He stared at her. 'But what the heck — ?'

'I want you to find out if the store is controlled by Black's Chain Stores, my

346

late brother's concern. Also find out if the girl's parents are really dead: I understand that they are. In other words find out everything you can and telephone me from Columbus at the first opportunity.'

'Okay.' He stuffed the money in his pocket. 'If I go by train it may be tomorrow before I can give you the lowdown. If I went by plane I could find out much quicker.'

'Tomorrow will do: I have other matters to attend to in between,' Maria said. 'But find out all you can. How long will it be before you can tell Joey?'

Pulp grinned and released an ear-splitting whistle. Joey's taxi appeared from round a side street and drew to a halt against the curb. Maria gave a complacent smile.

'Good! Joey, take me to the same East Side spot as last night.'

'Okay, Black Maria. Hop in!'

Pulp held open the door for her and she clambered in. He slammed it shut and winked significantly. 'I'll phone the dope,' he said, then turned and strode off actively . . .

Joey started up the taxi and began to thread his way through the traffic.

'Well, Black Maria, how goes your murder case?' he asked, without turning his head from the front.

'Excellently!' Her voice was complacent. 'In fact I might go so far as to say I know exactly whom to single out as guilty. Only it would be dangerous without my final proofs . . . A moment, Joey! Is that a public library over there?'

'Sure is . . . ' He drew to the kerb and stopped the engine.

'I shan't be a minute,' Maria said, and hurried inside the building. She asked the clerk for the directory of businesses — English section. It was promptly placed on one of the tables for her and she waded through its massive pages, running her finger down the 'L' section.

'Laycock — Laythorn — Layton . . . Hmm!'

When she closed the book her lips were tight. She returned to the taxi.

'Drive on, Joey,' she announced, and for the rest of the trip lay back in the cushions and thought deeply. There was an uncommonly cruel glint in her blue eyes.

'Here we are, Maria . . . '

She climbed out at almost exactly the same spot as on the previous night.

'You'd better keep me in sight at a respectful distance,' she said. 'I don't expect much to happen henceforth, especially in daylight — but no harm in making sure.'

'Leave it to me! You'll never be out of my sight until you reach wherever you're going.'

Maria nodded and started off, walking resolutely through the twisting streets and finally on to the wharf. This time she had no real anxieties. The brilliant sunshine lessened any chance of an attack, and the only living things in sight were two children with a fishing rod and a rowboat in the harbour itself. She went on steadily, reached the tenement house at last and continued up the stairs to the second landing. She rapped sharply on the door at which Janet had stopped on the previous occasion.

The door opened suddenly and Peter

Wade stood there. He looked amazed as he saw Maria standing before him.

'Why — Miss Black! Janet's Aunt, of course! But what — '

'Do you mind if I have a word or two with you, Mr. Wade?'

'Why, no! Come right in . . . ' He backed inside and rather hastily sought to tidy the place up a little. Maria cast a glance around her. Everything was clean enough even though it was in a state of complete masculine disorder. The table was littered with draft musical scores.

'Take a seat, Miss Black,' he invited, then as she sat down he asked seriously, 'Is there anything wrong?'

'No, Mr. Wade, there is nothing wrong. I just want a chat with you. Tell me, has Janet ever told you of the circumstances surrounding her father's death?'

'I know that most of the family now believe he was murdered,' he replied. 'I know too that you are trying to find the murderer. Janet told me that.'

'That saves me a lot of unnecessary talking. It has now become vital for me to check up on certain details concerning you, and if my questions are a little pointed I hope you will forgive it.'

He smiled faintly. 'Of course. I suppose Jan told you I could be found in this dump?'

'I found it out for myself by following Janet last night. Don't worry, young man, Janet has not betrayed your romance to anybody — nor will I. I'm here purely on business — '

'In a little while,' he broke in eagerly, 'it won't matter if all the world knows of our romance. I have — ' He checked himself. 'But never mind! How can I help you?'

'Can you tell me where you were on the afternoon of June fourth?' Maria asked quietly. 'That of course was the day on which Janet's father died . . . Can you recall what you did on that day between noon and teatime? Above all, can you prove what you did?'

He smiled and nodded to the year calendar on the wall. Maria glanced at it then raised her eyebrows at beholding blue-penciled rings round the dates of June 4, July 4, and August 4. She looked at him questioningly.

'Those are dates on which to find out about my musical revue from the publishers,' he explained. 'They take a month about to complete a reading; then I call in and get the verdict. On June fourth I spent the afternoon in the offices of Jacob Benson Incorporated trying to talk the big fellow into giving my revue a ride . . . But he wouldn't bite. You have only to ring him up in order to prove it.'

Maria wrote the name down on a slip of paper and put it in her bag.

'As Jan may have told you,' he went on, 'I've been working on a musical revue to try and regain something of my lost glory . . . And I've got a big surprise coming to her! Last night I was about sunk in the doldrums — but this morning I heard from Heath's, the biggest producers in the business, that they are going to give me a break — and put Jan in the star part! What do you think of that? That is why August 4 is ringed on the calendar. I was going to call on Heath's at that date, but now it won't be necessary — It's bucked me up no end, Miss Black!'

'It's certainly going to be a grand surprise for Janet,' Maria admitted.

'I'll say!' Then Wade looked at her earnestly. 'Only don't tell her a thing, will you? I want to surprise her . . . It means the end of the bad patch, end of all this enforced penury . . . Yes, I know what you are probably thinking — Jan has plenty of money, enough for both of us. But that isn't my way. I want it my way, or nothing. I knew I'd get back one day — on top!'

Maria sat studying his eager face for a moment. 'Janet has a beautiful voice, has she not?' she said, somewhat irrelevantly.

'Extra good!' he enthused; then he fell to reflection. 'At least she seems to have got it back to perfection now. I listened in to her last night and she was superb — far better than on her last night during the other recital.'

'Other recital? You mean the one that terminated so tragically in her father's death?' Maria was all attention again.

'Yes. I was listening to her on the last

night over the radio and it struck me that her voice was tired — or else she was. Her high notes had no clarity — But last night she was divine again. Probably she just needed a rest.'

'Yes . . . probably. About what time did that last concert end?'

'Oh, about nine o'clock . . . at least the radio version did. We only got an excerpt of course. We were faded out just as the applause was sounding for Jan's *Alleluia* encore, then the announcer said it was nine o'clock. I remember that. That's how I'm sure of the time.'

'I see.' Maria rose and held out her hand. 'Well, Mr. Wade, thank you for being so helpful . . . And don't worry, I shall not forestall your little surprise for Janet; and I do congratulate you most sincerely.'

'Thanks.' He shook hands and at the door regarded her seriously. 'Have you any idea who did this thing? The murder?'

'Yes, I know,' she said quietly. 'Probably you will too before long . . . '

With that she left him and went out on to the wharf thoughtfully. At the first street 'phone kiosk she came to she went inside and rang up Jacob Benson Incorporated. It took her only a few minutes to verify Wade's statement from the callers' register.

Maria was smiling when she emerged into the street again. It was that smile of approaching triumph that all Roseway College knew . . .

At the taxi Joey rejoined her. 'Well, nothing happened that time,' he grinned. 'Where to now?'

'Home, Joey, if you please.'

Sunk in the cushions at the back as Joey drove through the city, Maria's face registered a variety of expressions and finally ended in one of granite hardness. Even Joey noticed it as Maria got out of the taxi at the journey's end.

'Found something vital?' he asked keenly.

'I believe,' she said grimly, 'I have come to the end of the trail, Joey. I have just one more point to check up with Mr. Martin when he 'phones from Columbus . . . ' She paid his double fare and added, 'I don't know when I shall need you again, Joey — if at all. But in any case

I can always get into touch with you.'

'Always ready,' he said amiably. 'And good hunting!'

Maria went into the house and was crossing the hall when Dick hurried from the lounge and intercepted her.

'Aunt, just a minute . . . ' His face was serious. 'I've been waiting to catch you . . . I have found something,' he said, his voice deadly quiet.

She waited, eyeing him.

'This!' He opened his wallet and took out a sheet of folded paper. It revealed itself as thin copying paper — a carbon copy of single-spaced typing. Maria took it and read slowly.

'But Richard, this is an exact plot outline of the play you and Jean Conway are writing!' she exclaimed.

'Just that,' he assented grimly. 'And of all the value in the world to dad's murderer! Don't you see? This has been taken somehow from among my own papers concerning our plot! It shows the murderer the exact method we planned — enough anyway to put ideas into her head . . . '

'Her head?' Maria repeated, her lips tightening.

'Yes, I should have said murderess,' Dick said ominously. 'I found this copy in Pat's room! It was accidental, really. I've been doing some work this morning and I needed more paper. I was working in my room upstairs and rather than come downstairs after more paper I slipped into Pat's room for some. I knew she had a ream or two in that little desk she's got. I found this amongst the paper. Pretty obvious that she had put it there intending to lock it away and then forgot all about it — or else it was the police caught up on her and she just couldn't do it anyway.'

'And this carbon was missing from among your own papers?' Maria asked slowly.

'I made a check up at once. I had them — still have as a matter of fact — in the drawer in my room. This carbon plot outline, not since I had the whole idea in my mind, was never needed, so I didn't miss it . . . ' Dick stopped and shook his head. 'This is damnable, Aunt, I know

357

— but I thought I'd better tell you. It might help.'

She took the carbon copy and folded it slowly. 'I'd like to keep it for a while, if I may . . . Does Jean know of this?'

'Not yet. I'm going to tell her the moment I see her.'

'Perhaps you had better not,' Maria reflected. 'At least not until I want you to . . . Well, thanks very much, Richard. I think this is going to help me a great deal. Now I must get tidied for lunch.'

She went on upstairs with her face still set and determined. As the dressed she thought over every detail she had collected, finally tabulated everything in her diary as usual.

'I know who killed Ralph! It is the most amazing discovery! I have every fact save one — and on this I have no doubts. Mr. Martin will telephone me tomorrow and then I shall start to unravel this extraordinary web.

'The time is 12.10 p.m. And possibly this is my last entry for this particular case . . . '

'The end of the trail,' she muttered, putting the book away. 'And now . . . Ten minutes!' She frowned as a sudden thought struck her. 'Yes, about ten minutes. I wonder if it is possible in that space of time?'

She made up her mind to her own satisfaction and went down to lunch. But the moment it was over, during which she had only indulged in small talk, she headed for the library. The household was fairly quiet. Dick had gone upstairs to rest and Janet had left for the theatre with the intention of shopping on the way.

Within the library Maria glanced at her watch, then with methodical movements went to work putting cushions on top of the nearest chair, climbed up within reach of the crossed guns, went through several pantomime movements intended to represent the placing of a second gun — the .38 — in position. At the end of her activities she climbed down, put back the cushions and chair, then looked at her watch. She smiled grimly . . .

Next she strolled with apparent unconcern into the lounge. For the first time in her hectic exploits she felt that she could relax — and it was a revelation that astounded Alice as she sat on the terrace reading. She came in with book in hand to where Maria reclined in an armchair.

'Maria dear, is it really you sitting here taking your ease?'

Maria looked up. 'Do you never sit and think, Alice? Do you never pause amidst a torrent of events and piece together all the things you have encountered?'

'Yes . . . sometimes.' Alice frowned. 'Does this mean your search has come to a blank wall?'

'No. It means I know who killed Ralph!'

'What!' Alice laid her book down and reached for a chair, her face suddenly pale. 'You — you know?'

'By tomorrow morning I shall have the last piece in the jigsaw . . . ' Then in a softer tone Maria went on, 'Alice, I want you to do something. Tomorrow afternoon you are going to be hostess to a little party, whether you like it or not. I am going to give you a list of guests so you will know how many to prepare for, and you can leave the actual inviting to me. Here they are — Janet, Janet's maid, Mary — yes, I insist on it! A young man named Peter Wade whose identity Janet and I will make clear tomorrow. Then there will be Richard, and a young lady friend of his named Jean Conway — and Mr. Johnson, the lawyer. Walters and the staff will be here in any case . . . That completes the party.'

'Who are these strangers you mention?' Alice demanded.

'You'll soon know; take my word for it. I absolutely insist on all this, Alice. And it will have to be in the afternoon because Janet and Richard, and Mary the maid, will be unable to be here on an evening — and for me the morning will be unsuitable. Is all this quite clear?'

'Well, I'll have to take your word for it,' Alice replied irritably. 'I'll arrange it, of course — but I wish you'd tell me a little more.'

'Tomorrow you'll know all you need,' Maria promised, with a grim smile. 'My one regret is that Patricia and her husband will not be able to be here — but that of course is impossible. However . . . ' She rose to her feet. 'That is as far as I can go for now. At the moment I'm beginning to feel rather tired after my exertions. I think I shall go up for a rest, Alice.'

'Yes, do . . . ' Alice started out of a preoccupation.

Maria had her rest, but made no effort to sleep. The moment she heard Dick leave his room next door she hurried out and intercepted him in the corridor.

'Hallo there, Aunt!' he smiled. 'Bit of a change to see you around in the afternoon. Trying to rest?'

'I have been,' Maria acknowledged. 'Actually I was waiting to catch you. I want you to do something for me. Tomorrow afternoon I am calling together quite a number of people whom I have pestered with my suspicions — and I want you to bring Jean along about half-past three.'

'But I can't do that!' he protested. 'We're keeping our acquaintance a secret in any case . . . ' He stopped and gave a shrug. 'Well, maybe it doesn't matter this time. Okay, I'll bring her — but you will have to explain things to mother.'

'I have every intention of doing so,' Maria assured him.

He hesitated. 'Are you by any chance going to prove who did it?'

'I am, yes!'

'Rely on me,' he nodded. 'I'm all for it. Pity Pat can't be here as well; it would make it a full house . . . On the other hand maybe she is only in the place where she'd be anyway when all this is cleared up.'

With that he went on his way, leaving Maria staring after him with her watch-chain twirling in her fingers.

10

During the evening Alice was in a restless, anxious mood — a fact that Maria noticed silently. But she said nothing and spent the evening listening to the radio, glancing through magazines, doing everything with such a calm deliberation that it was clear she knew exactly what her plan of campaign was going to be. Alice looked quite relieved when Maria finally announced her intention of retiring early.

She slept soundly all through the night, and was glad of it: she felt in tremendous form for the task that lay ahead of her. Before breakfast she took the opportunity of catching Janet alone and making a request of her similar to the one she had made of Dick. The girl's acquiescence was surprisingly prompt.

'I saw Peter again last night, Aunt,' she smiled. 'He told me you had been to see him — and he also told me the good news about his musical comedy. That

364

means we hit the top together. I don't mind coming into the open in the least now. Montagu can't do a thing about it since I'll be leaving him anyway — But why Mary?' she frowned. 'Bit of an unusual request, is it not?

'I assure you I have a very definite reason,' Maria replied. 'I want you, Mr. Wade, and Mary. I'll leave it to you to contact them during this morning. Your mother knows the arrangement: I will explain everything later on.'

Janet nodded slowly, looking vaguely puzzled, and with that Maria left the bedroom and went on her way downstairs. During breakfast Dick caught her eye and nodded, obviously to signify that he had contacted Jean and obtained her consent to the invitation. Alice still maintained a complex kind of silence, speaking only when spoken to — and then very absently.

After breakfast Maria paced up and down the lounge impatiently. She almost forgot her dignity and ran for it when Walters announced that she was wanted on the hall telephone.

'Yes — yes? Hallo! You do all the talking . . . '

'Okay, lady, this is Pulp,' Pulp said needlessly. 'I'm at Columbus like you told me. Right now I'm at a railroad station — '

'To the point, Mr. Martin, please! What did you discover?'

'I got to Columbus and found the store — but it ain't anything like the same as it was. It's a branch of the Black Provision Network Stores — Anything to do with you, lady? Name being the same, I mean.'

'Did you find out what happened to the former owners?' Maria demanded.

'Sure. The old folks died and the daughter blew town — nobody knows where to: figure she must have gotten a job with that niece of yours, like you said. Seems like the business got bust up — the hardware one, I mean — and the old folks just got the skids under them and passed out . . . Guess I couldn't find much more.'

'You didn't need to,' Maria said tensely. 'In fact you have found out just what I expected you would. I'll contact you again through Mr. Three-Shot when I want you. Goodbye.'

She hung up, rubbing her slender hands. The one thing she was waiting for now was the afternoon . . .

★　★　★

It was towards mid-afternoon when the party began to gather. As they arrived Walters conducted them to the library, until at last every requested guest was present. With her usual weakness for a dramatic entrance Maria arrived last, motioned Walters and Lucy the house-maid inside the room, then closed the door. She walked to the desk, sat down, and interlocked her fingers. Her cold blue eyes looked at each of the faces in turn, from Lawyer Johnson's pince-nezed visage to Alice's troubled features.

'Each one of you, in some way or other — with the exception of Mr. Johnson here — has been the victim of my rather inquisitive activities recently,' Maria said in a quiet voice. 'For that reason each one of you is entitled to an explanation. That is why you are here . . . '

She got up, began to pace slowly up and down while she tugged at her watchchain.

'I have been singularly impressed throughout my whole search by the fact that my brother Ralph was a most disliked man. It seems more than obvious, now that I have heard it from so many sources, that he was a tyrant — a ruthless businessman with little or no regard for anything save his own advancement and standing. Of all of you gathered here, you, Janet, seemed the least bitter — and you, Alice, threw me off the scent for a long time with your professed love for Ralph. I realize now that you had no such love — that you did it for another reason. But Patricia — honest, outspoken, headstrong, said outright on the first day I came here that she hated her father. Had you all been so frank in your condemnation I might have been saved a lot of trouble . . . Patricia is a girl of sterling decency.'

The assembly glanced at each other. Then Alice cleared her throat. 'Yes, Maria

dear, you are right. Ralph was not all
— all a husband should have been . . . '

'On the night I found you in this
library, Alice,' Maria resumed, 'you were
not seeking to recall past events and
memories — even though you had
cleverly built up to that impression in
your earlier conversation as a safeguard
against being caught in the library later.
So, I found you in here, searching for one
thing only — a spring! You had realized
I was determined to solve the mystery of
Ralph's death — and only the finding
of that spring, which had originally
graced some kind of mechanism, possibly
a typewriter — could throw a spanner in
the works from the start. I do not
presume it was the first time you had
looked for it, but I do realize — and did
— that it suddenly became a matter of
extreme urgency when you saw how
determined I was . . . You did not find it,
but I did, lodging in a crevice . . . You,
Alice, have known from the very start
who killed my brother!'

'Isn't that a dangerous accusation?'
Janet demanded hotly. 'After all — '

'Sit down!' Maria commanded, as the girl half rose. 'I will come to you later . . . ' She looked round again on the faces. 'Excluding Mr. Johnson, who is here solely to see and hear my explanation of the mystery, it is clear that each one of you have known from the very start who killed my brother! Only one was absent from this circle of crime, and that one was Patricia, who at first I was inclined to suspect more than any of you. Yes, you have protected each other by common assent, believing my brother was worthy of death.'

The silence fell again. Johnson adjusted his glasses and breathed a little more quickly.

Maria turned. 'First, Mr. Wade, I will come to you. You hated my brother because he found out by subtle methods that you and Janet were as good as engaged; and had he wished to do so my brother could have done to you what he did to Arthur Salter — but he didn't. He died before he had the chance.'

'He deserved to die, Miss Black!' Wade retorted. 'But I give you my solemn word that I did not kill him.'

'I know you didn't kill him,' Maria replied. 'But you know who did, through Janet. I believe that had you not been forestalled you would have killed my brother one day. As it is you are innocent, and your alibi checks exactly. When my brother died you knew — as you did too, Janet — that the chance of him crushing either or both of you was gone for good. You, Janet, felt free to go on with your own career and pursue your romance in your leisure moments, defeating Montagu by a simple disguise. Your father, fanatically determined to maintain his high social standing at all costs, was dead . . . '

'I had different views to father, Aunt,' Janet said seriously. 'Peter and I were afraid of dad jumping on us in the way he had jumped on Pat's boy friend, just because he didn't like her associating with somebody whom he thought to be of a lower social standing.'

'But Patricia has much of her father in her,' Maria mused. 'She refused to obey his dictatorial methods and married her young man just the same, secretly. When he was sent to prison she even got him out of that and worked desperately to try and clear his name. Patricia, who had the most real cause to loathe her father, was the one who did not think of personal retaliation — and because of her frank, honest outlook you left her out of your council of crime — though it was her misadventures that fired the lot of you into action. You knew that the blows her father had struck at her might just as easily strike at any of you. You realized that over this family there hung a shadow — a rod of iron from which only sudden death or murder could release you . . . The power of my brother extended not only over his family but to all the branches beyond it . . . to Mr. Wade, to Miss Conway, to Hugo Ransome . . . Never has Patricia known who really killed her father, nor I fancy does her husband. Her antipathy towards me when I first came was purely because she thought I might find out about her efforts connected with her husband's escape from the prison farm.'

Maria turned and walked over to where

Mary, Janet's maid, was seated.

'Mary, you are another victim of my brother's activities. At one time you and your parents had a prosperous hardware business in Columbus, Ohio, had you not?'

She looked surprised. 'Why, yes. But — but Mr. Black opened up a store there. He bought out my father and mother, failed to give the full amount of compensation, and — Well, I guess they died from hardship and disappointments,' she added grimly. 'I made up my mind to kill Black. I made everything tend that way! When Miss Black came on a singing tour I asked her for the job of maid, and got it, having heard of it through a friend of mine. I got the job, but I did it with the sole intention of furthering my way to smashing Black if I could ever get near enough.'

'Until you found that Miss Black had as much of a grievance against her father as you had?' Maria demanded.

Mary nodded slowly. 'I had far more of a grievance than her. But how do you know all this?

'I remembered Janet telling me where she had first met you, and I also remembered her telling me that your parents were dead. I pieced the whole thing together with a little outside aid . . . ' Maria pondered a moment. 'Tell me, Mary, how did you know exactly what was wrong with Miss Black's typewriter? You knew for instance that it had a missing spring. How did you know it was the spring?'

'Oh, I — I just knew, that's all.' The girl looked rather startled. 'From my earlier business life I know a bit about machines and when I looked at the typewriter I saw what was wrong. I told that to the typewriter people — ' She broke off. 'Listen, I know what you're thinking! But I didn't do it! Honest I didn't!'

'But you do know that the spring from that machine was the self-same one instrumental in murdering my brother!' Maria snapped. 'And I will go further . . . When in the dressing room at the theatre the other night I mentioned to your mistress that her voice could smash a wineglass, what did you do? You became agitated, dropped the hairbrush. You were, to use your own expression, 'all thumbs'! That little display of emotion convinced me you fitted into the pattern somewhere — But you, Janet' — Maria swung to her — 'never lost your nerve. Not that I expected you to. Your composure is a marvellous quality, my dear.'

'Are you implying — ' Janet began, but Maria cut her short.

'I am not implying, Janet; I am telling you that you have always known your voice could do tricks! You knew because you had been told so long before I found it out . . . You, Janet, as surely murdered your father as though you had stuck the gun at his head! You loaned your voice in order that he might die! When you reached high C your father's .38 automatic was fired by the snapping of a taut wire, while a typewriter spring pulled the trigger . . . ' Maria shrugged, her face like granite. 'But I have no need to detail the method used: you know all about it, every one of you in the family!'

'Supposing I did use my voice to kill

him?' Janet cried bitterly. 'He had to die, I tell you! He tyrannized us all! He was merciless . . . But I didn't kill him!' she shouted. 'I did not kill him, you hear?'

'But you knew that when you reached high C you had provided the means of killing him!' Maria snapped back. She stood for a moment glaring down on the girl, then she relaxed a little and added coldly, 'No, Janet, you did not plan the murder, I know that. That was your work, Miss Conway!'

Jean Conway looked surprised, then her brightly intelligent face became strained. 'I? But how could I have — '

'I repeat, you planned it! You found a plot for a play, and in finding it you also found the perfect way of disposing of my brother; even more so when you knew his daughter was a singer with a high C voice. You met Richard and fell in love with him . . . But first things first, Miss Conway. You told me the other afternoon that your brother Alfred had taken up a position with Edward Layton and Associates of England, the big steel people . . . '

'Right!' Jean nodded.

'It is not right!' Maria retorted. 'The directory assures me — even as I thought at first from my own knowledge of England — that there is no such firm as Edward Layton and Associates in England. Again, no English firm ever uses the term 'Associates,' that is exclusively American. I suspected that you were flying away from the truth the moment you mentioned the 'Associates.' For that you have your lack of English knowledge to thank . . . Your brother died, Miss Conway! That is the only solution. And that vengeance which you said you had retracted still smouldered inside you. Am I right?'

As the girl remained silent, biting her lip, Maria went on:

'You were torn between two things, as I see it. On the one hand you loved Richard sincerely, and on the other you wanted to destroy his father — '

'Right, I did!' Jean said defiantly, flinging up her head. 'And when I saw the way to do it — when I knew how he had ruled this whole family with such despotic power — I too felt it was right that he should die. And he did die! I planned it! I came to see Dick on the day of the 'suicide' if you remember. I sent up a needless note to him and then came into this library and fixed up the gun and taut wire. Only I could do it, knowing the science of sound.'

'You fixed the gun, the wire, the spring — everything?' Maria asked quietly.

'Everything! By the time Walters came back I was in the hall again and nobody was any the wiser.'

'And, I believe you said, you heard the typewriter clicking in the lounge?'

'Quite clearly. I've told you that before.'

'I know,' Maria said calmly, 'and that is where your story fell to pieces. Janet was using Patricia's machine on that day, and that machine is *noiseless!*'

'Noiseless!' The colour ebbed from Jean's cheeks. 'But — but I — '

'You did not hear it, and you did not enter this library,' Maria stated implacably. 'I have satisfied myself that it would be quite impossible to fix up that gun in anything under half an hour at least, not to make a thorough job of it. You had only ten minutes at the most. No, Miss

Conway, you realized the other day that I was looking into things. You realized that there was a slim chance that you might be able to take the blame on yourself by turning your quite legitimate call on Richard that afternoon to account. It was not a needless note you sent up to him: the whole thing was quite normal. But you have tried to turn it to account to save another ... You did plan it out, however. I pieced the whole thing together when you let slip the comment about a 'taut wire' the other afternoon. Obviously it was uppermost in your mind and you had said it before you realized it. Your sudden change of subject did not throw me off, Miss Conway.'

She made a helpless little gesture. 'Yes — yes, I guess it did slip out ... I'm afraid you are too smart for me, Miss Black.'

'The one who fixed the gun is, in a sense, no more of a murderer than any of you — and yet in a point of law might be considered the real culprit. You — Richard! I'm afraid Jean's efforts to shield you have proved unavailing.'

'Me?' He sat up with a start; then he looked contemptuous. 'Don't be absurd, Aunt! Don't you think this farce has gone far enough?'

'Probably you hope it has,' she answered, unsmiling. 'Do you recall that upon the day Jean called and sent up a note to you concerning your joint play, you told Walters to fetch you a book from the library; then on second thoughts decided to get it for yourself?'

His expression began to change. 'Yes — sure,' he said slowly. 'I suppose Walters told you?'

'He did. You came down here later for the book, I suppose?'

'Yes.'

'It was *Electrical Reactions*, was it not?'

'Yes,' he said shortly. 'But I don't see — '

'But I did when I read that book!' Maria retorted. 'You and Jean both withheld the title from me — but you had mentioned it to Walters, Richard, so I made it my business to read it. There, set out perfectly, was the more technical side of sound, explaining in detail how a taut wire can be snapped by a sound wave. It even gave the calibre of the wire — all the details. I realized then that you and Jean had worked together from this textbook and hatched your plot. It seemed to me that the point you wanted to correct — in the note Jean had sent up to you — demanded this book. It was too obvious a clue to miss. You told Walters unthinkingly to get the book. Then you thought better of it — However, you did finally get the book, and then what did you do?'

'I gave it to Jean,' he said quickly. 'I guess she still has it.'

'You have a bad memory, Richard, or else are a poor liar. I have just told you I read it myself. It is there on the shelf!'

He gestured impatiently. 'So what? I remember now — Jean brought it back.'

'Maybe I can save you the trouble of further invention, Richard. You did not lend the book to Jean at all. You no doubt checked up on the point at issue and then told her personally. That does not concern me. What *does* concern me is that you gave the story of the book to

Walters in order to provide yourself with a pretext for entering the library for some time during the afternoon. You made a mistake in mentioning the title of the book, though, for it got back to me — Though Walters, as you imagined, would think no more of it. You came in here later on in the afternoon and fixed the gun, arranged every detail. You needed a chair and a cushion to stand on . . .'

Dick opened his mouth to speak, then shut it again.

'You tried to confuse your trail where you could — for that matter all of you have done so.' Maria looked round slowly on the set faces. 'You, Richard, outdid yourself when you thought I was getting dangerously close. You tried to switch things over to Patricia by producing a carbon copy of the plot presumably found among her papers. I realized that that was a hasty move on your part because, had you reflected, you would have remembered that on the day of the 'suicide' Patricia was helping her husband to escape from Jamestown . . . You tried to pin the guilt on her at the last moment because you knew that with her out of the way in prison I was not in a position to question her! It was a despicable thing to do — even though I suppose you had some other plan for detaching her from the main issue later on when she was freed from the law.'

Dick drummed on the arms of his chair for a moment. Then he said shortly:

'And you think that I would have sent for you, that I would even say it was murder, if I had had a hand in it? Be reasonable, Aunt!'

'I'll tell you why you did that,' Maria replied. 'You realized — all of you realized — from Mr. Johnson's remarks when the will was read that he would state it as his private opinion that my brother was murdered. You knew, probably because my brother had often mentioned the fact, that I have a penchant for criminology. You knew I might look into it! You took the offensive by coming right out into the open with the admission that it was murder, thereby hoping to take me off my guard right at the start. From then on all of you followed a prearranged plan, each one of you confusing the others' trail in the hope that I would finally lose myself in a blind alley. I cannot believe that you devised all this for my especial benefit, however. The obvious solution is that you planned it that way in case the police questioned the suicide theory ... And indeed all would have gone well for you had you been able to find that missing spring. I would probably never have got started. But I *did* find the spring and moved right through the maze you had all so cunningly prepared in advance for a possible police enquiry. Even Janet invented a reporter who never existed in the hope of tripping me up. She too, used the 'Patricia' angle — giving her mythical reporter thick glasses in order to hint at the fact that said reporter was Patricia in disguise, using the thick glasses to hide her rather rare shade of eyes ...

'But that did not ring true to me, Janet, because I had long since convinced myself that of all the people in on this — this council of death, Patricia alone was an absentee. Your studied efforts to throw guilt on to her was the main hole in the defence . . . As I had hoped, my move of putting her in police custody made two of you — you, Janet, and you, Richard — try and pin blame on her because she was out of my reach. And since it was not part of your original plan it was hasty in both cases and did a good deal to let you down . . . '

Maria moved slowly back to her desk to allow her long statement to penetrate. Then as the assembly looked at each other soberly she went on:

'In regard to your two secret affiances — yours, Richard and Jean; and yours, Janet and Mr. Wade — I can understand partly your reasons for wishing to keep secrecy while my brother lived . . . But after his death it struck me as insincere. Now I know why. You all kept as much separated as possible because you could not rely on yourselves to tell a straight story if you all assembled. That has been proven this afternoon . . . You, Richard, must have told Jean on that fated afternoon that Janet was using her typewriter, but you did not say which.

Jean would not think of a noiseless one, and you no doubt — being used to the fact that Janet usually used Patricia's machine — never thought to mention it . . . There is one example of the holes in your scheme. Had you all gathered together as you are now anything might have happened!'

'You've got it all worked out, haven't you?' Dick asked after a long pause.

'All!' Maria agreed. 'But there is still a more personal matter for me to clear up . . . One of you tried to kill me last night — and so far as I can make out it was you — Mary!'

Mary's face was white. 'Yes . . . Yes, it was me, Miss Black. I heard all you said at the theatre and I thought — Well, I realized things were getting dangerous and I didn't want to be involved in a murder charge so . . . I must have lost my head! When I saw you leave in a taxi behind Miss Black's car I followed in another taxi and . . . I must have been crazy!'

'Yes, I think you must,' Maria agreed, eyeing her grimly. Then she shrugged and asked quietly, 'Well, what have all of you to say?'

'What is there to say?' Alice asked, in a low voice. 'You are right, Maria, absolutely right. There is nothing to be gained by denying it, that's obvious. For one thing, most of us needed money for various things and Ralph wouldn't part with any. But the main trouble was his vicious domination over us. Somehow, we felt, we had got to break it! It was when we saw what happened to Arthur Salter that the red light went up for us. We had got to do something . . .

'About that time Mary came into the picture and we all learned how she too had suffered at Ralph's hands. When Richard met Jean Conway and we realized that she also had a grievance we realized it was time to act — time to take the law into our own hands. Jean had the method, culled originally from the book *Electrical Reactions* — not the one in the library here but a copy of it. Janet had the voice. Dick said he had the courage to fix the device, knowing all about where Ralph sat and all that. Mary and Mr. Wade had nothing to offer materially but they agreed to support the plan we had worked out to confuse the trail if there should ever be a police enquiry. We felt that we were on safe ground so far as Ralph was concerned, for he had frequently said that if he ever was struck down it would be by business enemies. We relied on that to keep us out of suspicion. So it was arranged — in an effort to release ourselves from his control and avenge the merciless way he had treated Pat's love affair.

'Pat herself we kept out of it, thinking she had enough trouble for one thing, and because her forthright nature might prove the undoing of the lot of us. We were genuinely staggered when you discovered her efforts at helping her husband to escape. Up to the time of your coming she had taken care to keep all newspapers referring to her husband's escape out of sight . . . The rest you know. We had no sooner done the job and had the verdict of suicide when we realized Mr. Johnson would probably tell you it was murder. Dick said he'd come into the open . . . We *had* to find that spring. But search though we did, we couldn't locate it . . . '

Alice stopped. 'That's all there is, Maria. But I warn you, we will support each other if you carry this thing to law.'

Maria gave a slow, grim smile and glanced across at Johnson. He was wiping his glasses and looking round rather dazedly.

'Well, Mr. Johnson?' Maria asked calmly. 'Have I conformed to the requirements of the will?'

'Quite! Quite!' He replaced his glasses. 'I never heard a more astounding story of a — a suicide in all my life!'

Maria got to her feet. 'You are satisfied that I have proven the form of murder and named the culprits?'

'Entirely — though I would like a fuller demonstration of this gun fired by sound.'

'You shall have it later, I assure you . . . At the moment I must be certain that I am entitled now to my bequest.'

'Definitely!' he nodded. 'As to this affair, I am compelled to inform the police that — '

'No!' Maria shook her head firmly.

As the others looked at her in growing relief she held her watch-chain firmly and looked round on them.

'I have done my part,' she said quietly. 'I have proven exactly what your plan was — I have shown you how you fully think it took place . . . But perhaps it was a hand of Providence that saved you from committing this crime . . . *Ralph was his own slayer!*'

'What!'

'That's impossible!' Dick cried. 'We arranged it and — '

'A moment!' Maria said, raising her hand. 'Let me finish. It is all a matter of timing — the difference being so slight that none of you noticed it. But I did, being especially concerned. On that fated night Janet was faded out at exactly nine o'clock on the radio, after the completion of her song . . . Right, Janet?'

'So Peter told me,' she acknowledged.

'And yet,' Maria said quietly, 'your father rang for his wine at ten minutes past nine! Walters is sure of it.'

'Correct, madam,' Walters agreed, as she looked at him for confirmation.

'But . . . ' Janet looked bewildered. 'I — Then he was still alive after I had finished singing? But what could have gone wrong? That gun should have gone off, and I know he would listen to me — He must have done because the radio was still on when Walters broke in.'

'Not the radio — the *gramophone*!' Maria corrected. 'In that cabinet, on the turntable, was the second of six of your records. This record had stopped in the middle with the needle still on it. That happened when Walters switched off. He in the confusion thought it was still the ordinary radio programme playing. The record that *had* been played had been automatically put aside, and that one was your *Alleluia*, which *did* kill your father.'

'But why should he play records of my voice when he had just listened to the original?' Janet demanded.

'That,' Maria said, 'is the vital point! When it came to it, Janet, your voice lacked its fire. You could not bring yourself to sing that death note on high C. Mr. Wade here remarked that your voice was not at all good on that night.

You never reached the required tone and purity in your last note that should have fired the gun, though you thought you had because of circumstances afterwards. Your father — as I see it — wanting to hear that note more than anything else played your record of that aria. So he rang for his wine and then set the radiogram playing your records, starting with *Alleluia*. In that record was the pure high C note. It snapped the wire, fired the gun, and your father died . . . So, you never really succeeded in your intention. You murdered, it might be said, by proxy. It might also be said that your father killed himself.'

There was a long stunned silence. It was Dick who broke it.

'Then — then we didn't murder him at all! Don't you understand, all of you?'

'It was attempted murder,' Maria said. 'But how is one ever to prove it when the real method has been disclosed?'

'Meaning what?' Alice asked, low-voiced.

'It still looks like suicide. Doesn't it, Mr. Johnson?'

He reflected. 'Tell me, why should Mr.

Black ring for his wine and yet not unlock the library door for Walters to enter? Are we to assume that he went back to his armchair after putting on the radiogram?'

'I believe so,' Maria nodded. 'Knowing Walters would knock in any case, and not wishing to risk a disturbance until he came, he forgot all about the door being locked. He sat down and listened to the record and . . . died.'

'Then it was certainly very like suicide,' Johnson admitted, fetching a sigh.

Janet said slowly, 'You mean you are going to let it go at that, Aunt?'

'I am something of a fatalist, Janet. If this plan failed because of lack of courage on the part of the originators — for your bad singing was really nervousness, Janet, and yet it succeeded because of the hand of the marked man himself, I — Well, so be it! Besides, it seems there was plenty of motive . . . But Patricia must never know. When she and her husband are acquitted, as they will be soon, it must still be suicide.'

Heads nodded slowly. Then Maria smiled faintly.

'What?' Dick asked quickly

'Nothing, Richard. I was just thinking that the rest of my vacation is going to seem dreadfully quiet, and as for when I go back to my college . . . Ah, well, there it is.'

'One thing I do know,' Dick said, rising and gripping her arm. 'I was certainly right when I called you my favourite Aunt. From now on that goes double . . . '

THE END